At the Mercy of the Sea

Other Books by Amanda M. Cetas

Thrown to the Wind

A Home in the Wilderness

Charting a New Course

Join her newsletter list at

https://books.bookfunnel.com/CFC_Free_Gifts

to receive a free short story that takes place between books 1 & 3

as well as updates on her latest projects.

A Country for Castoffs
Book 3

At the Mercy of the Sea

Amanda M. Cetas

Windy Sea Publishing

At the Mercy of the Sea

Book 3 of the Series,

Country for Castoffs

Windy Sea Publishing, LLC

ISBN-13: 978-1-956277-10-4 (E-book)
ISBN-13: 978-1-956277-09-8 (Paperback)
ISBN-13: 978-1-956277-14-2 (Hardback)

Library of Congress Control Number: 2023910786

Story Consultant/Dev. Editor: Laura Edge
Line Editor: Melissa W. Kelly
Cover Design by nskvsky

Author Image: Jim Irish, 2019

Publisher: Windy Sea Publishing, LLC: Tucson, Arizona

Dedication

To Jeremiah, the stalwart defender and supporter of his family and a man of integrity, and to Isabelle, whose care and wisdom heals all wounds.

Note

While this is a work of fiction, many of the people encountered, and the major events described are true to the historical records uncovered. While the personalities are made up, I have tried to do justice to the real people portrayed in this story. All Native American myths and traditions recorded here are accurate according to the records obtained from Native American sources. A complete annotated bibliography is available on my website at www.amandamcetas.com.

Map on next two pages: *Atlantic Ocean, or, North Sea: where the route from Europe to the West Indies is exactly observed, and from the West in Europe, drawn up on the newest relationships, 1700.*
New York Public Library, Public Domain.

OCEAN
ATLANTIQUE,
OU MER DU
NORD.
Ou sont Exactement observée
le Route d'Europe aux Indes Occidentales
et des Indes Occidentales en Europe.
Dressé sur les Relations les plus Nouvelles
A AMSTERDAM
Chez PIERRE MORTIER Libraire
Avec Privilege de nos Seigneurs les Etats.
AMERIQUE SEPTENTRIONALE
CANADA, ou
NOUVELLE
FRANCE.
NOUVELLE
ECOSSE
NOUVELLE
ANGLETERRE.
NOUVEAU
PAYS BAS.
VIRGINIE.
CAROLINE.
FLORIDE.
MEXIQUE.
GOLFE DE
MEXIQUE.
Isles Lucayes.
Providence
CUBA
Isles Antilles
HISPANIOLA
JAMAICA
ILE
ESPAGNE
JUCATAN
HONDURAS
NICARAGUA
COSTARICA
TERRE FERME.
MER
DE SUD
PEROU
AMAZONES.
AMERIQUE MERI
NOUV BRETAGNE

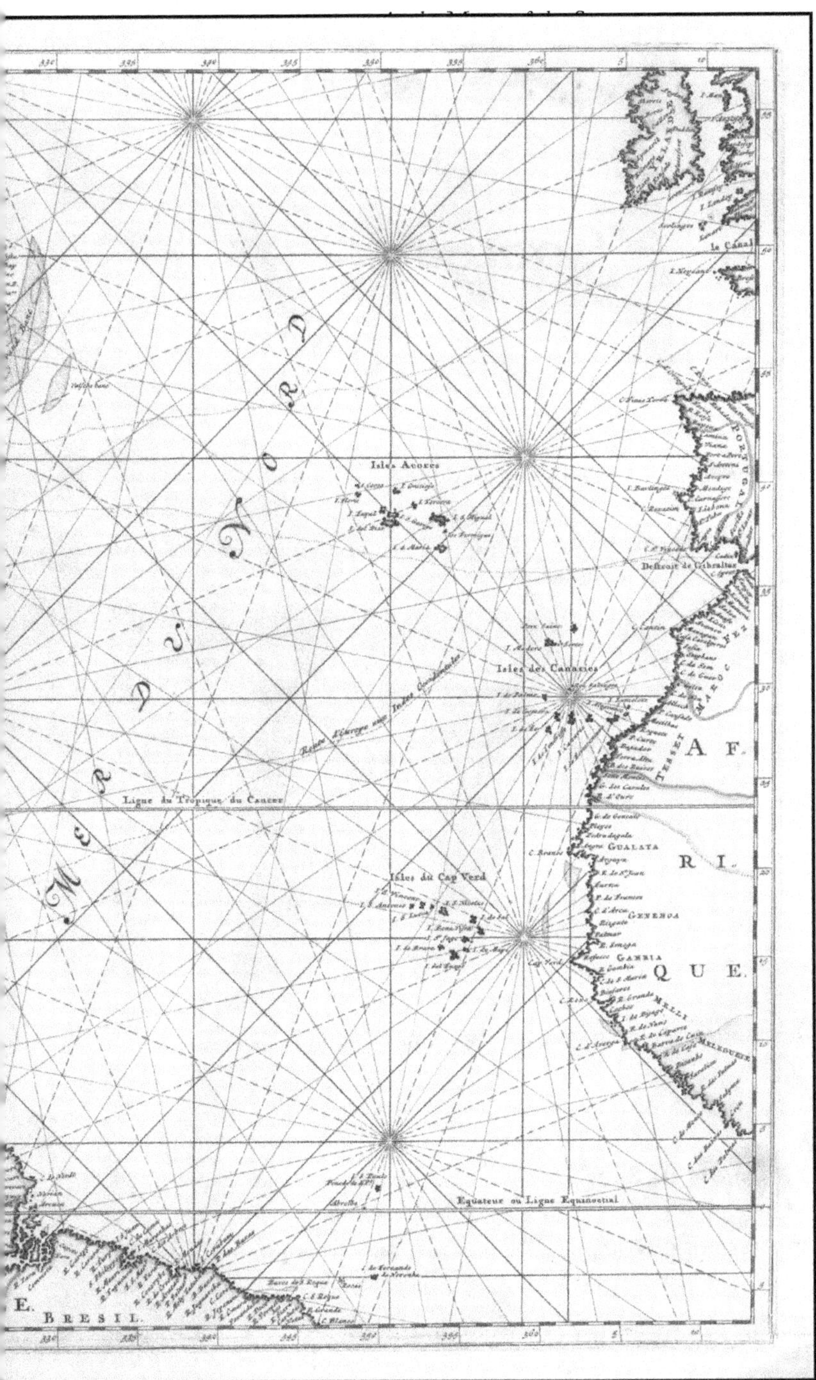

Contents

Amanda M. Cetas

Prologue

Alsoomse, September 18, 1663

Alsoomse fumed as she rowed toward the dock. *Why was he leaving without even saying goodbye? He calls himself a friend!* She steered the boat up to the dock and tied it to a mooring. Etienne was standing a few paces away talking to a younger boy. She leapt out of the boat and stalked over to her friend frowning.

"Why did you leave without telling me?" she asked in her native tongue, studying his reactions. He looked like a startled deer. "You said you were my friend, but you couldn't even tell me you were leaving!"

"Your mother has kept you so busy lately, trying to keep us apart. How could I interfere?" Etienne looked uncomfortable as his hands twitched nervously at his sides.

"You should have at least tried," she said and noticed the boy beside Etienne studying them.

"I'm sorry. How did you find out?"

Etienne's face looked so sad, her heart softened, and she

grinned. "I snuck away when mother was distracted with the little ones. When you didn't come to our meeting place, I went to your home. Your mother told me that you were leaving to work on one of the big merchant ships. So, I came to find you." She paused and frowned. "Why didn't you tell me your plan?"

Etienne had sold the precious dugout she and her brother Kitchi had helped him make. He'd said it was to help his family repay some debt, and now he was leaving to cross the great sea, and for how long?

The boy beside Etienne smirked and she turned to face him. She recognized his facial features as those of the neighboring Montauk allies. She addressed him in her native tongue. "What are you laughing at? Our conversation is none of your business!"

"That's fine with me. I don't care what you do," the boy replied.

"Why are you here?"

"My father is negotiating a trip to Boston on his captain's ship. What are you doing here?" The boy scowled and tried to look fierce, but she could see the insecurity in his eyes.

"My name is Etienne," her friend interrupted. He spoke slowly and deliberately in Algonquian. "And this is my friend, Alsoomse."

The boy stifled a laugh and stuck out his right hand. "My name is Abraham."

The captain returned and addressed Etienne. They spoke briefly, during which time another man approached. Finally, the captain and the other man left. Etienne turned back to her.

"I'm sorry," Etienne said. "I should have told you, but I really didn't have time. And I didn't know what to say."

Finally, the truth! What would he do without her out on the

great sea where she couldn't protect him? She feared for his safety and tried to put on a brave face. "I am glad I got to see you before you left. Don't worry, I will keep an eye on Lidie until you return. I must go too. Mother will have noticed I am gone and will be angry."

"What will you do?" Etienne's eyes were filled with concern.

"I will make some excuse," she replied and flicked her hand as if to brush away a troublesome fly.

Etienne dug into his purse and handed her a few Dutch coins.

"Thank you, Etienne! I will buy an iron pot for mother with this. Then she will not be so angry."

"There should be enough for you to buy some glass beads for yourself too."

A wave of emotion washed over her, she impulsively took Etienne's face in her hands, and kissed him. "Be safe and come back."

"I will," he said.

She watched him leave with Abraham. He turned, waved at her, and then hurried after the captain. A feeling of dread clutched at her heart. *He will be alright*, she thought trying to convince herself that it was true.

Her eyes strayed to the boy. He had tried to look tough, but she had seen the fear and sadness behind his eyes. *Who is he? And what is troubling him so?* She knew Etienne would look after him as long as he could. *But who will look after Etienne?*

Amanda M Cetas

Part 1
New Ventures

September 1663

Eastern Coast of North America

"Bright glows the morn, I pace the shining sands, And watch the children, as with eager hands They gather driftwood for the evening fire. Their merry laughter, ringing loud and clear, Resounds like sweetest music to my ear, As swift they toil, each with the same desire." ➻ "Driftwood," Olivia Ward Bush-Banks

Ball-Play Dance, by George Catlin (-1872), Wikimedia Commons. Public Domain

Chapter 1

Le Dauphin

Abraham, September 20, 1663

Abraham stared up at the ceiling of their cabin. The undulation of the waves was soothing, rocking him gently back and forth enveloped in the narrow bunk, as if he were still a baby in a cradle. Da, stretched out in the bunk below him, was snoring. They'd been on the ship for several days now, and he was coming to recognize the routine sounds of the vessel and what those sounds meant. He heard a bell ring followed by the thumping of many feet moving back and forth across the deck and understood that it was the changing of the watch. It was the morning shift. Etienne would be on duty. He yawned, stretched, and climbed out of the bunk. He dressed quickly, carefully retrieved the jug he promised Da he'd protect, left the cabin, and made his way onto the deck.

The sea was calm as Abraham emerged into the early morning glow. He walked to the railing and stared out over the water. Gulls circled overhead, taking turns diving into the rolling waves, as they hunted for their breakfast. He turned, leaned against the railing, and watched the men climb up the masts on ropes and dangle precariously from the yard arms.

He searched the men for several minutes before he found the young, French seaman. The boy, older than him but not yet a man, was barefooted and scrambled up the rope like a squirrel. Abraham watched as Etienne reached the crossbeam and walked out along it to release the sail. It made a snapping sound as it unfurled and swelled in the breeze. Abraham could feel the ship pick up speed.

Etienne was tall for a seaman and broad shouldered. Abraham thought about the first time he'd met the French boy. He'd been at the docks loading beaver pelts into a rowboat. Abraham had been wary of him at first, as he was of all Europeans. Some were honorable, but others were unpredictable, especially now with all the recent attacks by the Esopus. But Etienne's blue eyes were kind. The Lenape girl had befriended him, so that was also a good sign. Abraham smiled again, as he remembered how surprised Etienne had been when the Lenape girl had suddenly addressed him in Algonquian.

But why was Etienne friends with a *girl?* Abraham scrunched up his nose in disgust. Still, she was from a neighboring tribe and he was a colonist. Their friendship meant that he couldn't be all bad.

The sails set, he watched as Etienne descended the rope and landed on the deck with a soft thump.

"Is there something you want?" Etienne asked as he walked over to him.

Abraham held the jug tightly to his chest. "No."

Etienne eyed him closely. "What's in the jug?"

"Nothing! None of your business anyway."

"Okay. Have it your own way. I saw you watching me." Etienne turned toward the sea and leaned on the railing. "Have you ever been on a ship like this before?"

Abraham was caught off guard by the young man's easy tone.

"I … no. I've been in boats before, but only small fishing boats."

Etienne nodded and continued to look out over the sea. "I was pretty impressed my first time too."

"Who said I'm impressed?" Abraham snapped.

Etienne cocked his head to look at him, and a huge grin spread across his face. He raised his eyebrows and shrugged. "I've got to get back to my duties, but I'm sure I'll see you around later."

Abraham watched him go with a touch of disappointment and went to find a place to sit down out of the way.

Several hours later a bell rang and Abraham looked up from where he was sitting in a nook between the foremast and a large barrel. He spotted Etienne as he climbed down the rope ladder on the main mast and watched him approach.

"How are you fairing this afternoon?"

"I'm fine."

"You don't look fine." Etienne squatted down beside him and studied his face. "You look sad. Is something bothering you? I only ask because you remind me of my little brother, Louis. He used to make that same face when he was upset or frustrated. He'd have been about your age now too, I think."

"Where is your bother now? Did something happen to him?"

"He died when he was little."

"Oh. I'm sorry."

Etienne shrugged. "It wasn't your fault. It happened years ago. I still miss him though sometimes."

"I miss my little brothers too. They're at home with Mum, and sometimes they can be a pain, but …" Abraham smiled. "I especially miss Caleb. He's only four years old and he follows me around all the time and that can get annoying. But he's adorable and he always wants to give me presents … bird feathers, round stones, flowers, and other things he finds. He can always make me laugh when I get grumpy."

"He must love you a lot." Etienne quirked a smile at him. "How many brothers do you have?"

"Two older brothers and three younger. Caleb is the youngest. I don't have any sisters though."

"I have three younger sisters and a baby brother."

Abraham nodded.

"Have you explored the ship yet?"

"No."

"Do you want to? I'll take you below and show you around, if you want."

"Don't you have duties?"

"I'm off now. Did you hear the bell just now?"

Abraham nodded.

"That was signaling the end of the watch, so I have a little time off. Come on, I'll show you around."

Etienne led him below deck to the bunk room and showed him his hammock and trunk. Abraham was impressed. "Why do you all sleep in those?" he asked. "Da and I have bunk beds nailed to the wall."

"We can fit more hammocks into the space, and they are also more comfortable. They rock and sway better with the movements of the ship."

"Then why don't Da and I have hammocks too?"

"Most of our guests aren't used to sailing and are used to actual beds," Etienne replied.

"But maybe they wouldn't get so seasick if they were in hammocks?" Abraham asked, earnestly.

Etienne laughed. "They'd probably still get sick. It's the movement of the ship that messes with their sense of equilibrium. But you want to know something ironic?"

"Yes."

"Sailors who've been at sea a long time can have trouble walking on dry land because they're so used to the rocking of the ship. The solid ground seems to be moving when they first set foot on it!"

Abraham grinned. "Has that ever happened to you?"

"Sure has! Once I even leapt out of the rowboat trying to show I was as good as the other sailors and ended up slipping on moss and landing hard on my backside."

Abraham laughed. "Weren't you embarrassed?"

"I sure was!" Etienne's cheeks flushed pink. "Are you hungry?"

Abraham nodded.

"Let's visit the cook and see if we can talk him out of some bread and cheese."

Etienne led the way to the kitchen and greeted the broad-shouldered Irishman, who filled the small galley like a bear in its den.

"Ah, hello young Etienne. What can I be getting for ye now?" the cook asked, as they approached. "And who's y'er friend there?"

"This is Abraham. Abraham, this is Paddy, our cook. This is Abraham's first time on a masted ship like this, so I was showing him around."

"I've some boiled sausages, if y'er hungry." Without waiting for an answer, Paddy reached into a large kettle simmering over the stove and plucked out two steaming logs. He wrapped them each in a slice of bread and handed them to them.

"Thanks," Etienne said, taking them and handing one over to Abraham. They ate as they finished the tour of the holds and returned to the midship deck.

"Have you ever been to England?" Abraham asked.

"No. Why?"

"Da's English. He came here with my grandsire when he was about my age. He's told me stories about what it was like there, how different it was. I was just wondering … if you'd been there and what you thought of it?"

"I've never been to England, at least not yet. I was born in France."

"Oh. Is France far from England?"

"England is an island, like Long Island is but much larger. France is on the mainland of Europe. They are separated by the English Channel. It is much larger than the North River or Long Island Sound, though with a ship like this one, you can sail across it in a day or less, but from where I lived it took nearly a week to sail the distance up the coast."

Abraham jerked his head in acknowledgement.

They found an out-of-the-way place to sit on the lower deck and finished their sausages. Then Etienne pulled out a knife and a piece of wood he'd been carving and set to work.

Abraham watched him. "What are you making?"

"A dolphin," he replied and showed him the creature. "When I was about your age, I wanted to be a musketeer, and one of them gave me a carving he'd made of himself."

"Do you still have the figurine?"

"No. I gave it to a friend of mine on Manhattan Island three years ago."

"Why are you making a dolphin now?" Abraham asked. Etienne's eyes had not left his work through this whole discourse.

"My dreams have changed, so I decided it was time to make a new symbol of that. I've decided to become a sailor. I've watched the dolphins that often follow the ship. I think they represent a good life at sea. They always work as a team, like the sailors on a ship. I've even seen them work together to surround and kill sharks. They have the freedom of the seas and I've seen them at play. They seem to have so much fun! You should see the men when they are off-duty and the weather is calm. They know how to have fun too!" He smiled and a wave of sadness crossed his face.

"What's wrong?"

"I was remembering some of the sailor songs. Some are about the winds, the seas, and shipmates, but many also speak longingly of visiting or leaving women. I thought of Alsoomse and felt a pang of regret for leaving her behind."

"She seems nice … for a girl." Abraham said.

Etienne laughed. "You'll understand some day." He looked down at his carving. "The old seamen also say dolphins can provide help and guidance to sailors in trouble. I love to watch the dolphins as I work; it can be quite boring in the down times, so it's nice to have something to do. And dolphins are easier to carve than people!"

Abraham looked up startled and laughed. "You're doing a fine job."

"Thank you! I've been working on it since we boarded."

They sat in silence for a time before Abraham spoke again. "So, you have sailed on ships like this one before?"

"I have. I even worked on one before this." He told Abraham about his first voyage, where he'd had to flee France in the middle of the night and about the boarding and the storm. All the while, Abraham watched him eagerly.

"But you said you worked on another ship too. What about that one?"

Etienne laughed again. "You are so much like Louis – never satisfied with one story – always wanting more!" He described a trip across the Atlantic, being chased by Pirates, more storms, the fishing accident, scurvy, and getting beached on a sand bar. "The sea can be a dangerous place," he said, finally.

"It sounds exciting!" Abraham said. Then he looked up, gasped, and jumped to his feet.

Etienne followed his gaze and saw Abraham's father watching them.

"Thanks for the tour and the stories, but I should be going now."

"See you tomorrow?"

Abraham smiled and nodded.

Abraham joined his father.

"Who was that boy you were talking to?"

"His name is Etienne. He took me on a tour of the ship."

"I'm glad you've made a friend. I was wondering where you'd gotten to."

When they reached their cabin, Da sat down heavily in a wooden chair at the desk and opened a ledger book he'd brought with them on the trip. There was a soft knock at the door and Abraham went to answer it. A sailor was there holding a tray with two bowls of steaming stew. Abraham took them and thanked the man. He set one down on the desk for his father and sat on the floor to eat the other.

When he finished, he went to door and pulled the latch.

"Where are you going?" Da asked.

"I'm just going to explore a little more."

"Fine but leave the oil here. And don't be too long. It will be getting dark soon, and you can never trust sailors."

Abraham started to ask why, but then he shrugged and set the jug on the desk. He wandered to the kitchen where he found Paddy still at his stove.

"What can I do for ye, lad?" the big man asked.

"Do you know where there is a spare piece of wood I could have for carving?"

The man watched him for a moment and then nodded. He reached down to the wood pile he used to stoke his cooking fire and picked up a short, somewhat straight piece and handed it over. "Do you have a knife?"

"No."

Paddy smiled. "Then how'd ye expect to do much carving, lad?"

Abraham shrugged. "That's my next problem."

Paddy chuckled to himself and rummaged around in a box of odd bits and pieces until he found what he was looking for. He pulled up an old, beat-up knife. It was rusted and worn.

"The edge is dull, but we can fix that," he said. He pulled out a small porous stone and ran it along the edge of the blade. It took a while, but when he was satisfied, he picked up an old cloth and poured some oil into it. "Now you must oil the blade to keep it clean and free of rust," he said and handed the blade to Abraham.

"Thank you, sir!" Abraham said. He took the knife and held it carefully.

"I'm no sir!" Paddy said, laughing. "Be careful, you don't cut yer'self."

"I won't!" Abraham wrapped the blade in the oiled cloth and tucked it into his pocket. Then holding the piece of wood, he returned to his cabin.

When he entered, he saw Da hunched over the small desk pouring over his ledgers and journals. The bowl of stew, untouched and cold, sat beside him. Da grunted as Abraham shut the door behind him and climbed into his bunk. He turned the wood around in different directions to see how he might make a whale out of it. He started whittling the edges to remove the sharp corners and shape it so that it was larger at one end and narrower at the other.

Da stood up and stretched.

"What are you working on?" he asked and walked over to the bunk.

Abraham showed him. Da took the piece and rotated it in his hands. Then he looked at the knife and tested the edge. He handed them back. "Be sure to cut away from yourself, so you don't slice your hand."

"I will," Abraham replied.

"What are you trying to make?"

"A whale."

Da snorted and returned to the desk.

Abraham looked at the wood. He ran his hand along the edge and frowned. He let out a frustrated sigh as he wrapped the piece of wood and his knife into the cloth and slipped the bundle under his pillow. Da blew out the light and he was cloaked in darkness.

He lay listening to the creaking of the ship, the footfalls of the men above deck, and the waves hitting the hull as he fell asleep.

Chapter 2

Carvings and Hopes

When Abraham awoke the next morning, he dressed and accompanied Da to the galley for a bowl of porridge. Then he climbed the steps to the deck. He found a corner between the railing and the upper deck where he could sit and watch the sailors swarming over the ship like busy ants. He found a quiet spot and sat down to work on his whale.

By midday, Etienne again walked over and sat down beside him. "What are you working on?"

"It is supposed to be a whale," Abraham said as he showed Etienne the wood.

"It's coming along," Etienne said. He ran his hand along the larger end. "When the head's finished, you can use the tip of the blade to dig out the eyes, here and here." He pointed to places well back from the end.

Abraham smiled and looked at the carved block of wood. It still didn't look like much.

"Don't be discouraged. It will take time and patience," Etienne said and patted him on the shoulder.

"I don't know how to make the body, or the flukes, or the tail."

"You need to tapper the wood as you get to the other end, like this …" Etienne used his own knife to demonstrate. "And remember, whales have tails that are horizontal like dolphins, not vertical like fish."

Abraham nodded and took back his carving. Etienne took out his own carving and they worked together in silence for a while.

"Have you ever seen pirates up close?" Abraham asked. "I … I know they pursued your ship for a while, but, I mean, have you seen them in person?"

"Yes."

Abraham's eyes grew wide. "Really? What are they like?"

"They look like ordinary seamen, but they're dangerous. You'd best watch out for them, or they might try to kidnap you!"

"Kidnap me?" Abraham asked, skeptically.

"I know it sounds crazy, but believe me, there are more of them than you'd think."

"But if they don't look different from other sailors, how can you know who they are?" Abraham asked.

Etienne thought about it for a moment. "You can tell by the way they act. They are always looking at you to see what they can get from you. On the sea, you can tell by the way the ship behaves. Are they trying to cut you off and board you or just acknowledge your presence?"

Abraham considered this. "I don't see how you'd know just by looking at them."

Etienne smiled. "Well, in truth it is hard to tell. I worked for one, even lived in his home for months before I knew what he was."

"Really?" Abraham scrutinized Etienne's face dubiously.

Etienne grimaced. "My whole family lived in his house in Amsterdam. *Maman* cooked and cleaned, and Papa and I built him a stove. Then one day he had two of his henchmen kidnap me and take me to his ship."

"I don't believe you. You're making that up!"

"I am not! His name was Jacob Janssen van den Burgh. He smuggled slaves and sold them where he wasn't allowed."

"Then how'd you get away?"

Etienne told him the story of his escape from the storage room and flight up the mast, even his leap into the sea. As he talked, he found it easy to embellish certain aspects of his escape. The storage closet became a dungeon-like hold, the ropes became manacles and chains. Abraham followed his words with growing awe. Etienne was so brave and confident.

The wind picked up and the sailors were summoned to adjust the sails. Etienne hurried off to attend to his duties. Abraham watched him go. He seemed to know who he was and what he wanted to do. It must be great fun to be a sailor.

Later that afternoon, Abraham spotted Etienne sitting by himself sharpening his knife. He walked over to him. "That's a fine blade."

Etienne looked up at him and nodded. "My father bought it for me in Amsterdam before we came here."

"Europe must be an exciting place," Abraham said. "Nothing ever happens on Long Island though."

"What do you mean nothing ever happens?" Etienne asked, surprised. "Didn't you hear about how the Esopus attacked the Dutch settlement up north? Everyone on Manhattan was afraid of Indian attacks and was building fortifications. I can't believe they didn't hear about it on Long Island!"

"Oh, they did. The Shinnecock and Montauks were talking about what they'd do if the conflict moved south. And Da went to a meeting with the other English colonists to discuss it, but not much came of it."

"I'm surprised. I even had to go help rescue a couple of women and some children."

"Wow," Abraham said, his eyes getting big. "Did you kill anyone?"

"No, but I very nearly got caught by the warriors guarding the prisoners. If Alsoomse and her brother hadn't led them away, I'd have been caught for sure."

Abraham grinned. "Alsoomse isn't like most Indian girls. I've never known a Montauk girl to make friends with a boy. They don't even talk to boys that aren't family, until they are courted."

"You are right about that. Her mother doesn't like me and doesn't want her to be my friend. She is always trying to keep her home, but Alsoomse doesn't want to be confined. She's not like typical European girls either!"

They both laughed. Then Abraham said, "Someday I want to have adventures like you. All I get to do is help Mum in the fields. Da won't even let me help him in the shop. He is a cordwainer; he makes new shoes, like my grandsire did before him, though sometimes he does the cobber's job of repairing old shoes."

"Why doesn't your father let you help him?"

"He says that I'm just in the way. He has my two older brothers to help him, and there isn't a lot of business anyway."

"Do you want to be a cordwainer?"

Abraham thought for a moment. "I'd much rather be a sailor or an explorer and visit strange lands."

Etienne looked at Abraham and smiled. "Four years ago, all I wanted was to become a musketeer. I wanted to have adventures too, but my Papa made cooking stoves out of stone for wealthy families. I knew I was going to have to be a stove-maker merchant, just like him. But now I'm a sailor and I don't regret not becoming a musketeer. Who knows what will happen for you in a few years?"

Abraham gripped his jug tighter and turned to look off over the water. He thought about his prospects. They'd never had much. Mum raised crops in the traditional Indian way. Da and his older brothers fished and hunted, and Da made small sums of money from making or fixing shoes for the things they couldn't make themselves. It was never enough though, and that was why they were traveling to Boston to get the money for a new business.

He glanced at Etienne. He too seemed lost in his own thoughts as they both stared out over the water. Abraham took a deep breath. This new venture was his only hope for adventure. It *had* to succeed!

A bell rang, and Etienne bobbed his head at Abraham and darted off. Abraham watched the older boy as he ran up the mast and moved along the cross beams. He heard a puff, turned, and gazed out over the water. The large grey back of a whale slid beneath the waves.

Last February a whale had washed up on the shore near Southampton on the southeastern coast of Long Island where Abraham and his family lived. Months later, he remembered coming home from helping Mum with the harvest to find Da sitting at the kitchen table with his older brothers Sam and Ralph. His great-uncle Ahanu, whose name meant *One Who Laughs*, and his cousin Japhet, who was a few years older than he, were also there. As Abraham had approached, he saw a long wooden spear with a barbed point carved out of whale rib. A length of cedar rope was tied to the other end of the harpoon. A clay jar filled with the whale oil also sat on the table.

The men looked up at him as he'd come to stand beside the table.

"Abraham, your uncle was telling us about how his people have hunted whales in large dug-out canoes that each held a hundred men. They used harpoons like this one," he'd pointed to the long spear. "East Hampton is already developing a whaling industry. There's a lot of money to be made in selling whale oil and baleen. Drift whales must be shared by the whole community, but if we were to hunt them, then the rights to the whale would be ours alone. All we need is startup funds so we can purchase boats, harpoons, vats to render the blubber into oil, and to pay a cooper to supply the barrels."

"How will we get the money?" he'd asked.

"My father knew an investor in Boston that we might persuade to front the money," Da replied.

"We'll need more men too," Sam said.

"I can find men to help us," Uncle Ahanu said. "Our people are becoming dependent on the goods your people make. They will readily agree to the work for the opportunity to make the money to buy them."

It'd been true; before Abraham and Da packed to leave for Boston, Uncle Ahanu had lined up enough Montaukett and Shinnecock men to fill three large rowboats. Now they just needed the money to purchase the tools and supplies.

After several more days of sailing, the coast of New England was visible in the distance. It looked like they were rounding a thin hook-shaped peninsula of land. Etienne said they'd arrive in Boston soon. Again, Abraham was on deck watching Etienne. The older boy talked to him whenever his duties permitted it. With Etienne's help, the carving he was making though crude, was starting to look like a whale. Etienne had finished his dolphin and oiled it up nicely.

A few hours later the ship slid into the bay. Abraham watched as Etienne hurried to help take in the sails and ready the ship for anchor. As Etienne passed him, he held out his hand and slipped the carved dolphin into his hand.

"Good luck on whatever business brings you to Boston. Maybe we'll meet again sometime."

Abraham looked down and the dolphin, smiled up at him, and hurried off to join his father. He was still clutching his jar in his other hand as he stood beside his father and waited for the rowboat that would carry them to shore. Abraham looked up at Etienne, as he tied up the jib sail. Then the young seaman turned and smiled back at him.

After the ship was anchored, Captain Jolls called upon Etienne to help row Abraham and his father to shore. The harbor was crowded with sailors, merchants, and their customers, many of whom were wearing somber, unadorned clothing, like a flock of ravens greedily hunting for shiny baubles or brightly colored berries. As the captain and Etienne stated to leave them, Da called out to Captain Jolls.

"Do you know, Sir, where we might find iron whaling harpoons?"

"You won't find any of those here," Captain Jolls said, "but after we pick up some more cargo, we're heading to Europe. We will be stopping in London first. I could inquire there, or if not there, Texel is a whaling town in Holland. I could easily acquire harpoons there for you. I am on my way to meet with my brother, Robert, but if you would walk with me, we can discuss the terms?"

"But Da ..." Abraham started to protest, but his father held up a hand to silence him.

"Abraham you may stay here with that young seaman. I will be back directly."

Abraham scowled and clutched the jar tighter as he watched his father's retreating form.

"So, you want to hunt whales?" Etienne asked.

"Yes. Da says there is a lot of money to be made from whale oil." Abraham replied.

"Isn't it dangerous? I mean, have you ever seen a whale up close? I've seen many on the trip over the Atlantic. One came right alongside us. It was as large as our whole ship – maybe larger. I didn't see the whole thing since it'd been partly submerged."

"Of course, I've seen a whale! I bet I've even seen more than you have! One washed onto the beach near our town. We butchered it and boiled its blubber into oil." He thrust the jar out to show him. "My Montauk family has been hunting them in dugout canoes for generations. We even have a ceremony we perform on the whale before we cut into it. My uncle Ahanu says that *mishe podtap*, the great whale, has great significance to our people. It's a gift from the Great Spirit and has sustained our people's need for nourishment and spirit for many generations. That's why we honor the spirit of the animal and give thanks to the Great Spirit for its creation."

Etienne raised his eyebrows. "That's amazing! I bet you are proud to be Montauk."

"I am. And this jar of oil," Abraham continued, holding out the jar he was carrying, "is all my family has left of the barrel of oil we were allotted."

Etienne smiled and nodded respectfully. "Will you be going out with the boats too?"

Abraham snorted. "Of course, I will. I am nearly a man grown."

Abraham saw the corners of Etienne's mouth lift into a grin. "Well, then, good luck to you. I wish you great success. I hope someday you'll tell me all about it."

Just then Abraham's father returned and called for him to go. Before he left, he said, "I hope I see you again. Then you can also tell me of your voyage to Europe."

Etienne nodded, smiled, and watched them as they retreated along the street.

Amanda M Cetas

Chapter 3

Spilled Oil

Abraham hurried after his father, still clutching the jar of precious whale oil. He hoped he would see the young seaman again someday.

"Do not, ever, question my actions before others," his father said. He sounded angry.

"I wasn't trying to …"

"I know what I am doing. It is not your place to question me."

"But I just thought we should be sure of getting the money first."

"I don't care what you thought. You are just a boy. You don't know how things work. We must get those harpoons. And we will get the money if I must mortgage everything I own."

"But Uncle Ahanu could show us how to make harpoons like my Indian ancestors did. They wouldn't cost anything."

Da slowed down and turned to look at him. "You want us to go out to hunt the great beasts with fragile bone-tipped spears on flimsy wooden shafts that could easily break or pull free? What is the matter with you?"

"But if my ancestors could do it, why can't we?"

"You are English. Your ancestors were skilled tradesmen and entrepreneurs who would not risk their lives needlessly with inferior tools!"

Abraham felt a burning in his eyes but angrily forced it away. "But Mum is …"

"I know who your mother is, and we will not speak of it here."

He felt anger and shame both welling up inside him and stopped abruptly. He refused to go farther.

"You're ashamed of her. That's why you insist she wears the English-style clothing when we go out…"

"Enough! Now is not the time to have his conversation. Come, we must find this investor."

Frowning, Abraham followed his father. After inquiring of several locals, they finally found the investor ensconced in his office at one of the few brick buildings. The sign read *Investments and Loans*. They climbed the steps and pushed open the door.

They entered a small reception room with wooden benches standing in front of the windows on the street-side of the room. A young man sat opposite them at a tall desk pouring over a large bound ledger. He dipped his quill into a jar of ink, scratched something into the ledger, and then looked up to acknowledge them.

"We are looking for a Mr. Jonathan King," Da said, stepping forward. "Is he in?"

The young man's eyes drifted up and down, assessing Da. He rubbed his nose, smearing ink across it in a dark smudge. He was an odd sort and reminded Abraham of the blue herons that hunted for clams in the tidal waters along Peconic Bay.

"Do you have an appointment?" The man's voice was high-pitched like a girl's and cracked on the last word.

"No. I have only just arrived from Long Island."

"Then excuse me for a moment and I will inquire whether he will see you."

The man climbed off his stool and ambled off towards a side door. Abraham nearly laughed from surprise. The man even walked like a heron, his head bobbing on the end of his long neck as he walked. The man rapped on the door, and after a pause, entered and closed it firmly behind him. After a few moments, he returned and motioned for them to follow.

"Mr. King will see you now," he said and held the door open for them to enter. Then he turned and close the door again.

The room was dominated by a large oak desk with two wooden chairs standing in front of it. Behind it sat a stout man in a starched white shirt and ruby colored vest stretched over his ample belly. He motioned for them to sit in the wooden chairs. The man was clean-shaven and wore a wig of brown curls that hung to his shoulders.

He stood and held out his hand. Da took it, shook it, and then settled onto the hard, wooden seat.

"What may I do for you?"

"I need to take out a loan," Da said.

"Indeed? And the purpose of this loan?"

"I wish to start a whaling venture off the coast of Long Island. I will need to purchase the boats, harpoons, other necessary tools and supplies."

"You know how to do this thing?" Mr. King eyed my father skeptically.

"Show him, son."

Abraham placed the jar of oil on the desk and pushed it toward Mr. King. He took it, broke the wax seal, and opened the jar. He sniffed it, stuck his finger in the jar, brought out a bit of oil, and rubbed it between his fingers. Then he held the oil up to the light and examined its buttery color. Mr. King nodded in approval, replaced the stopper on the jar, and handed it back.

"This is of fine quality. How much money do you need?"

"Fifteen pounds," Da replied.

"That is a lot to risk, unsecured," Mr. King said and rubbed his chin. "Do you have any collateral?"

"I have my house and lot at North Sea, near the town of Southampton on Long Island."

"And there are no current liens on the property?"

"No, sir."

"I will consider your request. Return in a week and I will have an answer for you."

Da stood and shook hands with Mr. King. Then he turned and headed toward the door with Abraham following closely behind him. After they left Mr. King's office, they went to arrange a room for the night in one of the tavern houses near the pier. Then they went back to the docks to book their return voyage. Captain Thomas Jolls was there with Etienne loading a small rowboat with supplies for their voyage.

"Excuse me, sir," Da said. "Do you know where we might find a ship heading back to Long Island?"

"My brother, Robert, is working on a small ketch that trades up and down the coast. Come, I'll show you."

Abraham followed the captain and his father as they walked along the deck. Etienne tossed the last item into the boat and ran to catch up with him.

"Did you and your father get the money you needed for the whaling venture?"

"Maybe. The investor said he would consider our request," Abraham replied.

"Are you worried he won't give you the loan?"

"Mr. King seemed happy with the oil." Abraham paused. "I don't know. Something feels wrong, but I don't know what it is."

"Like a premonition?" Etienne asked.

"Maybe. I thought I'd felt an evil manitou cross my path when we left the investor's office." Abraham paused again and looked up at the young sailor. "You must think I'm crazy."

"Alsoomse says they are like evil spirits that try to make trouble for people. I guess we'd call them demons."

"We? Do you think I am Christian like you?"

"Aren't you? I mean you are English, and most English are Protestants too, though the Anglicans and Calvinists don't always agree...."

"My father is English, but he ... Da takes us to church because it is expected."

Etienne cocked his head to look at him.

"I meant no offense. Do you practice your mother's Indian religion then?"

"No! I mean ..." Abraham sighed. He took a deep breath and let it out slowly, and felt the anger subside. "Mum has converted to Christianity. I don't know ... I go because I must."

Etienne nodded and gave him a sympathetic look. Abraham felt the anger rising again. They'd reached a second, smaller pier and turned onto it. As he followed the men, Abraham stumbled, caught his toe on the wooden lip, and crashed face down onto the greying boards. He cried out in horror as the jar of precious oil shattered beneath him and the pale-yellow oil ran between the wooden slats and dripped into the foamy, green saltwater.

He saw Etienne flinch as the curse slipped out of lips before he could pull them back. Then he heard footsteps hurrying towards him. Da yanked him to his feet and slapped him hard across the face.

"I'm sorry, Da! I didn't mean to break it."

"Break it?" Da said, sounding startled.

Abraham watched his father survey the broken pottery shards and oil-soaked deck. He looked down and saw that his shirt was ruined and blood was dripping from a deep cut in his left hand. He frowned and stared hard at the deck trying with all his will to drill a hole in it to suck him down into the lapping water below.

He heard his father sigh, and Da lifted his head with a calloused hand so that their eyes met.

"That was not for the spilt oil, Son. That was for taking the Lord's name in vain. The oil's served its purpose. Lord willing, we will have the money soon. We'll have more oil soon enough." Da looked him up and down again and said, "Stay here and collect yourself, while I go book our voyage home."

"I'm such a fool!" Abraham said, angrily and kicked at a mooring.

"Here, let me see your hand," Etienne said, gently.

Abraham turned to look at him and held out his hand. It did hurt. Blood was running freely mixing with the oil on the pier.

Etienne pulled the bandana from around his throat and folded it into a long strip, which he then wrapped tightly around the injured hand and tied it off neatly.

"There, that'll keep the dirt out and stop the bleeding."

"Thank you." Abraham felt foolish and embarrassed.

"Come on, I've some money. Let's get a quick bite to eat."

Etienne led them to a small tavern where they each ordered clam soup and a pint of cider. While they ate, Etienne told him of his cousin, Nicolas, and how they'd fenced together in his cousin's back courtyard. He told him how he'd had to leave, and about Magdalena and Amsterdam.

"I'm hoping to have time to look for her when we get back there."

"I'm sure she'd like that," Abraham said. "Tell me how it goes when you get back."

Etienne smiled. "I will."

Just then Da came into the doorway. "There you are. Good. I've secured a place for us on the *Sparrow*. I'll need your help getting the rest of the supplies."

"Coming." He turned to Etienne and extended his uninjured right hand, which Etienne took. "Thank you for the bandage and the meal. I hope I see you again."

Etienne smiled and nodded.

Abraham nodded in return and left with his father to arrange for the rest of the supplies they would need for their new business — large iron try pots for boiling blubber, long lengths of rope to tie to the harpoons, barrels for the oil, and cleavers for cutting up the flesh. It was late when they finally returned to the tavern for a warm supper and a bed for the night.

Chapter 4

Recognition

Etienne, September 27, 1663

I t smelled like rain, but it didn't look like it. The clouds were still wispy and sparse, though I could see them building off in the distance. I thought again of the young boy, Abraham, whom I'd met on the voyage to Boston. I thought about how fiercely he'd protected the jug of oil when I'd first met him, as if I would try to steal it from him. Maybe that fierceness was what remined me of my brother. *Abraham is so determined to go out whaling with his father.* I shook my head as I swabbed the deck. How does the boy think he will be able to take on the great behemoths of the sea? But he seems to have no fear....

"Etienne, quit your daydreaming and get back to work!"

I jerked my head up and saw Mr. Palmer approaching. He was studying me as he came to stand inches from my face. Suddenly, I saw the recognition spread across his features, and his lips curled up into a sneer that showed his crooked yellow teeth.

"So, you are *lazy,* as well as a thief. I will have to keep a sharp eye on you."

I could feel anger rising inside of me and clenched my jaw.

"I'm not lazy, and I'm not a thief," I said between my teeth.

Mr. Palmer leaned in close, and I could smell his foul breath. "Don't argue with me, Boy. I will have a word with the captain, and if I see you put one foot out of line, you will answer for it!"

Mr. Palmer turned on his heal and strode off.

I grimaced and returned to work. The wind was growing colder, and the clouds were darkening. It might rain after all.

Chapter 5

Pretense and Omens

Abraham, October 4, 1663

Abraham and his father left the Three Cranes Tavern where they had been staying for the past week and walked along the busy town docks to the bustling market center. As they approached the Boston Meeting Hall, he saw the red brick building with the sign that read *Investments and Loans*. The bell tinkled as Da pushed the door open. Once again, the gangly-looking, young man was sitting at the high table at the back of the room. The man looked up from his ledger.

"So, you're back," the man said in his high-pitched, girlish voice.

"We are here to see Mr. King," Da said.

"Do you have an appointment?" The young man said and looked them over.

"Yes," Da said confidently.

Abraham smiled at the man's awkward gait as he crossed the

floor towards Mr. King's office. The young apprentice knocked on the door, opened it, and thrust his head inside. After a moment he pulled his head back out, bobbed up and down, and then motioned them over. As they entered the room, Mr. King hefted his immense bulk up from his seat behind the massive oak desk. He leaned forward to shake Da's hand, nearly bursting the buttons from his velvet jade vest.

"Good afternoon, Mr. Dayton. It is good to see you again," Mr. King said, smiling broadly. "Please have a seat."

Da and Abraham sat in the two wooden chairs proffered across the desk from Mr. King, as he took out a sheet of paper. He stared at some scribbles he had written there for a moment and scratched his cleanly shaven chin in thought.

Abraham listened to a ticking sound coming from behind them. He turned to see a tall, narrow oak tower on the back wall. It was a curious device with a round disc near the top and two small arrows that seemed to be moving around from a center point. Numbers from one to twelve had been spaced out around the disc. As Abraham turned back around, Mr. King looked up from his notes.

"After some consideration, I have decided to loan you the money you requested to start your business venture," Mr. King said. "I am offering terms at 15% interest to be repaid in full by the first of December next year. Is this acceptable?"

"Yes, sir. Thank you," Da said, smiling broadly.

Mr. King scratched out some calculations on a slip of paper. When he finished, he looked up again and said, "For the loan of fifteen pounds, I will expect repayment in the amount of seventeen pounds, two shillings, seven pennies. Are we agreed?"

Da nodded. Then he stood and shook Mr. King's hand.

"Very good. Then I will have Henry draw up the mortgage papers." Mr. King excused himself and left the room; Da sank back into his chair to wait.

The device on the back wall continued to tick. Abraham found himself counting them. One … two … three … the sound was hypnotic, and he felt his eyes growing heavy. He looked over at Da. He was sitting immobile and erect, staring out of the window, lost in thought. Worry lines creased his forehead. Sixty-seven … sixty-eight …the noise of horses, wagons, and vendors calling out their wares drifted in through the open window. Sea gulls screeched in the distance, and a dog barked. Da wiped a bead of sweat from his brow, even though a cool breeze was blowing through the window rustling the papers on Mr. King's desk. One hundred twenty-three … the door opened, and Da took a deep breath.

Mr. King entered with a written document in his hand. Da plastered a smile onto his face as Mr. King resumed his seat. He handed the document to Da, who carefully looked it over. Then Da nodded and took up the quill Mr. King offered. He signed his name at the bottom and slid the document back over to Mr. King, who also signed his name with a flourish. Mr. King counted out the fifteen pounds and pushed them towards Da, who collected the money and stowed it in his small leather purse. Then he rose and shook hands with Mr. King again. He turned, placed a hand on Abraham's shoulder, and directed him out of the office.

As they walked out into the afternoon sun, Abraham heard a screech and looked up. A crow was staring at him cockeyed from the sign over the doorway. He felt a shiver as an evil omen seemed to pass over him. There was no doubt now that trouble was coming.

"Da, look!" Abraham pointed at the crow.

Da paused and looked at the bird. "It's just a crow. Come. We have much to do."

"But Da, it's a bad omen," Abraham protested.

"Nonsense! Silly superstition."

Abraham huffed angrily and hurried to catch up. As he fell in beside Da, he fingered the strand of wampum that hung around his neck and thought of his mother. Last time he'd seen her, she was in the fields harvesting the ears of corn from the now-brown stalks. The beans that had eagerly climbed up the stalks in the spring had been harvested weeks ago; the remaining vines were brittle and dry. In the valleys between the corn mounds, the squash and melon leaves were yellowed and wilting, revealing the large dark green watermelons, large green and yellow striped squash, and sandy-colored gourds with long heron-like necks.

He smiled as he remembered how Mum had looked up at him and smiled, with the large basket of corn in her arms. He had gone to help her, but she had shaken her head and her long black braid had slipped over her shoulder.

This is woman's work, Abraham. Your father is resoling a pair of shoes. Go and see if he will let you help.

He looked over at his father as they walked. His brown velvet jacket was showing its age. He had trimmed his beard into a neat point at his chin and waxed his full mustache. Grandda had come from a wealthy family, from somewhere back in England. Now his father was just a poor man clinging to a life that no longer existed. But at least Da knew who he was and what he wanted to become. Abraham grimaced and looked down at his tanned hands. Soon, they would return home. It would be good to go home.

The journey home was not nearly as interesting without Etienne. The young seaman was only a couple of years older than him, but he had already experienced many great adventures.

Abraham longed for his own great adventure. He hoped this whaling business would be his chance. Whales were a gift from the Great Spirit. Uncle Ahanu had told him so.

Abraham stood by the railing and stared out at the sea. He could see where schools of fish must be clustered because of the large flocks of birds circling and diving overhead. He'd also seen sharks prowling the water between the ship and the shore. Sharks were another bad omen. Abraham fingered the carved dolphin Etienne had given him and searched the waters. Dolphins were known to chase sharks away. They were often seen in these waters too, but they could be elusive.

As the ship rounded the eastern end of Long Island, Abraham thought about jumping overboard and swimming home. It would be easy and certainly quicker than sailing all the way back to New Amsterdam just to row back out here. He couldn't wait to see his mum and his brothers again … and to put an end to this enduring silence.

As he brooded, a shadow fell across him, and he looked up to see his Da standing there.

"Almost home."

Abraham nodded.

"I'll have to commission the barrels we need before we head home; there are more coopers in the city than in Southampton."

Abraham nodded again.

"Then we'll have to start work on the lookout tower."

"I can't wait to go hunting for whales," Abraham said softly, imagining the excitement of the chase.

Da only grunted and turned away. "Come, we must retrieve our belongings before we reach the docks."

Abraham turned and followed his father back to their cabin.

Several days later, they arrived back in New Amsterdam harbor and Da went to make arrangements to have the barrels made. Abraham was relegated to watching over the boxes and bundles that held the other supplies they'd purchased in Boston. As he stood looking out over the tumbling waves, he scowled in frustration. Why couldn't he be more like his older brothers, Ralph and Sam?

He felt a presence come up beside him and turned to see the tall Lenape girl he'd seen with Etienne before they'd left. *What was her name? Oh right, Alsoomse.* He smiled at her.

She smiled back and turned to look out over the sea. "Is Etienne well, do you think?"

He nodded. "I think so. He's bound for England on *The Dolphin*. I haven't seen him for seventeen days now. But he was well when I last saw him."

Alsoomse nodded. "When do you think he will return?"

"Da says that we won't see any ships coming back from Europe until spring, at the earliest."

She nodded again. "My people are leaving soon for our winter village, but I am worried for him. I've had a recurring dream about a dolphin that is eaten by a shark."

Abraham turned to look at her. "Usually, the dolphins chase away the sharks."

"That's true," she replied and continued to stare out over the sea. "That's why I am afraid for him."

"I will keep watch for him while you are gone."

At this, she turned to look at him. She gave him a small smile.

"Thank you, Abraham. I will find you when we return to *Manahatta.*"

"Then I'll watch out for both of you," Abraham said and smiled.

She nodded again and left just as Da approached.

Together they retrieved their rowboat and loaded the whaling supplies into the hull. Then they took up the oars to take themselves home. They rowed in silence, the uneasy stillness broken only by the screeching of the sea gulls and the lapping of the surf. It took three days before they arrived on the shore near East Hampton. As they landed, Abraham's brothers Ralph and Sam came to greet them.

"Hello Sons," Da said and smiled. He climbed out of the boat and embraced Ralph and then Sam. "I trust everything is in order at home?"

"Yes," Ralph replied and held out a coin. "Mr. Gregor came to have his shoes repaired, but it wasn't difficult. The shoe just needed restitching."

Da took the coin, nodded, and turned toward Sam. "How was the fishing?"

"Good. We caught several large bass. Mum is smoking them now."

Abraham climbed out of the boat and Ralph came over to help him pull it farther up onto the shore so that it wouldn't get swept away at the high tide.

Smiling, Ralph reached out a hand and mussed up Abraham's hair. "How was Boston?"

Abraham thought for a moment. "Da got the money we need, and I made a new friend on the ship. But I have a feeling that something bad is going to happen."

Ralph eyed him. "You're probably worrying over nothing."

Abraham shrugged. "Maybe."

Da interrupted their conversation and told them to take care of the supplies. Then he mumbled something about going to find Uncle Ahanu and, left the three boys standing on the beach.

Sam scowled and grabbed some of the supplies from the boat and headed up the path to their farm. Ralph and Abraham took up the remaining bags and, they followed their brother more slowly.

"Tell me what the city was like. I'm a little jealous that Da took you instead of me," Ralph said as they walked.

"It was busy, noisy, and smelled of stale fish and tobacco. Not much different from New Amsterdam, except it didn't have any canals and most everyone was English. There were one or two Africans, but I didn't see any Indians in town. I think Da is ashamed of me."

"He is not ashamed of you," Ralph said. His tone was serious. "Da is worried about how people will treat you. There are many who look down on halfbreeds."

"Why?"

"I don't know. Some people fear what they don't understand."

Abraham was quiet for a moment. "It's more than that. Da barely spoke to me the whole trip. And then I broke the jug of whale oil. I suppose he's still mad at me for that too."

"Da loves you, Abraham. He just doesn't know how to talk to you." Ralph laughed. "Don't worry about it. You are always so serious!"

Ralph ran to catch up with Sam, and Abraham walked home alone. After dropping his burden off at the barn, he went to find Mum. She was in the fields harvesting.

Abraham paused for a moment to watch as his mother gathered the large, hook-necked squash from their withered vines. The large striped fruit were scattered over the ground among bright green watermelons, orange pumpkins, and sandy-colored gourds, like giant beads from a broken necklace. As he approached, Mum turned to face him with a large squash resting on each hip. He hurried over to take them from her.

"How was Boston?"

"Fine, I guess."

"Did your *noshi* get what he needed?"

Abraham looked down at the ground. "Yes."

"What's wrong?" Mum asked. An edge of concern cut through her words.

"I broke the jug and spilled the oil into the sea."

Mum blew out a breath and smiled to reassure him. "It is good to give an offering back to Great Spirit who gave us the whale. I am sure God is pleased, even if your *noshi* is not. Now let's get these to the root cellars."

Abraham helped Mum make many trips carrying the squash from the fields to the pits dug in the ground behind the house. Together they stacked them beside tightly woven and lidded baskets filled with beautiful multi-colored corn kernels and others filled with black or tan beans. Soon the melons, and gourds would be added filling any remaining space. Some of the harvest would fill the shelves in the pantry off the kitchen, but the rest would be stored here until needed. The pit would be covered with a lattice work of young saplings and branches, and then topped with leaves and earth to preserve the food stores through the winter.

Ralph and Sam had already begun chopping down trees for the lumber needed for the whale lookout tower. It had been piled along the beach beyond the water line. The lookout tower would have to be built farther back on the grassy dunes for the best vantage point. Once all the lumber was gathered, the lookout tower would go up quickly, reaching over twelve feet into the sky. A platform would be built on top with a ladder to reach it. The design would resemble those his mother's people made near their fields, where children would perch to watch over the crops and scare the birds away, only this tower would be much taller.

Abraham returned to the fields for another load of squash. Whaling season couldn't come fast enough!

Chapter 6

Celebrations

Abraham was helping his mum prepare and pack up a portion of the harvested corn, squash, and melons to bring to the harvest festival they celebrated each fall with her Montaukett people. As he packed the food into large baskets set on top of the long kitchen table, the door on the far wall opened and Ralph and Sam walked inside. The smell of fish clung to them, and they removed their heavy aprons and hung them on pegs by the door.

"The fish has been cleaned and loaded into the wagon, Mum," Ralph said, brushing something off his breeches. He'd rolled up his shirt sleeves to the elbows, showing his muscular forearms.

"Thank you, Boys," Mum said as she wiped her brow with the back of her hand. "Could you load these baskets into the wagon for me?" Then she stretched and rubbed the small of her back, her swollen belly protruding over the table.

Ralph and Sam both nodded and walked over to retrieve a large basket apiece. There was one left on the table, so Abraham quickly picked it up and followed his brothers outside. Da was adjusting the harness on the horse as they approached the wagon and stowed the baskets in the back beside the barrel of fish.

"Aren't you going to change before we go?" Abraham asked Sam.

"Why? What's wrong with what I'm wearing?" He looked down at himself.

"You can't play in the ball game wearing that," Abraham replied.

"We'll change before it begins," Ralph said. He patted Abraham on the shoulder. "Besides the games don't start until tomorrow morning."

"Well, you could try to look less … English!" Abraham said, frowning. "You'll look out of place."

But Ralph and Sam both laughed and went back into the house. Abraham walked over to Da. "Can I play in the ball game this year? I'm as old now as Sam was when he started playing."

"Sam was bigger than you are. You'll get hurt. Better wait another year or two."

"But Da, that's not fair. I am old enough …"

"You aren't ready, and I won't hear any more about it."

Abraham turned to see his younger brothers, Isaac, Jacob, and Caleb, laughing and chasing each other around the front yard. All three were dressed, like he was, in the traditional Montaukett clothing with breech cloths and leggings, though with English-style cotton shirts. Only Caleb shared his and his mother's dark complexion, hair, and eyes.

"Quit running around. We will be leaving soon." Abraham yelled at his little brothers.

"Why are you so grumpy?" Isaac asked. "We're just playing tag while we wait."

Isaac was eight now, nearly three years younger than he was, since he would turn eleven in December. Jacob was six, and Caleb was only four years old.

"Someone's going to get hurt!"

"You're just mad because Da won't let you play in the ball game!"

Ralph and Sam had finished loading the wagon and were standing with Da discussing the plans for the whaling venture. They were fourteen and twelve now and were considered men by both sides of his family. Abraham both envied and resented the special privileges and treatment they received as befitting their positions in the family. As he walked over to join the discussion, Ralph turned to him.

"Have the boat crews been chosen yet?" Abraham asked.

"Yes," Ralph replied. "We'll start with three teams. Da and Sammy will lead one, Japhet and his father another, and I will take the third."

"Then does that mean I will be with you?" Abraham asked.

Ralph shook his head. "Da said you're not going out in the boats. I will be going with one of Da's friends from East Hampton."

"Why can't I go? I've been out fishing before. I know the sea as well as Sam does and I'm nearly his age too."

"You are not ready for men's work," Sam scoffed. "And besides, you're a mama's boy."

"I am not!" Abraham felt his face flush with anger.

"You're too young and too small. You would only get hurt, or worse, you'd get us all killed," Ralph said.

"I would not!" He stepped forward, his hands balled into fists.

"Abraham, get your little brothers into the wagon," Da said.

"Why did you take me to Boston if you didn't plan on letting me help?" Abraham asked, turning to Da.

"Because your mother asked me to. Now go and do as I said."

Abraham turned on his heel and stalked off to round up his brothers. Most other boys had already started apprenticing by now. It wasn't fair! "Isaac, time to go. Bring Caleb with you. Jacob, let's go!"

"You don't need to yell," Jacob grumbled. He ran over and climbed into the wagon.

Isaac came too, dragging Caleb behind him. He scowled at Abraham as he passed.

Abraham bent down and helped Caleb into the wagon.

"I'm sorry, Abram. Don't be mad," Caleb said.

"I didn't mean to yell at you," Abraham said. He brushed hair from Caleb's face. "I'm not mad at you anyway."

Caleb smiled up at him and hugged him. Then he sat down in the wagon with the other two brothers. Mum came out of the house carrying a large iron pot. Abraham quickly went over to take the pot from her and stowed it in the wagon. She was wearing a beaded deerskin dress and had braided her hair into two cords resting on each shoulder. Strands of beads and feathers were woven into tiny braids that were then woven into the larger ones. She looked beautiful. Mum always looked forward to the festival and spending time with her family.

Da offered to help Mum into the wagon, but she shook her head.

"I will walk with Abraham, Husband," she said. "It will make the baby strong."

Da nodded and climbed into the wagon; Sam took the seat beside him. The wagon was fully loaded with food, supplies, and his younger brothers. Ralph mounted his own horse, and Abraham and Mum walked behind the wagon.

His mother stooped to catch a feather as it twirled and spun on the breeze. It was a large brown feather with a white tip. "An eagle feather for you, *Aranck*," Mum said, smiling at Abraham. She quickly knotted it into his hair. "It is good luck."

The wagon had moved a little distance from them now. Mum took his face in her hands and looked directly into his eyes. "You must be patient with your father. He does not understand you. You are not like Ralph and Sammy in disposition, but he *is* trying. He took you to Boston with him so that he might get to know you better."

"Yes, but only because you made him do it, and he hardly spoke to me the whole time!" Abraham pulled away.

"Your father is a man of dreams and ambition, but not a man of words. He sees what he wants the world to be like but does not always see it as it truly is. He sees empathy as weakness, not as the great gift it is."

Abraham scowled and looked down at the dirt road as they walked on in silence.

The family arrived at the Montauk village amid a flurry of activity. Women were preparing vegetables in the cooking shelter and adding them to large clay pots simmering over small fires along the edges. The shelter was a large rectangular area with a roof made of young saplings and straight branches laid across each other, but without walls, designed to give shade and to allow cooling breezes to blow through. Men sat in groups talking and smoking in the men's lean-tos. Da and Abraham's older brothers tied up the horses and went to join them. His younger brothers quickly jumped out of the wagon and ran off to play games with the other boys in the lean-to on the far side of the village. Abraham sighed and started to help his mother unload the wagon.

"I don't see why they can't help too."

"It is not men's work, Abraham. You know this. I do not expect you to help me either."

"You don't have any daughters to help you. I don't mind."

"Medlen! I am so happy to see you, Daughter."

Abraham looked up to see his grandmother approaching. Her long hair was still mostly black, though streaks of grey ran through it, like a skunk's pelt, and several eagle feathers were woven into it. Her face and hands looked like old leather, but her eyes were welcoming and joyful. She wore a fine white deerskin dress with a large wampum belt cinched at her waist. Half a dozen strands of the purple and white beads hung around her neck as befitted her important position in the tribe.

Grandmother greeted Mum by taking her arms in her own.

"How is the child?" she asked.

"It is strong. It keeps me awake at night with its constant moving."

Grandmother smiled. "It sits lower than your others. I think it will be a girl."

"That would be nice," Mum replied, placing a hand gently on her belly.

Grandmother turned and smiled at Abraham. Then she made a shooing motion with her hands.

"It is good to see you too, Grandson. Now go and join the other boys. I will help your mother. I think they are playing a game of moccasins."

With that grandmother took Mum's arm and pulled her over to

the cooking harbor. Abraham was left to wander through the village alone. He noticed the younger girls playing with their dolls in the shadow of a *wetu*, a small summer house. At the back of the village a knot of older boys huddled together in a close circle beneath another lean-to. As Abraham approached, his cousin, Japhet, nodded to him and he went to join him.

Japhet stood and embraced Abraham.

"It is good to see you Cousin! You are taller than the last time I saw you."

Abraham smiled and stood up straighter. "Do you think so?"

Japhet nodded and slapped him on the shoulder. "Come let's watch the game."

The boys were playing the Moccasin Game. Four moccasins sat in the middle of the circle. The boys were staring intently at them while one boy had his hand out ready to choose. The singer on his team was offering encouragements, while the singer on the other team berated the seeker with taunts. The seeker picked up one of the moccasins and turned it over. Nothing. The other team erupted with cheers, while his singer offered encouragements. He picked up another moccasin. Again nothing. The opposing side was becoming quite unruly now. The boy picked up the third moccasin and turned it over. A pebble dropped out onto the ground. His team cheered and the keeper picked up the pebble and held it in his hand. The drumbeat started and he waved his hands over the moccasins quickly. The drum stopped and he opened his hands to show that he no longer had the pebble. Now Japhet stepped up as seeker. He looked at the moccasins and reached out to pick one up. He grinned broadly and turned it over. Out dropped the pebble. His team erupted in cheers, and thumped Japhet on the back.

The other boys now noticed Abraham and one older boy named Pannoowau spoke, "What are you doing here? Why aren't you helping the other women with the food?"

The others laughed. Pannoowau was the largest boy in the circle and one of the oldest. Soon he and Japhet would be joining the men's circles.

Abraham smiled as sweetly as he could and said, "I thought I was with the women."

Pannoowau stood up and thrust out his chest. "What did you call me?"

"A beautiful little *squaw* playing with her friends in the dirt," Abraham replied, scowling.

Pannoowau's face grew dark, and he moved forward aggressively, but Abraham was ready. He bent down, lunged at the boy, grabbed him around the middle, and tackled him. They fell over and landed with a thud in the circle. Pannoowau twisted and turned, trying to get up, but Abraham held him pinned to the ground. But Pannoowau was stronger and managed to gain some leverage. He flipped Abraham off, and both boys leapt to their feet. Pannoowau swung at Abraham, who ducked and struck back, connecting his fist to the boy's nose. The boy bellowed and backed away; fire burned in his eyes.

Japhet stepped between them and looked at each in turn. Then he spoke so quietly that his words were barely heard. "Enough!"

Pannoowau paced, but then he backed off and wiped his nose. "I am not done with you, Sissy Boy!" Then he turned and stalked off.

Japhet turned to Abraham, put his arm across his shoulders, and ushered him away from the circle of boys.

"That was a very bad thing to say to him. Do you know what it means? No decent woman should ever be called that, let alone a warrior!"

"I know," Abraham sighed. "But it was out of my mouth before I could pull it back."

"I know he taunted you, but you came looking for a fight."

Abraham looked up to see Japhet watching him.

"You have humiliated him. He will not let it go unanswered."

"I know," Abraham said softly.

Together they walked over to Uncle Ahanu's *wetu*, where Japhet and his parents also lived. Japhet took Abraham inside and showed him the large game stick he'd been working on. Abraham admired the straightness of the shaft and the graceful curve of the hoop at the top. The sinew netting that formed a bowl around the hoop was neat and tight. He looked at his cousin and nodded his approval.

"I could show you how to make one of your own," Japhet said.

"Da thinks I'm too young to play this year," Abraham replied.

"You aren't too young to start practicing. Here, I still have the one I used when I was your age." Japhet stood and walked over to his bunk. Reaching above it he pulled a slightly smaller game stick out of the netting hanging there. He returned and handed it to Abraham.

Abraham looked at the greyed shaft. A pod of dolphins was carved along its length, swimming toward the netting at the top. It was beautiful work. He looked up at Japhet and tried to hide his excitement.

"It needs to be oiled, but it's yours if you want it."

"Thank you," Abraham said and smiled.

Japhet retrieved a clay pot of fish oil and together they rubbed oil into the wood of their sticks.

"I haven't had time to carve anything into my new stick yet," Japhet said.

"Will you carve dolphins again?"

"I don't know. Maybe I'll make a whale instead."

Abraham smiled, "That would be great." He sighed. "I wish I could play with you all tomorrow."

"You should play with us," Japhet said. He looked over to Abraham. "No one will notice you amid the crowd of men."

"I can't. Da would be angry when he found out."

"You will cheer for us though and jeer the Shinnecock? It's an important part of the game. We play better when we can hear your support."

Abraham nodded sadly.

Japhet slapped him on the back. "Are you sure you won't play?"

Abraham nodded, unable to speak for the lump in his throat.

"It won't be long before you are out there with us, Abraham," Japhet said. "Don't worry."

A welcome breeze floated through the open doorway. Japhet hung his stick back on the wall and rose to lead Abraham back outside. They found a lean-to that wasn't being used and sat down on the logs placed there as seating to wait out the afternoon.

A few women were grinding corn mixed with ashes to make hominy and corn cakes, while others were plucking and cleaning quails which they stuffed with chopped garlic and onion and strung on sticks to roast over the fire. Large turkeys were also being prepared and strung on large spits, where older girls slowly rotated them over the fire. The women were laughing and chattering together as they worked. Abraham spotted his mother across the way. She looked happy and younger than she had in a while.

As the afternoon wore on, the smells of roasting fowl, garlic and onion, smoked fish, cooked squash, and other complex aromas wafted on the breeze. Abraham's stomach was growling impatiently, and his mouth was watering. Finally, as the sun began to slip below the horizon, the meal was laid out and the men were invited to eat first, followed by the boys, then the women and young children. The food was amazing! Abraham was ready to take a second helping when he noticed that Japhet had only taken a small portion.

"Don't you like it?"

"It's very good, but I have to be careful what I eat the night before the game," he replied. Then Japhet carefully looked around them, leaned in conspiratorially, and whispered, "Come to my *wetu* early tomorrow morning. I think I have a way to get you into the game."

Abraham smiled and set his bowl down.

After dinner, men and women dressed in their ceremonial regalia, danced around poles erected in a ring around the fire. His older brothers had donned their traditional garments too. Only Da stood out as an outsider in his English garments. Sacrifices of quail were made to the Great Spirit and the men gathered to yell sacred blessings for their teammates and intimidations for the Shinnecock. The ceremony lasted well past dark. As the women and children retired to bed, the men stayed up a little longer and discussed the rules that had been agreed upon. A two-mile stretch of grazing field to the north of East Hampton would be used for the game. Two posts had been erected at each end for the goals. There would be no out-of-bounds. The game would start just after sunrise.

Chapter 7

Ball Game

Japhet woke Abraham before sunrise. They quickly dressed in loin cloths and then Japhet added a beaded belt with large feathers attached to it, like the tail feathers of a great bird. Then he donned a red head band with feathers standing up from the top and more feathers affixed so that they hung down on each side and covered his ears. Japhet took out a jar of red paint. Abraham watched as he dipped his fingers in and he drew four horizontal lines across each of his cheeks. Then he drew two lines across his forehead and one down his nose.

Abraham tried to be happy for his cousin, but he couldn't help feeling sad and nervous. Japhet had said he might be able to get him into the game, but Abraham also worried about what Da would do if he did play.

Japhet stood and walked over to his bunk and rummaged through a basket hanging overhead. He drew out another feathered belt and a red headband. This headband was smaller and held fewer feathers, but it was similar to the one he now wore. Japhet blew dust from the belt and headband, straightened a few of the feathers, and then handed them to Abraham.

Abraham raised his eyebrows in surprise.

Japhet nodded encouragement. "Put them on," he said. "I wore these in my first game. I want you to wear them now."

Abraham ran his hand gently over the feathers. "Are you sure no one will notice if I play?"

"No one will notice. And think how proud your father will be when he discovers you played a man's game."

Abraham sighed. "More likely he will be angry, but …" He ran his hand over the feathers again. Then he squared his shoulders and set his jaw. "Once it's done, he will have to admit I am ready." His hands trembled as he carefully tied on the belt and then the headdress.

Japhet smiled at him and again dipped his fingers in to the paint and drew two stripes down each side of Abraham's face. Then Japhet used his thumbs to make a large circular smudge in the center of Abraham's forehead. He sat back, studied his work, and smiled.

Standing up, he said, "Hurry, we must join the others."

Abraham followed his cousin outside and over to the cooking harbor. Silently they ate a small bowl of *sappen* and then stood and grabbed their sticks.

The men were moving in clusters towards the shore of Napeague Bay that lay just north of the Montauk village. Uncle Ahanu, as shaman for the village, was there standing up to his knees in the water. The men were lining up along the shore. Abraham took his place squeezing in beside Japhet and another man. They stood there as the men continued to file in and jostle to find a place along the water. Finally, everyone settled, and it grew quiet with anticipation. The sky was lightening with a rosy glow, though the sun had not yet appeared over the horizon.

Uncle Ahanu caught sight of Abraham and his old eyes darkened in acknowledgement of what Abraham was doing. His lips pursed almost imperceptibly as he turned back to the crowd of men and raised his arms. In silence, the men walked forward together into the water just past their ankles and stopped. Abraham could feel the tension and excitement building in the men around him. His own heart was beating fast, though he knew if Da caught him, he would not be allowed to play. The tension grew; it felt like everyone was holding their breath together, waiting.

Uncle Ahanu turned his palms downward, and everyone stooped to dip their sticks into the water. Then Uncle Ahanu sang out a prayer to the Great Spirit and asked for strength, courage, and skill to defeat their enemies. As he spoke, he became more animated and the men too became energetic. They lifted their sticks above their heads and chanted. The sound rose and grew until it reached a roar. Then with a great whoop, it was over. The men turned and headed to the shore talking and slapping each other on backs and shoulders. Some men clustered together to give each other ceremonial scratches on their arms and torsos.

The sky continued to lighten, and everyone moved as a great herd towards the field. The women and children had already gathered along the perimeter. As the men approached, they let out a loud volley of cheers and whoops. Abraham looked across the field and saw the Shinnecock approaching in the distance. They looked like a plague of grasshoppers swarming over the land. He looked around at the Montauk. There must be hundreds of men on each side spreading out over the field.

Uncle Ahanu moved slowly, limping slightly. As he passed Abraham and Japhet he gave Abraham a knowing look but continued walking. Abraham felt guilt rising inside him and sighed. He began to move towards the edge of the field to join the women, but Japhet grabbed his arm and moved him in the opposite direction.

"You can't leave now," he said.

"But what of your grandfather? I think Uncle Ahanu knows Da does not want me to play today. Did you see the look he gave me?"

"Grandfather will sort it out."

Abraham watched dubiously as Uncle Ahanu approached his mum, dad and grandmother standing along the sidelines. Da shifted on his feet and looked uncomfortable as he watched the men taking to the field. Da did not seem to notice Abraham's absence until Uncle Ahanu walked over to him and said something to him. Da began to scan the faces of the players and Abraham sucked in a breath. He was caught! Uncle Ahanu was still talking and placed a hand on Da's shoulder. Just then their eyes met. Da did not seem angry or anxious, and turned his attention back to the shaman. He nodded slightly at the old man and met Abraham's eyes once more. Abraham saw resignation there, but no anger or encouragement. Abraham smiled and gripped his stick with determination.

"Just remember to catch the ball with your stick," Japhet reminded Abraham. "It is a penalty to touch it with your hands."

They approached their goal where two posts had been sunk into the ground several paces apart. Abraham looked up. They were as tall as three men, each standing on the shoulders of another. Marks had been made on each about chest height for a large man and then higher up, well above an arm's length, strips of colored cloth were tied. At the very top of the pole large whales were carved.

"We need to get the ball." Japhet held up a small wooden ball about the size of a small apple. "Above this first mark for one point. Below this mark no points are awarded. If you can get the ball above the flags, it is worth two points. Send a ball above the whale and we score three points."

Abraham nodded.

"Wagers! Place your wagers," Uncle Ahanu called out. He moved toward a railing that had been erected along the side of the field.

"Hurry, all players must put up a wager," Japhet said and led him over to the railing. Men were placing all sorts of objects there: colonial-style jackets, belts, hatchets and knives. Japhet slipped his knife and sheath off his belt, placed it on the railing, and turned to Abraham. He removed the string of purple and white wampum beads his mother had made for him and placed it beside the knife. Japhet nodded and turned to jog towards the center of the field. Abraham followed.

"Remember it is good trickery to pass the ball, but cowardly to dodge an opponent. Stand your ground and take it."

Abraham nodded. "Got it."

The sun had risen by now and men were gathering on each side of center field. The Shinnecock chief stepped forward into the center. It grew quiet as the chief scanned the Montauks.

"What are we waiting for?" Abraham whispered to Japhet.

"Watch," Japhet replied.

Abraham looked and saw his grandmother walk out onto the field. She approached the Shinnecock chief, and they grasped each other's forearms in greeting. They spoke briefly together, then turned each to their own team to admonish them to play fairly, and finally, after turning to acknowledge the watching crowd, they walked off the field together. A loud whoop broke the tension, and a ball was thrown into the air. Pandemonium ensued as mobs of men ran and shoved each other trying to reach the ball.

Abraham followed the groups of men running back and forth across the field following the flight of the ball as it sailed from one player to another. The ball sailed past him towards the Montauk goal, only to be stopped by a large warrior and hurtled back. The ball was caught by a Shinnecock and hurtled back again. Men ran and dodged. The mass of painted warriors ebbed and flowed back and forth across the field. Suddenly, a great cheer went up from the Shinnecock and Abraham spun around to see a huddle of their warriors jumping and hugging each other.

"They scored two points," Japhet said in his ear.

The ball was brought back to the center of the field and thrown into the air. The mobs of men moved out again, slowly advancing the ball toward the Shinnecock goal. Abraham saw the ball fly straight towards him. He braced himself and suddenly Pannoowau darted by, snatched the ball from the air, and hurtled it to another Montauk player. Men were moving with speed towards the Shinnecock goal. Whoops and cheers erupted as they scored two points. The game was now tied. A short break was called, and the women hurried onto the field with skins of water for the players.

The game continued through the morning with points being scored on both sides. A longer break was taken at midday before the final half of the game resumed. Abraham had never run so much in his life, but he felt no pain. Neither had he ever felt so alive! Again, the ball was flung toward him. He was following the course of the ball so intently he didn't notice Pannoowau run up beside him, until suddenly, he sprinted by him. Abraham felt a sharp whack on his ear, stumbled, and felt his ankle twist and give way beneath him. Somehow, he managed to catch the ball. He looked around and caught the eye of a Montauk warrior off to his left. He drew back his arm and chucked the ball just before he was tackled by half a dozen men. He hit the ground in a jumble of arms and legs, and pain like he'd never felt before shot up his leg. The fall knocked the breath from him, and as he lay there a moment trying to catch his breath, the men leapt off in pursuit of the ball. A cry of anger and pain erupted from his lips unbidden.

Japhet appeared at his side. "That was amazing!"

Abraham couldn't talk for the pain. He closed his eyes and rocked back and forth holding his leg. He couldn't tell how much time had passed before he felt strong arms lift him up and carry him off the field. Each step jostled his aching ankle and sent pain jolting through him. He bit his lip and tried not to cry. He closed his eyes and tried to imagine himself far away on a tall ship, climbing the ladder to the crow's nest ...

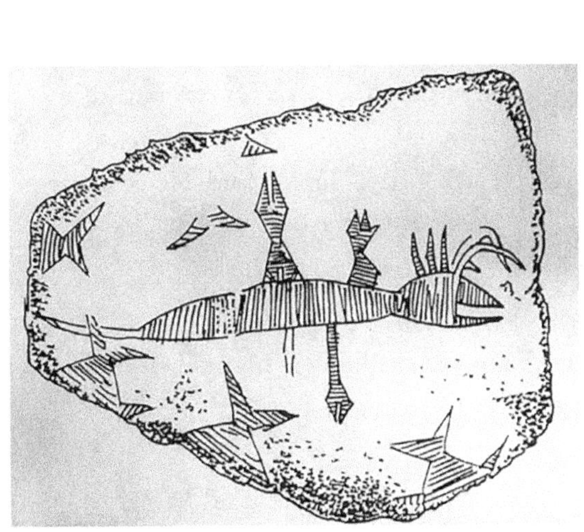

Late Woodland Mica Tablet found in Brookhaven in the 1840s. New York State Museum collections, Albany, N.Y.

The game continued through the afternoon, but Abraham had missed it all. It was now evening and Japhet had come to see him in his grandmother's *wetu*. In his hand Japhet held the wampum beads Abraham had wagered along with another pendant of mica tied to a leather thong.

"So, we won?"

Japhet smiled broadly. "24 to 22! It was a great game. I wish you could have been there for the ending."

Abraham took the proffered beads and pendant and traced the pattern with a finger. In the center of the large piece of dark mica was carved an elaborate dolphin with two horns bending over the animal's open snout. Three spikes stood up on the back of the head, two flippers protruded from each side of the body, and the large top fin stood erect in the center of the body. The tail was a thin horizontal line, like dolphins have, made to go up and down, rather than side to side, like shark tails. Thin stripes filled in the body of the dolphin. The carved marks had been filled with white paint so that the lines stood out against the dark background. It was a stunning piece of artwork.

"You played well today," Japhet said. He took the pendant and placed it and the beads around Abraham's neck.

"Pannoowau did it on purpose."

"I know. We can't prove it though."

"Uncle Ahanu said the bone in my ankle is broken. I may never walk right again."

"I'm sorry."

"Da is furious I played. He said it serves me right for disobeying."

"Don't worry about your father. He's really proud of you. He's been bragging to everyone about the great save you made today."

Abraham snorted. "Mum's been fussing at me all afternoon. I finally told her I needed to sleep. I couldn't take it anymore." His leg throbbed, and he scowled.

"There's going to be a big feast and celebration tonight."

"My first official stickball game and I can't even go to the celebration!"

"Maybe I could help you out?"

Abraham could feel the branches that made up the bed platform through the fur coverings. He longed for his softer straw stuffed mattress at home as he adjusted his splinted foot slightly. Pain shot up his leg, and he grimaced.

"I could sit with you tonight."

"No. Go enjoy the celebration. You've earned it. Mum will bring me something to eat."

"You're sure?"

Abraham nodded. Japhet got up and started to leave.

"I'll come back later and check on you, okay?"

Abraham nodded again. As his cousin left, he lay back and thought of ways he could get back at Pannoowau.

The shadows were lengthening, and Abraham could smell the deer meat and turkeys roasting over the fires. His ankle hurt and he was angry. He would find a way to hurt Pannoowau. Maybe he would gouge his eyes out or lie in wait and attack him as he went to make water. His thoughts were interrupted when the doorway darkened. He tried to turn to see who was there, but another sharp pain shot up his leg. He gritted his teeth and uttered a curse under his breath.

"May I enter?" Uncle Ahanu asked quietly.

"Yes, Uncle." Abraham said. He took a deep breath to ease the pain.

Uncle Ahanu came in and sat down cross-legged beside his bed. His grey hair had been pulled back in a ponytail at the back of his head and several slender striped pheasant tail feathers hung down from it, while a roach of deer and porcupine hair encircled it on the crown of his head. He watched Abraham for several moments before he spoke.

"You are angry."

"Yes, I'm angry!" The words exploded from his mouth. "Pannoowau threw me off balance on purpose. And now I won't be able to go out with the men to hunt the whales."

"There will be time. You are still young."

"I will find a way to get back …" Ahanu held up a hand, silencing him mid-rant.

"Vengeance is not the way. It is ugly. It will eat your soul."

"But he …" Abraham began.

His uncle shook his head sadly.

"What am I supposed to do?" Abraham scowled.

"Forgive him."

"How? How can I forgive him after he …"

"Peace," Uncle Ahanu said. After a long pause, he continued. "When I was a boy, I too was angry."

"I have never seen you angry," Abraham said, surprised.

Uncle Ahanu smiled. "You did not know me when I was young, as you are."

"Then how did you stop being angry all the time?"

Uncle Ahanu smiled and looked thoughtful. "When I was a boy, my grandfather told me this tale about a battle between two wolves…．

There are two wolves inside each of us. One wolf is evil. It is anger, envy, jealousy, sorrow, regret, greed, arrogance, self-pity, guilt, resentment, inferiority, lies, false pride, superiority, and ego.

"The other is good. It is joy, peace, love, hope, sincerity, humility, kindness, benevolence, empathy, generosity, truth,

compassion, and faith.

Uncle Ahanu paused, looked at Abraham, and smiled. "I then asked my grandfather, 'Which wolf wins?'"

Abraham waited for him to continue. When his uncle remained silent, he asked, "What was the answer?"

Uncle Ahanu cocked an eyebrow at Abraham, exhaled slowly, and said, "The one you feed."

They were both quiet for several moments. Then Uncle Ahanu rose and came over to the bed. "Now it is time to celebrate. You have played a man's game today. You will celebrate with the men."

"But my ankle … I can't walk."

"I will carry you." Uncle Ahanu stooped down and lifted him in his arms as if he weighted nothing. Abraham watched his uncle's chest muscles flex beneath the tattoos that swirled from one side to the other in a sideways S, as he stooped to carry him through the doorway. His uncle's steps were steady, despite his slight limp, so that there was hardly any jarring. A mat had been laid out for him by the fire. Japhet was grinning at him as his uncle set him down gently beside him.

"Glad you decided to come after all!"

Abraham shrugged. "Not sure I had a choice."

Uncle Ahanu snorted but said nothing.

They ate roasted deer, turkey, corn, and squash. The food made him feel better and soon he was laughing at his cousin's retelling of their victory. As the night wore on drums made from deer hide stretched over wooden rings and gourd rattles were brought out and the men and women formed a circle around the fire. The dancing began. Abraham watched from the sidelines. It grew late and the women took the children to bed, while the men sat around the fire to smoke and tell stories. Abraham tried to stay awake, but his eyes kept closing of their own accord and his head nodded. Finally, Uncle Ahanu came and carried him off to his grandmother's *wetu* and laid him down in his bed.

"I'm sorry, I couldn't stay awake," he mumbled.

"You have had a long day and need much healing. It is good for you to rest now."

Abraham nodded, his eyes already closing.

Chapter 8

Mr. Palmer

We'd been out to sea several weeks now and so far, it had been a fairly smooth journey allowing for the one storm, or blow, that had nearly sunk us off the coast of Nova Scotia. The wind too, had favored our journey, but as we entered the more northernly waters, storms were an increasing possibility. Captain Jolls had sent me to check the hull for leaks and make repairs as necessary.

"Etienne, hurry up with that bucket!"

I carried a pail of oakum, a mixture of strands of old rope and tar. I'd spent several days beating the ropes to loosen the weavings. Then I'd used my fingers to pull the remaining strands apart into individual, shortened pieces. My fingers had bled the first day, but over time callouses had developed to protect them. Today I'd mixed the pieces of rope with hot tar, which gave out a pungent smell. I had to work quickly, before the tar cooled and formed a solid mass in the bottom of my pail.

I entered the crew's chamber, lantern in one hand and pail in the other. It was dark in the lower regions of the hull. I looked for any evidence of dampness, or leaking, between the strakes, the horizontal planks, of the hull. I found a place where a small trickle of water was running down the side and set the lantern down. I reached into the bucket, scooped up a wad of the warm sticky oakum, and worked it into the seam. I was so intent upon my work I didn't notice that several of the sailors had returned.

"There's the thief spreading his foul stench!"

I heard several men chuckle and turned to see Mr. Palmer staring at me and laughing.

"I'm not a thief," I replied evenly.

"Are ye not? Then why were ye stealing cherries from my trees?"

It had been two years, but still the sting of humiliation I'd felt from Palmer's beating and the subsequent arrest, flooded me. They weren't even his cherry trees, but Master Carteret's, and I'd had permission to pick them! I wanted to lash out, to yell obscenities and justify my actions, but I knew it would do no good.

"You are mistaken, sir." I said it quietly but knew as soon as the words left my mouth, that I should not have said them at all.

In an instant, Palmer grabbed my shoulder and wrenched me around to face him.

"Where do you get off telling me anything, thief?" Palmer said fiercely.

I raised my hand to wipe Palmer's spittle from my face and stared at him, trying to keep the emotions from showing on my face. "I stand corrected," I said. "If you don't mind, I must finish my work before the oakum dries."

"You will finish when I tell you, you may finish!"

I could sense the tension in the room. Many of the other men were muttering awkwardly, trying to cajole Palmer out of his rage, but Palmer only seemed to grow angrier.

"You think you are special, don't you? That you can do and say whatever you like without consequence. Well, you are mistaken. You will show me the respect I deserve."

Then Palmer walked to the side of hull, dug out the oakum I had just placed, and dumped it back into the bucket.

"Your work is faulty. Do it again."

I snorted and struggled to gain control of my temper.

"What did you say?" Mr. Palmer's voice was cold as ice.

"Nothing, sir," I said through clenched teeth.

Mr. Palmer moved within inches of my nose and flashed a malicious sneer. "I will be back to check on you soon." Then he turned and left.

Slowly I stooped to pick up more oakum and jammed it into the crack. But the oakum was cooling and simply slipped out and fell to the deck with a plop. I yelled and punched the hull. Pain shot up my arm and I yelled again cradling my fist in my other hand. After a few minutes I was able to breath normally again. I stooped and picked up the cold oakum and returned it to the pail. Then I picked up the pail and stomped off angrily to dump it back into the pot simmering over the fire on the main deck.

I thought of the rolling hills and forests at home and wondered what Alsoomse was doing now. When would I see her again? I sighed again. Best to get back to work before Palmer returned.

Chapter 9

Harpoons and Healing

Abraham, October 30, 1663

The next day, it was decided that Abraham would stay in Montauk Village until his ankle healed sufficiently that he could walk on it, while the rest of his family returned home. He watched the wagon pull away from his place in the lean-to and suddenly wished he were going with them. His cousin, Japhet, had left earlier that morning with the hunting party. He felt useless and angry.

Uncle Ahanu snorted. "It is good for you to stay here. Learn who you are."

Abraham scowled.

His uncle watched him for a time and then sighed. "Why are you so angry?"

"Why shouldn't I be angry? If Pannoowau hadn't tripped me, I could have gone hunting with the men." Abraham said.

"If your ankle was not hurt, you would have gone home with your parents."

That only made him angrier. He could see his uncle cock his head to study him.

"Da won't let me go hunting with my older brothers. He says I am too young, but then my brothers tease me for helping Mum in the fields. They say I am doing women's work. So, what should I do?"

"There is still work you can do. Hunting and fishing are only a part of men's work."

Uncle Ahanu picked up two leg bones from a large buck and handed one to Abraham. Then he picked up an old whale harpoon and showed him the barbs that had been cut into it. Using an iron hunting knife, Uncle Ahanu began to cut notches in the bone. It was a delicate, but difficult job.

After working on one barb for most of the morning, Abraham's knife slipped and broke off the tip of the barb. Abraham cursed and flung the length of bone away.

His uncle made a disapproving noise and slowly stood. Abraham watched him limp over to the discarded spearhead. He bent slowly to retrieve the bone and Abraham felt a pang of guilt. He hung his head as Uncle Ahanu limped back and handed him the unfinished spear tip.

"But it's ruined!" Abraham said. He felt a stinging behind his eyes.

"Make the barb shorter, but still sharp."

"But …"

"Patience, Boy. You will never be a hunter or a fisher until you learn patience.”

Abraham opened his mouth to argue, but then blew out a frustrated breath and bent back to the work. By the end of the day, his uncle had completed two harpoon tips. He had not even completed one. His uncle examined his work and nodded.

“This is good work.”

“But I haven’t even finished one today,” Abraham said. He frowned and threw his knife down.

“Speed is not needed, patience only,” Uncle Ahanu replied and stood. “Time now to eat.”

His uncle bent over, picked him up, and carried him to his grandmother’s fire. She had a savory turkey stew prepared for them. It smelled delicious. The hunters had not yet returned.

“Aren’t we going to wait for the men to come back?” Abraham asked as he accepted a bowl of the steaming stew.

“No. The hunters may be gone for many days,” his uncle said.

Abraham raised his eyebrows in surprise. When his Da and brothers went hunting, they came home every night, sometimes with a deer or other game and sometimes empty handed, but they always returned each evening. The meal was relaxed and casual. Young children ran around playing and groups of women sat talking and laughing around the small cook fires.

In the following days, Abraham became more skilled in his work and slowly they stockpiled several harpoon tips ready to be attached to shafts. After a week, the hunters returned in boisterous celebration. The men had killed a bear and carried back the meat and hide. That night they celebrated with a feast, stories, and smoking to honor the bear spirit.

After a couple of the hunters relayed the details of their adventure, Uncle Ahanu took up the pipe and took a long draw on it, puffing smoke into the air. The children, women, and men gathered in closer, waiting eagerly. After taking a second long puff and gathering his thoughts, Uncle Ahanu began his story.

The Great Creator Spirit taught us that all living things on land, in the sea, or in the air – plants, animals, birds, fish, and humans - are connected in a great circle. Each takes what it needs, and each must also give something back.

Moshup, the Giant, lived along the coast of the mainland when Earth was young. He loved whale meat and went out to catch them in his hands. He cooked them over fires he built along the shore. Moshup married Granny Squannit, medicine woman of the Little People, who lived in the forest. In this way, he united the land and the sea. But he had a bad temper, and once in a rage he stomped all over Long Island and left his footprints behind to form the peninsulas and bays on the east end of this island. He and Granny Squannit often fought and that caused bad weather to plague the coast.

Moshup befriended our ancient ancestors, and he shared his whale meat with them each time he caught one of the great creatures. In gratitude they brought all the tobacco they could carry to Moshup. He smoked the pipe creating the fog that rolls in from the sea each morning. But over time, our ancestors became lazy and relied on Moshup to provide whale meat, so they stopped hunting for themselves.

And so, the Great Creator Spirit came to Moshup and told him, "It is good to give to your younger brothers, but not so much that they stop providing for themselves. They are like little children who will never grow strong and become men. If they cannot care for themselves, how will they care for the rest of Creation?" Moshup agreed, so he said good-bye to his friends, and wished them well. They watched as he swam out to sea towards the east. As he swam, the Great Creator Spirit honored him by turning him into a white whale. If you ever see a white whale, it is Moshup coming to check on our progress. Good luck will always follow.

After Moshup left, the people didn't know what to do, so the Little People taught them how to use the things the forest provided and how to farm and hunt. In return, they left baskets of corn cakes, berries, and meat in the forest, and at night the Little People came and took them. In this way our Ancestors learned to be strong and provide for themselves and to be mindful of all of Creation. We must never forget to be grateful and give back from our bounty.

The fire was burning low and soon everyone returned to their homes for the night. The next morning, Abraham was again sitting under the lean-to working on a harpoon tip, when Pannoowau approached. He stopped a couple of feet away. Pannoowau glanced quickly over his shoulder and nodded to someone behind him who Abraham couldn't see. He then turned back to watch Abraham, but Abraham kept working and did not acknowledge him.

"I regret tripping you during the ball game," Pannoowau said. "I am sorry you injured your ankle." Then he waited.

Abraham's anger flared. Pannoowau was not *really* sorry. He was here only because someone had made him come. Pannoowau stood still and watched. Abraham gave a slight nod in acknowledgement but remained silent. Pannoowau remained standing and watching. Abraham frowned and concentrated on his work.

Finally, Pannoowau leaned over and whispered, "Watch yourself, Boy. Your rudeness will not be forgotten." Then he spun on his heel and walked away.

Uncle Ahanu put a hand on Abraham's shoulder and said, "Much trouble would be saved if you would forgive him."

"But he …"

Uncle Ahanu held up a hand to stop him, and after a long solemn look, went back to carving his own harpoon tip. Abraham fumed and grudgingly returned to his work. Several times afterwards, Abraham caught Pannoowau watching him from the lean-to across from them, where he was socializing with his friends. He tried to ignore him, but it was impossible. There was nothing he could do about it though, until his ankle healed, so he contented himself with his work. The weather was turning colder, and the sea was growing rough. Soon the whales would arrive, and he would be ready.

Chapter 10

Beads and Blood

Alsoomse, October 31, 1663

Alsoomse leaned over the long, narrow loom. She strung purple and white beads in rows and wove those rows into their proper place in the belt. The pattern was nearly finished. She'd started with a man on the left side, followed by the image of a wolf and the diamond shape that represented his tribe. The center place was reserved for a willow tree representing strength and stability in old age, experience, deep inner knowledge, and open-mindedness. Then on the right side, she placed the symbol for her tribe, then an eagle, and finally the figure of a woman. Two lines representing constancy connected them all.

She looked up, gazed over Long Island Sound, and searched the horizon for the white men's tall-masted ships with sails that looked like a flock of startled seagulls taking flight. She thought of Etienne and wondered once more where he was now and when he would return.

Her mother approached and leaned over her to examine her work critically. She made a small affirming sound and straightened back to her full height.

"This work is much better, Daughter."

Alsoomse felt the warmth of pride fill her chest as she watched her mother pick up her large basket and move off toward the cooking shelter. Her back ached and her feet longed to run, but she shook her head grimly and bent to finish the final row. She bound the ends. Then she removed the belt from the loom and sewed the wampum onto the strip of soft leather backing. She cut the leather she'd left on each end into long fringe and strung three alternating white and dark wooden beads onto the end of each strip, finishing it off with knot in the end. She stretched and stood to admire her work. She picked up the belt and moved toward the *nush wetu* to stow it in her dowry basket. As she walked, she felt something wet run down the inside of her leg. She reached down to wipe it away. As she brought her hand up, she gasped as she saw the scarlet smear. She nearly dropped the belt in dismay. Her days of freedom and independence were now gone forever!

"*Ókas!*" Alsoomse said and ran toward the cooking shelter.

She found her mother preparing to bake some of the large root vegetables they'd gathered to supplement the sparse corn crop they'd managed to harvest from the fields near their winter camp. The tribe had not arrived in their summer camp on Manahatta in time to plant the fields there. The previous year's hunting had been largely unproductive and so they had stayed longer than usual. Then the Esopus War had delayed them further. Now they would have to rely on the large tubers from the man of the earth vine, wild parsnips, and chestnuts to survive the winter.

Alsoomse held out her stained hand, and her mother looked at her and smiled. She left the tubers to the other women and hurried over to Alsoomse. She rushed her to their house and grabbed a large blanket which she threw over Alsoomse's head, covering her from head to ankle, and led her out of the village to the women's hut nestled on the edge of the woods. Once inside, her mother stripped her of her buckskin and sat her in a bed of old ashes. She placed the blanket back over her head like a hood and wrapped it around her body.

Her mother balanced a small clay pot on three rocks on the edge of the fire pit that lay in the center of the hut and started a small fire. She gave Alsoomse some water from a gourd ladle, and then added a handful of pungent herbs to the pot. Her mother left and returned with cornmeal which she also added to the pot to simmer.

"You are becoming a woman now, Daughter," her mother said as she stirred the pot. "It is time we find you a husband."

"I already know who I wish to marry."

"That is good! Who is this man? Is he from our tribe, or perhaps a Mohawk?" Her mother smiled, half to herself as she stirred the pot.

"My friend, Etienne, but he is still too young and is away at sea."

Her mother looked up and scowled. "You will not marry that French boy! You must marry someone who shares our culture, from our tribe or one of the neighboring tribes."

"But I love Etienne!"

"Why must you always dishonor me, Daughter? Your place is here. He does not understand our ways. ..."

"Why must I stay here?"

"Hush now! Your meal is ready." Her mother dished up a small bowl and held it out to her.

Alsoomse reached for the bowl, but her mother held onto it.

"This trial will be difficult, but it will make you stronger. I will be here to watch over you."

Alsoomse nodded and took the bowl. She was hungry and gulped the watery corn mash down quickly. She held out the bowl for more, but her mother shook her head sadly. Within minutes, Alsoomse was vomiting up the food she'd just consumed into a bowl her mother held out for her. Her mother stroked her hair as she retched and coughed, and then gently wiped her mouth clean. Her mother then offered her a little water and helped her to lay down in the ashes. Alsoomse was trembling and weak. Her mother covered her with an old bear skin and sat by to watch over her as she slept.

Alsoomse woke up hungry and again her mother offered her a bowl from the clay pot. Again, she became violently sick and again, her mother rinsed her mouth with a little water and lay her down to sleep. The patterned continued again and again. But even when Alsoomse tried to refuse the food, her mother made her eat it anyway.

"You must eat, Daughter."

"But it will make me sick."

Ókas sat, hugged Alsoomse, and brushed the hair from her face. "I know it is not pleasant. You are strong. It will be over soon. You must be purified in preparation for childbearing."

Alsoomse quickly lost track of the days and nights and sunk into a restless delirium. She was vaguely aware of her mother stroking her hair or arranging her blankets. The firelight flickered behind her eyelids, and she drifted in and out of consciousness.

Alsoomse was walking through the forest. It was late spring

or early summer. Flowers were blooming everywhere, their colors more vibrant than she'd thought possible. A young deer looked up at her from the bushes in fearless curiosity, and a bunny leisurely hopped across her path. A squirrel chattered happily to her from a branch above her head and then climbed down to take an acorn from her outstretched hand. She heard water burbling in a stream nearby and moved towards the sound. She didn't recognize this place.

As Alsoomse approached the stream she saw an old woman stooped over picking herbs along its edge. The woman stopped and stood with her back towards her. She was a medicine woman, for she wore the traditional medicine bag at her waist. The woman seemed to be listening and then turned around to meet her eyes. The woman looked strangely familiar. She was wearing an amulet made of a brilliant blue-green stone with black veins running through it which gave the impression of a willow tree swaying in the breeze. The stone was as long as her pinkie finger, three times as wide, and was tied to a leather thong around the old woman's neck. It was the most beautiful thing she'd ever seen!

The woman's face showed the creases of vast experience and her eyes sparkled with the deep wisdom only those who have lived long possess. The woman smiled, walked towards her, and slipped the medicine bag off her waist as she approached. Then the old woman handed the bag to Alsoomse. As Alsoomse took it, the woman clasped her hands firmly, and Alsoomse felt strength in the knurled hands and a warmth that seemed to flow into her. Then the woman turned away, transformed into an eagle, and launched herself into the air.

Alsoomse held the bag and looked up into the air. She watched the eagle retreat toward the horizon, and time seemed to stop. The forest quieted, and even the babbling of the creek stilled in reverence. As the eagle disappeared into the clouds, Alsoomse heard her mother calling her name. It was soft as if coming from some great distance. She turned towards the sound, and everything went black. ...

Chapter 11

Stars and More Stars

Etienne, November 1, 1663

It was cold in the crow's nest. Wind whipped though my hair pulling it from its binding. The glow of the moon reflected off the water. I'd been told to watch for white caps, an indication that we were getting close to the rocky shores of Ireland. I'd never thought of the moon as a place one could visit, but rather as the face of God watching us, protecting us. But now I wondered, was it a place more like the earth with its own rivers, gardens, and animals? Were Elijah and Enoch there?

I'd started reading the book I'd traded from Tomas. In it, Cyrano de Bergerac described how he'd made it from Paris to New France in mere hours by using glass globes filled with dew to lift him into the air. Then, by breaking them gradually he was set down in the colony of New France. The rotation of the earth had allowed him to rise up from one continent, only to land on another. I'd never been to New France, but I knew it lay to the northwest of New Netherland and his description was similar to what I'd seen traveling north to Wiltwyck.

Then de Bergerac described a machine propelled by fire-works that carried him up so high that when his machine was burned up, he fell onto the moon. Being of lesser size, the moon had a lesser pull, so that he fell more slowly and landed with less force. He described a garden presumed to be that of Eden after which he met with the prophets Elijah and Enoch.

I looked out over the waters. The waves were increasing in size and the strength of the wind was increasing. Was a storm coming? Way off in the distance I thought I saw a glint of white. I stared at the place where I'd seen the glint and searched the darkness. Yes, there it was again! Off to port to the northeast was the faintest glint of white foam. I made the call and was soon relieved by a more seasoned sailor.

I reached the deck, walked to the portside railing, and looked out over the water. Master Jolls came to stand beside me. He looked up as my relief crewman called down confirmation of the whitecaps.

"You have good eyes, Etienne."

"Yes, sir. Thank you, sir," I said and continued to stare out at the water.

"It is so beautiful tonight. I hope the weather holds."

"Yes, sir," I said. I listened to the water lapping at the hull and watched the reflection of the moon on the water. "Sir, do you believe the earth rotates, or that the stars are fixed and move about the earth?"

"What makes you ask that question?'

I told him about the book I was reading.

He looked at me and smiled. "What is easier to believe, that one body rotates or that hundreds of thousands of stars are fixed to some invisible firmament that rotates about us?"

"I suppose it would be easier to think that one body is moving. But then why don't we feel the movement?"

"Perhaps it moves slowly in comparison to its size. Just as seamen eventually get used to the constant movement of the ship, perhaps we are used to the movement of the earth."

I thought about that. It did make some sense.

"I need you to work with Palmer to finish the repairs on the ship. Please report to him in the lower hold in the morning."

"Yes, sir," I said and tried to hide my disappointment. I'd much rather climb the masts to set the yards or untangle the sheets, or sit in the crow's nest and keep watch, or swab the deck, or even clean the head. Anything would be preferable to being stuck in the bottom of the ship stuffing hot oakum in the cracks of the hull with Palmer hovering at my elbow and breathing his fowl breath in my face. But I resolved that I would do my best to get along with him, or at least to ignore his jibes.

As I retired to my hammock, I couldn't stop thinking of the things I'd read about. Finally, I went to my trunk and pulled out a piece of paper, quill, and ink, which I'd purchased in Boston. I sat on the floor and used the trunk as a desk and by the dim light of the lantern I wrote.

> *Dear Nicolas,*
>
> *I am sailing under Captain Jolls to London and then to Texel and Muscovy. I wish I could visit you. France is so close now, but it is not possible. How I wish I could use Cyrano de Bergerac's wonderful globes to come and visit with you! I've been reading his book, maybe you know it,* The Other World. *In it he writes that the Copernicus's claim that the earth moves about the sun is true and that the stars are all suns, like our own, with their other worlds moving about them. Do you believe it? My*

captain said that he'd heard of a Galileo Galilei, who also supported these claims, though he'd also heard that the Pope had forced him to recant them.

There is also a passage in the third chapter that says, "but as God could create the Soul Immortal, He could also make the World Infinite." De Bergerac claims that if the universe were finite, then God would also be finite since he would not exist beyond the limited boundary of the universe. What a wonderful time of discovery we live in! I wish I could discuss these things with you, Nicolas. I will write more later, but now I must get some sleep. It will be a busy day tomorrow.

Sweat ran down my back and dripped off my face as I worked. I'd removed my shirt and rolled up my pant legs trying to protect them from getting into the oakum. Tar was so difficult to get out, and I didn't want to ruin my clothes. My back had healed well, thanks to Alsoomse's ointment, but I could still feel the burn scars pulling and stretching as I worked. I remembered the fear in the children's faces as I'd pulled from the burning *wetu* and the burning smoke searing my nostrils and lungs. I'd gotten them out in time, but the house had collapsed on top of me. I remembered little else until I'd come to later, discovered I was in danger again, and fled for my life. I ran and ran, and in my delirium, had stumbled into Alsoomse. Again, she had saved me. But now she was half a world away. If I got into trouble now, I would have to save myself.

My pail now empty, I turned toward the ladder to go and refill it. My shadow moved on the far wall as Palmer held the lantern up behind me.

"What's that on yer back?" He came closer and I could feel the warmth of the lantern as Palmer moved in for a better look. "Been in some trouble have ye? Playing with fire?" He laughed.

I tensed. Every day I'd endured his insults and jabs. I took a deep breath and moved toward the ladder.

"Were ye involved in burning the Indian village on Manhattan? Did ye enjoy hearing the savages scream? I say, good riddance! Might be ye aren't so bad after all," he said, thoughtfully, and then chuckled.

Sudden anger welled up in me so violently that I immediately dropped the pail and spun on my heel. I felt my fist connect with Palmer's jaw before I knew what I'd done. In an instant he was on me. He slammed my head into the floorboards and smashed his knee into my gut. I swung again and harmlessly grazed his shoulder. Pain erupted behind my eyes as his fist made contact with my nose and blood ran into my mouth. I tried to push him off me, but he leaned harder into my gut. I was struggling to breathe. I started to see stars and I feared I would blackout. But then Palmer yanked me to my feet and propelled me across the cargo deck to the ladder, up the stairs and towards the captain's quarters where he banged on the door with a meaty fist.

The door opened and Thomas Jolls looked out at us and sized up the situation. Slowly, he motioned for me to step inside and take a seat at the small table. Then he stepped outside to talk to the wild-eyed Palmer. I could hear pieces of a muffled conversation but could not make any sense of it. Finally, after several agonizing minutes, Master Jolls returned and took a seat at the table opposite me.

"If I remember rightly, when I took you on, I'd asked you whether you'd be able to work with Mr. Palmer, given your history. You told me you could, but now I am not sure that you spoke truly."

I started to explain about our unpleasant first meeting in the cherry tree and its subsequent conflict, but Jolls held up his hand to silence me.

"I don't need to hear your explanation. I know Mr. Palmer can be difficult, but he is still your superior and worthy of your respect. You must not allow yourself to be baited."

With that, Master Jolls stood, opened his door, and summoned his first mate.

"Take Etienne to the main mast and give him ten lashes for insubordination. Afterwards, ensure that he finishes his caulking of the hull."

Chapter 12

Impressions of War

The *Dolphin* rose on a swell of wave. I stood on the bow of the deck and stared over the water. We'd made it across the Atlantic Ocean, around the dangerous southern coast of Ireland, and into the English Channel. The ship was now skirting the southeastern end of Britain and would soon reach the Strait of Dover. From there we would sail north and round the point to enter the mouth of the Thames River which would lead us up to London. The straight was at the narrowest portion of the English Channel, a mere eighteen nautical miles across. To starboard we would soon pass Calais. So close to France, though still a long way from La Rochelle and Nicolas.

Slowly, the white cliffs came into view off to port. As we neared, I could see castle towers rising from atop the cliffs that seemed to glow in the afternoon sun. The rounded fortifications reminded me of the two towers that flanked each side of the mouth of the inner harbor in La Rochelle having served both as guards and guardians. Some sailors claimed that Dover Castle was built by the Romans; others said it was William the Conqueror who'd built it.

Who manned it now, I wondered? And what purpose did it serve?

The great ship creaked as it slowly changed course and slid into the mouth of the Thames. I scrambled up the mast to help take in the main sail. It could be tricky entering a riverway, even one so large as this. The captain would want to go with caution.

The yard secured, I paused to look out over the unfamiliar landscape. A long stretch of beach shifted and moved with changing patterns of light and dark. I cupped my hands around my eyes to shade them from the sun and stared intently at the moving forms. As the ship moved closer, I could make them out – seals. Hundreds of them! Old, fat bulls lounged on all the high places overseeing the younger bulls vying with each other for the middling heights. Juveniles splashed and played along the shallows with their watchful mothers hovering along the edge of the water.

Slowly the ship crept up the river until rows of buildings could be seen crowding together like rats fleeing a burning barn. The smell of sewage reached my nostrils, and I wrinkled my nose in disgust, though in all honesty the lower decks of the ship smelled no better. Amsterdam, too, had smelled the same. I'd forgotten that until now. It was inevitable with so many people living in such close quarters. I hoped Manhattan would never become so crowded and rank. I realized how much I'd come to enjoy hunting quail and grouse in the tall grasses, and fishing in the burbling streams, or searching the woods to see if I'd caught any rabbits or foxes in my traps. I was learning to love the wilderness as much as I did the sea. Did I regret returning to the sea? Or did I just miss Alsoomse? I thought of her dark eyes sparkling as she played some trick on me and her hair as it moved in the breeze. A hand slid involuntarily to my belt and I stroked the uneven beads gently. I missed her.

I thought again of the book I'd been reading. The author had described how he had tried to reach the moon by filling numerous glass spheres with dew fixing them to himself. Then as the hot sun beat down on the spheres, the dew was attracted to the warm rays and rose to join the other clouds in the sky. The author had quickly been pulled up into the sky. But instead of reaching the moon he was afraid he would be pulled off course, so he started breaking the vials until he slowly dropped back to earth. How amazing would it be to fly halfway around the world in so little time!

The Dolphin was approaching the crowded London docks. I had never seen so many ships moored along the shore, not even in Texel Harbor. What could this mean? Master Jolls ordered the crew to haul in the remaining sails and drop anchor. I quickly scrambled to help the other sailors on the sheets. When the ship was secured, the rowboats were made ready and slowly lowered into the water.

"Etienne, come help with the resupply," the captain ordered. He strode toward one of the row boats, and I had to run to catch up to him.

I followed the captain down the ladder and took my place at one of the oars. There was no room left along the piers, so we had anchored the ship offshore. The foul smell of rot and decay grew stronger as we approached the docks. A cold mist was settling over the city.

As I rowed, I looked over my shoulder upriver; I could see a large bridge spanning the great waterway. Its length was crowded with houses, shops, and even a church, judging from the steeple. Its arches were so low to the water that only rowboats could pass beneath it. I wondered how anyone could pass along the bridge, cluttered as it was with buildings.

We made it to the dock and tied our rowboat to a mooring. As I climbed out, I looked up to see a large stone wall. Behind its imposing grey façade rose a tall square building with three rows of arched windows adorning each side. Three square towers and one round one rose from each of its corners. One large arched opening breached the wall facing us.

"That's the Traitors' Gate," Mr. Palmer said as he came up behind me. "London Tower has held some of the most notorious traitors over the years. Should I tell them to save a room fer ye, eh?"

I shivered, remembering how close Papa had come to meeting a similar fate four years ago in the Lantern Tower of La Rochelle when he'd been accused of religious heresy forcing us to flee in the dead of night.

Palmer laughed and I watched him saunter over to a tavern and slip inside. I stood silently as Master Jolls negotiated with a local merchant. They shook hands and Jolls turned to give the first mate instructions while the merchant hurried over to a large storehouse near the wharf and gave orders to his men.

As I started toward the storehouse to help with the crates and barrels, I caught sight of Master Jolls moving toward the Traitor's Gate. A cloaked man stood in the entranceway waiting. Jolls greeted him and they slipped into the shadow of the gateway. Curious, I moved closer. I inched along the wall to be out-of-sight from the men and as I approached, I could hear voices speaking low and urgently.

"Louis XIV has signed an alliance with the Stadtholder of the Netherlands to protect each other's trade routes. However, our good King Charles II is keen to disrupt that agreement ...."

"What will that mean for us and for the colonies?"

"Surely you can guess the result? A trade rivalry has been brewing with the Dutch and now it will likely lead to open warfare. Best not stay too long in port, or your ship will be commandeered for the king's fleet."

"How much time do we have?"

At that moment a hand clamped onto my neck, and I nearly jumped out of my skin. I was forcibly propelled back toward the wharf. I smelled Mr. Palmer's whiskey laden breath as he spoke in my ear.

"Spying on the captain are ye? Guess ye'll be needing that traitor's room after all."

Chapter 13

Blows

braham stared out over the rolling serf. A cold wind blew in numbing his nose and ears. He pulled his woolen cap lower and rubbed his mittens together to warm his hands. He'd been on lookout since well before dawn. There was a full moon and the sky was clear. That should make it easy to spot the whale blows, if there were any to see, but it also meant it would be cold since there were no clouds to hold down any residual heat from the day. And the hour just before dawn was always the coldest part of the night. He shivered again and wrapped his coat tighter around his body.

He'd been told to look for "right" whales as they started their migration south to warmer waters. They could be distinguished from other whales by their blow spouts. Unlike other whales in the area, which had a single blow spout, right whales had two. They were called right whales because they were slow moving behemoths, which would make them easier to chase down. The fat that protected them from the cold northern waters would be boiled down into an oil to be burned in lanterns. Instead of teeth, right whales strained their food through baleen which acted like a netting to catch small sea creatures. The baleen would also be harvested and used to make women's corsets.

Lookout duty was boring work and his mind kept wandering. He wondered what Etienne was doing now. His ship should be returning soon, and Abraham was growing anxious to see his new friend again and to hear of his adventures.

The harpoons he and Uncle Ahanu had made would have to suffice until the iron ones were brought back from Texel in the spring. Three eight-men row boats were lying on the beach below the wooden lookout platform where he lay stretched out on his belly. The men had set up a camp on the high ground along the shore, taking turns watching for the dual sprays of the whales as they surfaced on their journey south. Smoke snaked up from the chimney holes in the shelters the men had erected as sleeping lodges. Abraham wished he could be in his bed near the warm coals with his father and brothers instead of perched up on this bare wooden platform being frozen by the harsh northern wind.

Just then as the sun peaked over the horizon and cast its golden light across the water, he thought he saw two plumes of mist shoot into the air. He looked again to be sure his eyes weren't playing tricks on him. Nothing, then *wait* … there it was again!

"Blows! Blows!" he hollered and crawled to the edge of the platform.

Da was the first out of the shelter, followed closely by his brothers and the other men. Uncle Ahanu brought up the rear, moving slowly across the sand, limping on his bad leg. Da squinted up at him, and Abraham pointed in the direction the whales were traveling. Men rushed toward the water's edge, pulling on coats and fastening trousers as they ran to the boats. As his father looked away and started down the beach, Abraham slid down the ladder, using his arms and his one good leg to land upon. As he reached the bottom, he caught sight of Pannoowau running out of one of the shelters.

He couldn't believe it! Why was that … that arrogant, no-good *big man* here?

Pannoowau spotted him, loped over, and grinned. "Hunting whales is for men, not *squaws* like you," he said and ran off toward the nearest boat.

Abraham started to run after him, but as his weight came down on his injured ankle, pain shot up his leg and he yelped and landed in a heap on the sand. Japhet appeared at his side, grabbed him around the waist, and pulled him to his feet. Abraham reached out and clutched the ladder to steady himself. He looked out toward the boats and frowned as he saw Pannoowau leap into a boat as it slid out into the churning waves.

"Ignore him. He speaks only wind and bluster," Japhet said.

"Why is he here?" Abraham asked between clenched teeth.

"One of the others was sick, so Pannoowau came in his place."

Abraham scowled and watched the boat fight against the crashing waves.

"Patience, Cousin. You will join us soon." And with that Japhet ran off to take the last place in the final boat as it was shoved into the surf.

Uncle Ahanu came to stand beside Abraham. "It is cold today. I do not envy the fishermen."

Abraham frowned as he watched the boats retreat. He caught his uncle's sideways glance from the corner of his eye but continued to stare angrily at the boats. Uncle Ahanu chuckled and put a hand on his shoulder.

"Come, let's go up to the platform where we can watch them better."

Abraham slowly made his way back up the ladder after Uncle Ahanu and lay down on the platform to watch the boats as they bounced and plunged with each wave. The whales had a head start of several leagues, and progress was slow as the rowers fought to catch up to them.

Abraham watched the boat he knew held Pannoowau as it struggled to clear the white caps. He replayed the boy's words over and over in his mind and grew angrier with each rendition.

Abraham scanned the horizon. The whales were slipping further into the distance. He couldn't help hoping the rowers would not catch the whales this time, just to spite Pannoowau.

It was hours before the boats came back to shore, their crews dejected and soaked through. Abraham felt guilty over his silent curse but said nothing.

"Come, let us go and encourage the men," Uncle Ahanu said and moved toward the ladder.

Abraham followed him down and looked around as he reached the bottom. Da looked angry as he approached them.

"The beasts were too fast for us," Da grumbled as the men dragged their boats up to the dry sand above the tide line. "You didn't warn us soon enough, Abraham. You must stop daydreaming and keep better watch! You have cost me a lot of money today."

"I was watching!" Abraham blurted and instantly regretted it. Da spun on his heel and smacked him across the face with his open hand. Tears stung the back of his eyes as he watched Da's retreating form.

Just then Pannoowau approached. "Half-breeds can't do anything right!" he said as he passed.

Abraham's face and neck burned with anger. He felt a hand come to rest on his shoulder.

"Peace," Uncle Ahanu said.

"But it's not my fault!"

"It is only wind. The men are disappointed."

"Da always blames me when things go wrong. It's not my fault." Abraham scowled at the retreating men, trying to burn holes in the backs of their heads.

"Which wolf do you want to win?" Uncle Ahanu said softly.

Abraham paused. His anger made him feel strong, powerful, righteous. He didn't want to give it up. He stood in silence and listened to his uncle's steady breathing. Nothing ever seemed to upset him.

"Look!" Uncle Ahanu pointed up into the air. A large pelican soared on the wind, circling. "See how little effort the bird uses? He lets the wind carry him. How graceful he is and how strong his wings! He was created for flying, but have you seen it on the shore?"

Abraham nodded.

"On the shore it is ungainly, awkward, clumsy. But in the air … it is beautiful! It does not fight against the wind. It uses it to its advantage. You must learn to let your anger go. Let the wind blow under you to make you stronger. Use its energy to soar." Then after a long pause, his uncle continued, "Which wolf do you want to win?"

But his uncle didn't wait for an answer. Slowly, he limped toward the shelters to join the others. Abraham silently watched him go before turning back toward the sea. The sky had darkened, and clouds were building. A storm was coming.

Chapter 14

Reunions

Etienne, November 20, 1664

It took only a couple of days to sail to Texel Harbor from London. The weather had turned cold as November came to an end. I was glad for my wool sweater, skull cap, and stockings, though I longed for a warmer coat. I had been sent up the main mast to help bring in the sails. With that done, I looked out at the familiar coastline. Rows of houses with steeply pitched roofs lined the shore beyond the star-shaped fortress that overlooked the channel between the peninsula at the northernmost end of the mainland and Texel Island.

As I looked off toward the beach at the southern end of the island, I could see a flurry of activity. An enormous whale was lying on its side on the sand. Swarms of men were moving around it with large knives and spears preparing to cut it up. I thought of Abraham and wondered if he knew how dangerous his whaling venture could be.

Sand bars had filled much of the bay between Texel and Amsterdam. Only narrow and shallow passages remained for the smaller ships to pass through. As a result, the larger galleons had anchored in the deeper waters near Texel. Many smaller ships, like *Le Dauphin*, whose captains were unfamiliar with these waters had opted to do the same, as had Master Jolls. I heard a loud holler and looked down to see the crew gathering as Master Jolls prepared to address us. I scrambled down the ropes and took my place among them.

"We will be staying no more than three days, just long enough to order the harpoons and resupply. After that we set sail for the Baltic Sea and the Gulf of Finland. We must reach the Swedish settlement of Nyenschantz on the easternmost point of the gulf, where we will meet with the traders from Muscovy, and then return before the Gulf of Finland freezes over." He paused to scan the crowd. "So, take your leave on shore; you can collect your earnings as you disembark. But be sure to return by sunrise on the third day or you may find your own way home." With that the crew was dismissed.

I collected my pay, hurried toward the boats, and took the only available seat beside Mr. Palmer. He looked me over and I saw a sly smile cross his lips.

"Be sure you aren't late in returning, boy. As much as he may like you, he won't wait if you fail to return on time."

"I won't be late," I said, trying to keep my tone even.

It was not difficult to find a small boat leaving for Amsterdam. I paid my fare and before long I had arrived in the city of canals. It was just as I'd remembered it. The smell of pancakes reached my nostrils and it felt as if I'd never left. The canals were filled with rowboats shuttling people and goods about the city. Women swept off the stairs leading up to their front doors or carried bundles home from the markets. With the weather growing colder, there weren't as many children playing outside, only the occasional boy fishing in the frigid canals. They had not yet frozen over for the winter, but I guessed it wouldn't be long. The birch trees had long since lost their leaves and stood bare. They looked like frail old men, tired and starved.

I thought of Magdalena. It would be so good to see her again. I wondered what had happened to her father. When we'd left, he had been arrested for piracy. Was he still imprisoned, or had he been hanged? I hoped her father would not be at home, but if so, then maybe enough time had passed so that Jacob Janssen van den Burgh may forgive my childish indiscretions. His daughter and I had been friends, but he had disapproved of that friendship; I knew not why. Perhaps he'd thought, like so many others had, that I was not good enough for her. But Magdalena had not been dissuaded and Janssen had tried to kidnap me and impress me into service on his ship.

My pulse quickened as I hurried along the street toward the tavern of the Green Leviathan. I shuddered. This had been where I had first met Janssen and where I'd received the lead on my father's whereabouts when he'd gone missing. So much had changed since then. I had changed.

As I rounded the corner, I caught a glimpse of someone ducking into the doorway of the tavern. I felt a prickle run up my spine. Was I being followed? I shook it off. Who would want to follow me? I continued down the street and couldn't shake the feeling that someone was behind me. But each time I turned to look the street was empty. I crossed the bridge where Lena and I had gazed up at the stars and shared stories about the constellations. Then I turned toward the double-wide townhouse where I had once spent some of the best days of my life.

I was out of breath by the time I arrived and climbed the stairs to stand before the imposing wooden door. I paused to catch my wind and then gingerly reached for the brass ring and rapped on the door.

It was a few moments before the door opened a crack to reveal the familiar ebony face of Janssen's maidservant, Chloe. Her eyes widened in recognition, the whites of her eyes standing in stark contrast to the darkened parlor behind her. Her hand came to her mouth, and she quickly opened the door and ushered me inside.

"Master Etienne, how tall and broad you've grown! How came you here?"

"I'm working as a seaman now," I said and smiled. "I don't have much time, but I was hoping to visit with Po and to see if, well maybe, to ask whether …."

Chloe made a clicking sound with her tongue against her teeth and shook her head. "Po is working in the stables, but I know he will welcome a break. The Lady no is here now," she said and eyed me with the hint of a smile. "Come, I take you to Po."

"There's no need. I remember the way," I said and hurried off toward the kitchen at the back of the house. I crossed the kitchen floor and saw that the potager's stove Papa and I had made was well used. I smiled.

Wind was blowing the dried leaves across the courtyard making small eddies as they swirled past. The garden looked sad and desolate, striped of all life and warmth. It made me feel sad. The pot that had held the tulip I'd given Lena was lying empty on its side by the large elm tree where Lena had once kissed me. I lifted my hand to my cheek, remembering. What had happened since I'd been gone? Had the tulip died? Maybe she'd planted it in the ground and didn't need the pot anymore?

An uneasy feeling started crept up my spine. I forced myself to continue towards the stable. As I pushed open the door the warm smell of manure and hay filled my nose. A horse nickered as I entered. I heard a gasp and suddenly found myself enveloped in Po's arms. We hugged, patted each other's shoulders, and then stepped back to examine one another.

Po was taller too, though he was still skinny. His face split into a huge smile, and his teeth glowed in the dimness of the stable.

"You come back!" he said.

"I came back," I said, grinning. "How've you been?"

"Good! I be good. I kept your nine pins safe for you. See, I get them!"

He was off like a jackrabbit before I could tell him that wouldn't be necessary. He came back carrying the satchel before him like a prized crystal bowl.

I took the proffered bag and pulled out one of the pins. The wood had been waxed and polished so it reflected the light of the lantern on its smooth surface. The ball had had a small tear in one of its seams a casualty of one of our boisterous matches, but that too had been mended with care.

"You took very nice care of them," I said and handed them back.

"You no want?" Po asked and frowned.

I laughed. "I gave them to you to keep. They were a gift. They are yours now."

He nodded and smiled.

We spent the afternoon talking, remembering, as I helped him shovel manure and groom the horses. Finally, I'd worked up the courage to ask about Magdalena.

"She no here. Gone to a party in the countryside."

"Do you know when she will be back?"

He shook his head. "Maybe two or three days?"

I sighed.

"You will wait for her?"

I shook my head. "I have to get back to the ship tomorrow or the next day."

"But you stay tonight?" He looked so hopeful I couldn't help smiling.

"I will stay tonight."

Chloe made a cream soup with potatoes and fish. It was delicious and warmed me up inside. I stayed the night with Po in the little room he still shared with his mother above the stables. Po and I were now too big to share a single cot, so Chloe made up a mattress for me by the fireplace.

It was wonderful spending time with Po again, but when the morning came it was time for me to go. I bid him goodbye, and he hugged me again before I left. I felt badly that I'd not been able to see Lena again though. Slowly, I left the house and wandered back towards market square. I still needed a warmer jacket, and this would be a good place to purchase one. The square was bustling with people browsing the stalls and haggling with the vendors. I stopped to buy a *pannekock* and then climbed the steps of the municipal building. I sat down on the steps to enjoy the pancake's warm, sweet goodness. I smiled and remembered how Lena had stolen my toy musketeer and forced me to chase her down to the market. That had been the start of our friendship. We'd sat together along the canal and shared a pancake that day.

I looked out over the market square and watched the people going about their business. I was surrounded by crowds of people, and yet I felt so … alone. As I finished the last of my pancake, a young woman caught my attention. She seemed familiar. I searched the crowds for her and finally found her approaching a shop across the square from where I sat. She was beautiful! The lady paused and looked up and I saw her face. Suddenly, I recognized her. It was Magdalena! I couldn't believe it. I rubbed my eyes and looked again. She really was there!

Lena was dressed in a deep blue gown that peeked out from under her wool coat as she walked. She was smiling and walking with her hand in the arm of a darkly clad gentleman, her uncle maybe? I couldn't see his face as it was turned away from me. Her uncle had taken her in when her father had been arrested. He had seemed to be a nice man. He'd had the same build and similar look as her father too. It most likely was her uncle then; he didn't act like a suitor, and she was still too young for marriage.

As Lena looked toward me again, I caught a moment's recognition in her blue eyes, but she quickly turned away and led her escort over to the nearby shop. I stood and hurried after her, but she ducked into the shop before I could cross the square.

I was approaching the shop when a man stepped in front of me.

"Excuse me, sir," I said and tried to push past him.

"Wher' ya going in such a hurry?" The voice replied. I looked up to see Palmer blocking my path. He flashed his yellow teeth in a malicious smile and put a hand on my arm.

"What do you want?" I asked impatiently. "We are not aboard ship now. I don't need to obey your orders here."

"No, ya don't, Boy, but you should be 'ware of entangling yerself with pretty, young girls. Bad things oft 'appen."

I scowled at him. "What do you know about it?" I pulled my arm away and pushed past him. I hurried toward the shop, looked through the window, and tried to catch Lena's eye again. She saw me and quickly turned her back to me as she stooped to examine a rich blue and white patterned vase. Blond hair tumbled down her back in waves, like a jubilant waterfall, to pool at her narrow waist.

I knew she had seen me and recognized me. Why was she so obviously avoiding me? I stood awkwardly outside the shop and tried to decide what to do. I had just determined to enter the shop, when Lena again caught sight of me and shook her head ever so slightly. Just then her escort looked over toward her and smiled. Quickly, she turned away and led her escort toward the back of the shop, but not before I recognized him. It was her father. Jacob Janssen van den Burgh was not hanged. He was alive and here in Amsterdam. Judging from Lena's reaction, I'd have no hope of meeting with her now.

Sighing, I turned and slipped back into the crowd. I wandered aimlessly, cursed my luck, and wondered what to do next. Then I remembered I still needed a warmer coat. This was as good a place as any to buy one. I found a shop selling woolen garments and entered. The store smelled of warmth with the comforting odors of cedar and wool.

The shop owner approached and looked me up and down. I told him my need and he took some quick measurements and disappeared through a narrow door at the back of the shop. He returned carrying a long, navy coat.

"This coat is not new. It was my son's, but I think it will fit you nicely. It might fit your budget better, though I can show you a new one if you prefer." I took the coat and looked it over. It was heavy and in excellent condition.

"Why doesn't your son need it? It looks like it's hardly been worn. Has he outgrown it?" I asked and looked at the lining.

"My son died a few years back, young sir. He won't need it anymore." The shopkeeper looked down for a moment and took a ragged breath.

I nodded and paid for the coat. Then I returned to the Green Leviathan to inquire about a room for the night. I took a seat at the bar and ordered a meal and an ale. As I picked at my food, I overheard a conversation between several merchants sitting at a table behind me.

"I think it prudent to start arming our merchantmen," a deep voice said.

"Why? Do you know something I don't know?" The second voice had a nasal, squeaky edge to it.

"King Louis XIV has ambitions to take the Spanish Netherlands and benefit from their trade routes. He is looking for any excuse to invade. And I heard a rumor that the English are building their fleet to spring a surprise attack on the Dutch. Since King Louis signed the mutual defense treaty with the Dutch, a British attack will land us right in the middle of a war."

"War is never good for business," a melodic voice said.

"Success always leads others to envy the rewards," the nasally voice said.

"Well, I for one will not risk my cargo needlessly," the man with the deep voice said, decisively. "Take the warning as you will. I will take my leave. We sail early tomorrow."

I thought of the conversation I'd heard between Captain Jolls and the mysterious man. War would make the Atlantic crossing far more dangerous. And war between the English and Dutch might well reach the colonies. *What would that mean for my family and friends? Should I try to warn them?* I finished my meal. Any letter I sent had no hope of reaching them before my own ship arrived. I sighed. *It will have to wait until I return then.* I spent a considerable amount of time nursing my drink before finally heading up to bed. And so, I was late in rising the next day. It was well past noon when I finally left the tavern.

As I headed toward the docks, I again ran into Mr. Palmer. He flashed me one of his winning smiles and said, "The last ship leaving for Texel is readying to sail. Better hurry or ye'll miss it." Then he rushed past me.

Sighing heavily, I hurried after him and caught up to him at the docks. I followed him along the pier to a sleek-looking barque moored at the end. The name *Zeelandia* was painted in elegant writing on the side. We approached a sailor standing by the gangplank. He seemed to recognize Mr. Palmer and then he glanced over to me. Turning back to Palmer, the sailor nodded and stepped aside. Palmer nudged me up the gangplank and followed close behind me.

"How much is the fare?" I asked as we ascended.

"It's been taken care of," he said and stood beside me at the railing.

"Thank you," I muttered distractedly as I stared out over the city.

Did Lena still blame me for her father's arrest? I wondered. *Was that why she wouldn't acknowledge me?* I had so wanted to talk to her again. Who knew when I would be back this way again?

I walked toward the ship's bow, leaned on the rail, and stared out over the gathering crowd. I'd come all this way, and only God knew if I'd ever make it back again. It'd been my one chance. ... I was vaguely aware of other sailors boarding the ship.

Suddenly, I caught a glimpse of bright cobalt. I scanned the crowd and saw a flash of blond. I sighed and closed my eyes. Now I was imagining things!

When I opened my eyes, Magdalena was standing there on the

causeway. She looked up at me, smiled, and waved. She was so beautiful! I waved back, smiling broadly. I called out to her, but the wind swallowed my voice. She looked over her shoulder and as I followed her gaze, I saw the back of the same man that had accompanied her earlier. She grabbed the sleeve of a passing sailor and pulled a piece of paper out of her purse. She folded it, handed it to the sailor, and pointed up at me. The sailor took the note, nodded, and started up the gangplank. I turned back to Lena. She flashed me another brilliant smile and pointing at her chest she pantomimed the word love by crossing her arms across her chest and then pointed to me. She blew me a kiss and then turned and disappeared into the crowd.

I searched everywhere for her, but she was gone. Then I heard the call, "Captain's aboard, prepare to set sail!"

As I turned instinctively, ready to help, I saw Mr. Palmer hurry down the gangplank. The sailor at the bottom handed him a coin purse, hurried up the gangplank, and pulled it up behind him. I watched in confusion as Palmer darted along the pier and boarded a smaller gaff-fitted sailboat.

I watched the shoreline slip past and tried not to panic. I imagined the ship would stop briefly in Texel anyway, and I would be able to slip off then. I decided to go look for the sailor who had accepted Lena's note. Not finding him, I looked instead for the first mate and found him standing near the portside bow. He looked over at me as I approached.

"What are you doing standing here, Boy? Go and stow you bag and get your assignment from the officer of the watch."

"I am not part of the crew, sir. I only needed a ride back to Texel, where I will rejoin the crew of *Le Dauphin*."

"Is that so?" He stared hard at me and said, "Then I believe you have misunderstood. We are not stopping at Texel."

"But Mr. Palmer said he purchased passage for me to Texel only."

"Mr. Palmer sold your contract to us for the journey to the Caribbean, though we will be stopping off first in Offra to pick up cargo."

"Offra? Where is that?" I asked and tried to comprehend the situation.

"It is on the western coast of Africa."

I looked out over the bay. We were leaving the deeper waters near Amsterdam and were approaching the narrow neck leading into the Texel Roads. As we entered the neck, I saw that the deep grey waters were lighter. Large sand bars were visible on both sides of the ship.

I looked up to see the first mate give hand signals to the pilot manning the wheel on the back upper deck. I had to admit my admiration for the skill they showed in navigating the shallow draft ship through these treacherous waters.

I tried to think what to do. I had to get back to the *Dolphin*. I could jump overboard and swim. Last time I'd done that, I almost didn't make it. And this time of year, the water would be frigid. It was very likely I'd never reach the shore. The harbor was busy. Maybe a sailor on the smaller craft or an oarsman would see me and come to my aid, or maybe not. We approached Texel harbor and I could see the North Sea beyond it. If I was going to jump, it would have to be now.

I gripped the railing and readied myself for the plunge, when I felt two strong hands grab each of my shoulders and pull me back. They spun me around and I found myself looking into the familiar face of Jacob Janssen van den Burgh.

"Welcome aboard, Etienne. It has been a long time since I have had the pleasure of offering you my hospitality." His eyes narrowed and a sinister-looking smile crossed his lips. "Come, let me show you to your accommodations."

Part 2, Storms

December 1663

Long Island and the Atlantic Ocean

Within my mind there dwells this lingering thought, How oft from ill the greatest good is wrought, Perhaps some shattering wreck along the strand, Will help to make the fire burn more bright, And for some weary traveller to-night, 'Twill serve the purpose of a guiding hand. ➻ "Evening," *Driftwood* by Olivia Ward Bush-Banks

Long Island, Boston Harbor by Clement Drew (1808-1889). Image is in the Common Domain.

Chapter 15

Preparations

Abraham, December 2, 1663

Abraham stood at the long wooden table chopping root vegetables to add to the stew he and Mum were preparing for the whaling men. In the down time between whale sightings, they had built a small shack behind the rows of bunk houses to serve as a kitchen and storage space for the large barrels that hopefully would be filled with the precious whale oil soon. Mum had come to join them on the coast rather than stay in their home at North Sea alone, though her delivery date was fast approaching.

Abraham grew angry as he mulled over the events of the morning. A whale had been sighted while Sam was on watch. Abraham had tried to sneak onto one of the boats, but Pannoowau had alerted Da. In spite, Abraham had tried to trip his adversary as he ran for the boats, but had failed. Pannoowau had reeled on him and struck him in the face. That had led to the fight. Abraham had tackled the older boy to the ground and they had wrestled in the sand, until Da pulled them apart, slapped Abraham in the face, and sent him back to help Mum with the food.

It wasn't fair! It wasn't fair that he was stuck here with Mum and his little brothers, while the rest of the men were out there on the sea! How would he ever prove he was as capable as his brothers if he was never given the chance?

Mum stretched, ran a hand over her swollen belly, and sighed. "I must go make water again," she said and paused a moment to watch him. "Careful, *Anarak,* or you will cut yourself." Then she wrapped a wool blanket around her shoulders and walked to the door. "Be sure to finish your chores, boys."

Abraham watched his younger brothers as they sat on the floor near the fireplace. Isaac was trying to teach Jacob and Caleb how to play *My Ship Sails.* It was an easy game, based on luck, where the winner was the first person to collect seven cards of one suit. Seven cards were dealt out to each player. Then each player discarded one card from his hand and picked up the discard on his right to add to his hand. It continued in this manner until a player won and shouted, "My Ship Sails."

"We really need four players," Isaac said. "Abraham you should come and play with us."

"You could come and help me, so I'll be done sooner, and then we could all play," Abraham replied with an edge to his voice.

Isaac snorted. "I've already done my chores. I carried the water for the kettle and the stewpot. *And* I helped you chop wood for the fire."

Abraham dumped the rest of the vegetables into the pot and sat down next to Caleb to play a round of cards.

"No, don't play that card," Abraham said. He leaned over to help Caleb. "See, these are the same suit. Play that one instead."

Caleb grinned and played the card he suggested.

"Why are you helping him!" Isaac complained and retrieved the card Caleb discarded. "I could have used the other one more."

"He's still learning," Abraham said.

Just then the door opened with a gust of cold wind, and Mum entered. She shut the door behind her, sighed, and rubbed her lower back.

"I will never get anything done, at this rate," she said. She sounded tired. "I am ready for this child to be born."

The younger boys giggled and returned to their game.

"Oh, Abraham, thank you for finishing the vegetables," Mum said, noticing the table had been cleared. "Is there any deer meat left?"

"No. We used it up yesterday," Abraham replied.

"I hope the men are safe out there," Mum said. "The weather looks like it is taking a turn for the worse. What would we do if they run into trouble? They are really on their own out there."

Abraham looked up from the game and said, "Uncle Ahanu could send up an alarm to call for more canoes to rescue them."

Mum looked at him with worry in her eyes. Then she sighed. "The boats are a long way out and the sea is rough. If something goes wrong, no one could get to them in time. But I shouldn't worry you. God will look after them." She paused and stirred the vegetables in the pot. "You are such a help, *Anarak*! What would I do without you? Could you help me shuck the clams?"

Abraham stood and rejoined his mother in the kitchen. She used a short, thin knife to pull open the two shells. Then she scooped out the soft clam and dumped it into a bowl.

Abraham picked up a knife and worked with her in silence. As they neared the end of the bucket of clams, Abraham looked up at Mum timidly and said, "I know Da makes you go to church with the rest of us because it's expected, but what do you believe? Do you believe in God, or do you still worship the Great Spirit, like Uncle Ahanu?"

Mum wiped her hands on her apron. "Come and sit," she said. "My feet are hurting and my back aches." She picked up the bowl of shucked clams and dumped them into the simmering stew. Then she sighed and sank heavily into her rocking chair.

Abraham followed her to the hearth and sat down on a stool near her.

"Is not God the Great Creator Spirit?" Mum asked.

Abraham shrugged. "The Bible says God created the heavens and the earth and everything in them. He created the fish of the sea, the birds of the air, and all creatures that walk or crawl on the earth. Then he created mankind, male and female. The man, Adam, he formed from the dirt and then the woman, Eve, he formed from a rib he took from Adam's side." Abraham paused and took a deep breath before continuing. "But Uncle Ahanu says the Great Spirit first created the Little People, who live in the rocks. Then, he took his bow and shot arrows into the ash trees, causing humans to emerge from the bark. After creating people, *then* he created all the animals of every kind. The stories are different. Does that mean God and the Great Spirit are also different?"

Mum sat quietly rocking for a few moments. Finally, she smiled and looked Abraham directly in the eyes. "You ask good questions, *Anarak*. My people have another story too. It begins before the creation of humans. It goes like this:

A woman spirit fell from heaven and landed on the earth. The earth at that time was a gigantic turtle encased in darkness. The woman became pregnant and soon bore twin sons who displayed opposite personality traits. One, named Glooskap, *or*

Good Spirit, was blessed with good virtues. He wanted the earth to be light and pleasant. The other twin was named Nanabozho, or Bad Spirit, and he wanted only darkness to cover the earth.

Good Spirit started the work of creation by turning his mother's head into the sun and her body into the moon. Then he made beneficial plants and animals. He fashioned soil into two images, male and female, and gave them human souls by breathing into their nostrils. At the same time, Bad Spirit created poisonous plants and reptiles to threaten people's welfare. Bad Spirit also formed clay into two images that he intended to be humans, but they were deformed like apes.

The two brothers fought over which of their plans for the universe would prevail. It was a furious two-day battle. Bad Spirit killed Good Spirit, but Good Spirit could not stay dead, so he arose and breathed again. Then he defeated Bad Spirit and sent him into the netherworld for eternity. Bad Spirit still wants equal power and tries to influence people to this day.

Mum paused and looked at Abraham. "Many years ago, when I was a young girl a little older than you are now, your grandfather, Ralph Dayton, became an interpreter between my people and his own. He came often and spent many days and night with my family. My father was the chief then, and your grandfather worked hard to learn our words. As he learned our language, he also taught me his. I was able to learn his words easier than the rest of my family, so he worked more with me. He even taught me to read his English words using a Bible he always brought with him. Then he taught me to write. That was how I was able to help negotiate the land deals between my tribe and the English settlers who came here.

"He left a Bible for me to practice with and as I began to read it, I recognized the stories of creation, and of Eve and the Bad Spirit, who takes the shape of a serpent, just like in many of our stories. God told Eve there would be a battle between her descendant's son and the Bad Spirit, who the Bible calls Satan. The Serpent would strike his ankle, but he would strike the Serpent's head. And then Eve gave birth to twins, Cain and Abel. Cain killed his brother and went to live with the other people. *Who were those other people? Were they the deformed people created by Bad Spirit? Maybe*, I thought. And finally, Mary gives birth to Jesus, the descendant who would fight against the Bad Spirit, against Satan. He gives his life but is raised again to defeat Satan once and for all and send him into eternal damnation."

Abraham frowned. "But you are mixing up the stories. I don't understand what you're saying."

Mum smiled, gently. "Don't you see? Go and get your father's Bible."

Abraham signed but stood and went to fetch it. His ankle still hurt some and he limped over to the table by the bed where his father kept it.

As he returned, Mum said, "Read to me Psalm 19."

Abraham took a moment to find the place and began, "The heavens declare the glory of God; the skies proclaim the work of his hands. Day after day they pour forth speech; night after night they display his knowledge. There is no speech or language where their voice is not heard."

"That is enough," Mum said gently. "God has made himself known to all people. The stories of creation, the flood, the struggle between Good and Evil, they have been passed down by word of mouth for generations upon generations. Your grandfather's people learned to write many generations past and preserved the stories in the Bible. My people did not have writing, and so, the stories changed ever so slightly with each new generation, as each new

Shaman remembered what he had been told. But the truth is there, in those stories. In Romans 1:20 it says, 'For since the creation of the world God's invisible qualities – his eternal power and divine nature – have been clearly seen, being understood from what has been made, so that men are without excuse.'" Mum paused. "You asked if I believe in God or the Great Spirit. I believe in him."

Abraham nodded and stood awkwardly to return the Bible to Da's nightstand.

The tide had turned, and the sun had trekked across the sky, but still there was no word of the fishermen. So, Abraham gathered up a wool blanket and two bearskins and went to join his uncle on lookout.

Word had already spread to the Shinnecock and Montauk villages. Women, children, and old men began to gather on the shore as the whale was slowly washed up by the tide. The boats had finally arrived hauling their catch, the men clearly exhausted. It was fully dark now as Abraham joined the others in building a great fire in a large pit dug into the sand. A large try pot was set over it to boil the fat into oil.

As the whale came to rest on the damp sand, Uncle Ahanu approached and moved around the animal. He said prayers of thanks to the Great Spirit and blessings for the spirit of the whale. When he was finished, Abraham joined the older boys in removing the fins, while the men removed the tail. These were placed in a large ring of stones to be sacrificed to the Great Spirit. Abraham joined the men, who were gathering around the stone circle to sing and dance in celebration for the great gift of the whale. Smoke rose, curling up to the heavens, as the men continued to dance and sing. Abraham's ankle began to ache, but he kept going, and tried to ignore the pain. He would prove to his Da that he was ready to join the others in the boats.

They celebrated late into the night. Abraham collapsed onto his blankets as the fire burned low in the sand pit nearby and stars winked at him behind drifts of cloud. The night would be cold. He pulled another fur over himself and was soon asleep.

The morning broke through a thick hazy fog. Abraham's ankle was stiff and aching. He reached into his pack and pulled out some of the medicated fish oil Uncle Ahanu had given him. He scooped some up in his fingers, rubbed it between his hands to warm it, and then massaged it into the skin around his ankle. He looked out at the surf slapping against the bulk of the whale carcass lying dark and ominous on the beach. Today the hard work would begin.

Abraham ate and then joined the men in flensing, or cutting off the fat, or blubber, from the whale. Large strips of it were sliced off and given to the women who added it to the try pot. The women took turns stirring the oil so it would not burn as it boiled down into the valuable honey-colored oil. Impurities would be removed and then the oil would be sealed into wooden barrels to be shipped to Europe where it would fetch a good price.

The fat was slimy and caused the knife to slip in Abraham's hands. It would be easy to cut off his own finger if he weren't careful. And the smell was atrocious! The heavy acrid scent permeated his clothes, his hair, and his nostrils.

Once all the blubber was cut off and boiled, the meat would then be cut into strips and divided among the people. Even the bones would be removed and dried to make tools, ornaments for leather belts, and ceremonial items. Little would be wasted. It would take weeks of hard work with everyone helping to process the whale, but with luck they would make enough money from the sale of the oil and baleen so that Da could repay the loan he owed to Mr. King.

Chapter 16

Zeelandia

Etienne, December 2, 1664

I felt helpless as the *Zeelandia* sailed past Texel without stopping to enter the North Sea. From there we sailed through the English Channel and continued to follow the coastline south southwest. Captain Janssen allowed me the freedom of the ship, so long as I willingly served as one of his crew. What other choice did I have? I had no way of getting back to Texel, and even if I did, the *Dauphin* was long gone by now in the opposite direction, braving the frigid waters of the Baltic Sea and then the Sea of Finland. I knew Captain Jolls would not have waited for me. It would not be long before the Sea of Finland froze over and isolated the small settlement of Nyenschantz and sealed off all access to Muscovy for the long winter.

I was scrubbing the deck when a young timid sailor approached me. He looked around furtively, reached into his pocket and pulled out a folded piece of paper. He handed it to me quickly and then darted off.

I looked down at the paper. My name was written on it in a neat, elegant handwriting. I quickly opened the paper and read.

Dearest Etienne,

I am so happy to have seen you again, no matter how briefly! I never thought I would. A lot has changed since you left. As you discovered, Papa managed to escape the hangman's noose by paying off the West India Company for infringing on their monopoly. He is still sailing and trading, though I haven't inquired on the legality of his excursions. You mustn't be too hard on him for trying to make a living for us in these competitive times. He is not really a bad man at heart.

I am sorry I avoided you when I first recognized you. I was afraid of how Papa would react if he saw you. He still harbors anger toward you, but I have endeavored to convince him to forgive you. Which reminds me .... We ran into your friend, Mr. Palmer, after you left. He had a long, private conversation with Papa, after which Papa smiled and seemed eager to enlist you on his ship. I expect he will treat you fairly should your paths ever cross again.

I don't know if I will be able to find you, but I will look for you along the docks. I have missed you and look forward to seeing you again.

Love Lena

P.S. I still have the tulip you gave me. I planted it in the tulip bed in the back garden where it has spread, producing several more of its kind. I can't wait to show you when you return!

I quickly reread the letter and smiled at Lena's naivety, but then Janssen *was* her father. Of course, she must think the best of him. I folded the note and slipped it into my pocket with the one I had written to Nicolas hoping we might stop some place in France, if not, La Rochelle, where I could send it. Then I went back to mopping the deck.

Ominous clouds gathered as we sailed past Brest, the westernmost point of France, and then the rain began as we entered the Bay of Biscay. Janssen took his place at the wheel with the pilot. The waves were rising, and the men had to work together to hold the course. Janssen saw me standing on the lower deck and called me over.

"Etienne, go below decks and make sure that all the lanterns are extinguished. Stow any loose items. Now!"

"Yes, sir," I said and hurried to complete the task. When I returned, I saw Janssen and the pilot straining at the wheel.

"Etienne! Come here and help us hold the wheel," Janssen barked.

I hurried over and took up a place between the two men. I could feel the force of the wind and waves trying to pull the rudder out of our control. I had to use all my strength to keep the wheel from turning one way or another. Waves crashed onto the deck and men pulled on the sheets, trying to tame the flapping of the yards.

"Why don't you lower the sails?" I asked, breathing hard.

"If we lowered them, we would lose all control of the ship and we would be capsized," the pilot replied between grunts, as he strained at the wheel.

Suddenly, we heard a horrendous ripping sound. I looked up at the main topsail tearing. Sailors were shouting and scrambling to lower the sail as the tear increased. I looked up, at the yard. One side was flapping violently in the wind; the other side was entangled in one of the sheets.

"Get that sail down!" Janssen roared over the screaming wind.

The ship was rocking badly, bending so low the side of the ship was nearly lying prone. Then a surge of water broke over the hull, spilling gallons of water over the deck. The sail would not budge.

I made a split decision and let go of the wheel. The ship lurched as I did, and I heard Janssen curse. I ignored his order to return to my post and darted to the stairs. I slid down and grabbed the railing as I felt the ship start sway violently. I fought my way to the mainsail, grabbed the ratline, and climbed. The ship tipped over again, and I lost my footing. My feet swung out in an arc as I clung desperately to the ropes. I regained my footing and began to climb again. Rain was running down my hair and into my face, and it was nearly impossible to see. I felt my way out along the beam inching along with my feet wrapped tightly around the yard arm. I could feel the ship rising on the crest of a wave and braced myself. The ship plummeted off the peak violently and I fell forward and grabbed the beam with both hands. My heart was thumping wildly. I tried to breathe through the torrent, and regaining my position, crept forward again.

I reached the end of the beam and drew my knife. I hacked at the rope that entangled the sail nearly dropped the knife as another wave crashed onto the deck. Finally, I felt the sail fall away and looked down to see several crewmen hauling away at the sheets.

The ship was still rocking, but not quite so violently now. I closed my eyes. *Thank you, God.* Slowly, I made my way back to the mast and climbed down the ratline.

The storm continued for several hours and finally abated as we were approached the western-most peninsula of Brittany off the coast of France. Several lookouts were sent to the crow's nests and the bow to watch for white caps. I hadn't seen the sun in over twenty-four hours, but as the darkness intensified, I knew it must be getting late into the night. My arms and legs ached. I couldn't remember when I'd last eaten, and my clothes were drenched. It was as if I had swum from Texel.

I was sent to the forecastle deck near the bow sprit to look for white caps. As I stood squinting out at the black water, a hand clamped down on the back of my neck and spun me around. Captain Janssen was staring angrily into my eyes.

"You disobeyed a direct order, Etienne. Do you know the punishment for that?"

"No, sir." My empty stomach clenched. What would he do to me now? Wasn't it enough that I'd been kidnapped and dragged halfway around the world from my family and friends?

"For disobeying a direct order in emergency circumstances, I might have you thrown overboard!"

I swallowed hard and waited for the verdict.

The captain released my neck. "But since your quick reactions also may have saved the ship," he said, looking thoughtful, "I will order ten lashes to be given once we are through these dangerous shoals."

"Ten lashes for saving the bloody ship!" My hands balled into fists at my side.

Janssen's eyes narrowed and when he spoke, his voice held a dangerous tone, though it was barely audible over the sound of the waves beating into the hull. "Fifteen lashes then, and if you utter one more complaint, I will have you thrown overboard. Am I clear?"

"Yes, sir."

"Good." With that he turned on his heal and retreated aft.

I stared out over the water, fuming with anger. Suddenly, I saw white caps crashing onto the rocks up ahead. Should I report it? I'd been tricked by a sniveling, vindictive carpenter to work on a pirate ship – and not just any pirate ship – one captained by the very man who'd tried to abduct me three years ago! Why should I help him? But, then again, if we struck the rocks the ship might sink. I wanted to live. I wanted to see my family again. I turned and shouted the alarm, but it was drowned out by the warning from another lookout. As I looked again, I realized it might be too late. We were already dangerously close.

The pilot heaved on the wheel and Janssen ran to his aid. I heard an awful scrapping sound as the hull of the ship scraped against the rocks and cringed as the terrible teeth-clenching sound reverberated throughout the ship. The hull strained against the rocks, and still the sound of scraping, cracking, and splintering continued. I wanted to melt into the deck and disappear. Finally, we passed by the rocks, the grinding stopped, and we slipped out into deeper water.

Janssen sent another crewman to replace me as lookout on the bow and ordered me to accompany him to check out the damage. I followed him below decks and watched as he lit a lantern and turned to hand it to me. I reached out for it, and suddenly, Janssen struck me in the face. The blow rocked me backwards into the steps.

"Why didn't you alert me to the rocks? Your daydreaming may have cost me my ship and the crew their lives!"

Fear and remorse flooded me, and I struggled to speak. "I'm sorry," I finally managed to say.

I followed Janssen as he surveyed the hold. A large seam had ripped open along the length of the ship below the waterline. Water was pouring in through the breach.

"Go get the oakum and start filling these cracks. And be careful not to set the lantern too close, or you will set the oakum on fire." Then he turned and left me in the near dark. Fear, despair, and anger fought for dominance within me as I stood paralyzed, entombed in the belly of the ship.

The sound of water pouring onto the floorboards called me back. I took a deep, steadying breath. Then I hung the lantern from a hook in the ceiling and turned to examine the breach. There was so much water. What had I done? How could I possibly stop such a torrent?

Chapter 17

A Suitor Arrives

Alsoomse, December 12, 1664

The sun was setting as Alsoomse strode out of the woods carrying three bunnies she'd trapped, strung on a rope, and slung over her shoulder. She entered the *nush wetu*, their winter house, and sat by the fire to skin the rabbits. She added the meat to the clay pot simmering on the edge of the fire and began to clean and stretch the skins onto frames she had made from birch saplings. Her mother looked up at her and clicked her tongue in disapproval.

"You should not be traipsing about in the forest, Daughter. You are a woman now. It is time you learned to stitch properly." Her mother scolded as she sat sewing a new buckskin dress.

"Etienne doesn't mind me hunting and trapping," Alsoomse replied and set her jaw.

"You know what I said about that!" Her mother looked to her

father for support.

Noshi sighed, and said, "Daughter, your mother speaks true. It is better to marry a man of your own people, with similar culture and beliefs. It provides more harmony at home."

Alsoomse finished tying the skins to stretching fames and stood to hang them up to dry. Then grudgingly she pulled the white buckskin from the basket hanging over her bed along with a long needle and sinew thread and sat back down by the fire. Angrily, she jabbed the needle through the hide along the seam joining the front to the back.

"Ow!" She scowled and sucked the blood off her finger. "Why must I learn to make dresses anyway? Why is it so wrong to go hunting? This work is tedious and my stitches refuse to fall in line."

"Soon you will have a husband to hunt for you. You must learn to do women's work properly. One day you will have to make clothing for your own children."

"Why can't I just sell my skins in New Amsterdam and buy clothing from the merchants there?"

"Daughter! Why must you always test my patience?"

"But it makes no sense! We buy their iron pots, steel knives, and axe heads. And I have seen others starting to wear white men's clothing. Why shouldn't we?"

"This is our way! Do you want to become totally dependent upon the newcomers?"

"No! But they are just as dependent upon us as we are on them! They need us for scouting and navigating. They want our beaver and bear skins. They needed us to show them how to grow corn, how to track, and how to hunt. They like our wampum and our land. We can learn from each other and help each other too. Etienne has proved that."

"I won't hear any more about that boy. He is gone now, and you must forget him."

Suddenly, Kitchi rushed into the home. "Sister, a suitor has come," he gasped as he tried to catch his breath.

She looked up sharply. "A *what?*"

"Come." Kitchi grabbed her hand and pulled her up.

Alsoomse and her mother followed him outside. Her father also rose to meet the visitor. A young man wrapped in a new bear skin was standing before them. His arms held several woven blankets, a cured buckskin, and a long wampum belt. He turned to face Alsoomse as she approached and held out his gifts.

"A token from Chogan, who wishes to take you as his wife."

When Alsoomse didn't step forward to accept the gifts, her mother stepped in and took them from the young man. "We will consider your offer," her mother said and backed away.

"No!" Alsoomse turned on her heal and stalked back into the house.

"You remember Chogun?" Kitchi said as he followed her. "He's from the neighboring tribe; he often hunts with Hassun. It is said that he has killed two bears by himself, though I think they must have been *cubs*," Kitchi added and laughed.

"I *know* who he is! He looks like a bear himself and smells like one too!"

Her mother entered the *nush wetu* and laid the gifts down on her bed. "You behaved rudely, Daughter. Chogun would make a good husband, though your father and I had hoped another would have made his offer by now. Still, Chogun would be well able to provide for you."

Alsoomse bent back over her work.

"Won't you even look at the gifts? The blankets are nicely

woven…."

"I will *not* marry Chogun," Alsoomse said without looking up.

Her mother snorted. "You say that now."

"I will not change my mind," Alsoomse said sternly.

Her mother sorted again. "We will see about that, Daughter."

Alsoomse heard Kitchi snicker and glared at him.

"Shall I return the gift, *Ókas?*"

Their mother shook her head. "We must honor Chogun by considering his offer. We will wait a night or two before we return them." Then after a pause, she added, "Leave us. I wish to speak to your sister."

Kitchi stood and grinned at Alsoomse before he ducked through the doorway and disappeared.

"I really do not understand you, daughter," her mother said. She sat by the fire to resume her own work.

"Why must I marry now? There is so much I want to do yet."

"What could you possibly want to do that you cannot do as a married woman?"

"I want to travel to *Manahatta* in the spring to sell my beaver skins…."

"You want to find that white-eyed boy, Etienne," her mother snapped.

"Etienne is a good man and has helped to save our people many times! If not for him, we would not have received our men back last summer, nor been able to talk to the Dutch chief to bargain for our village on *Manahatta*, or even *had* homes to return to next year …."

"I know he is a good *boy*, Alsoomse, but he is not for you," her mother replied more gently. "Let him be friends with your brother, but he can no longer be your friend. Your path is with your own people. You are a woman now. You are no longer free to roam the woods and do as you please. You must take your place with the women of this tribe."

Alsoomse huffed angrily and pretended to study her sewing, though her eyes refused to focus. She heard her mother rise and approach her. She felt her mother's hand come to rest on her shoulder, as its mate lifted her face up to meet her mother's gaze.

"You must take your rightful place in the tribe, Alsoomse." Her mother paused and looked deep into her eyes. "But your place does not have to be the same as mine. Matoaka thought you had promise as a medicine woman. It would be better if her son took you to wife, but she may still be willing to train you, even if he does not."

Alsoomse thought of the handsome third son of the Mohawk sachem and his unusual fawn-colored eyes. She thought again of that day in mid-November when she'd met him. Her father had taken her north to witness the signing of the treaty between the Dutch of Wiltwyck, the Esopus, Mohawk, and her people. She'd thought her father was honoring her for her role in rescuing the Christian women and children kidnapped by the Esopus. But she later realized it had only been a ploy to introduce her to the Mohawk sachem's son.

Okwaho was broad-chested and muscular like Hassun, but not so stiff and serious. His dancing reminded her of a graceful, young stag leaping through the fields. He had a sense of humor too, like Kitchi, and seemed gentle.

"I have an idea …," her mother said, jolting her out of her thoughts. "All young male wolves must eventually leave their pack to establish their own. And every young Alpha must have a Luna, a mate worthy of him. If the young Alpha is not yet ready to leave his pack, we will give him incentive."

Alsoomse stared at her mother in confusion.

Ókas smiled. "We tempt him with the Luna. Have you had any more dreams about the medicine woman?"

"No," Alsoomse said, suspiciously.

"Come, Daughter, there are preparations we must make…."

Chapter 18

A Close Call

"Blow!" Abraham yelled through cupped hands. "There's a blow!"

Sam, Ralph, and his father ran out of the small shacks. Abraham pointed in the direction he'd seen the blow spout. Their eyes turned to look in that direction. Just then another whale breached, and his brothers joined in the call. Uncle Ahanu and Japhet came out of the shelters to join them, followed by a dozen other Indians. Da and his brothers, Japhet, and the others rushed to drag the boats into the water. Uncle Ahanu walked to the shore to offer up a prayer of safety and success to the whalers.

Abraham quickly slid down the ladder and moved toward the closest boat. He was just climbing over the side when Da grabbed him by the collar and dragged him out.

"I told you that you are not coming!" He roared over the crashing waves. "Go home to your mother. You are no longer needed. Go! Now!"

All Abraham could do was stand and watch as the men divided themselves between the boats and shoved them out into the breaking waves. They were wet to the waist as they hauled themselves into the boat, took their places at the oars, and strained to cut through the white foaming tumult. Da and two other men took up the rudders at the back of each boat, leaving Japhet, Sam, and Ralph at the bow of each boat with the harpoons as six other men in each boat strained at the oars.

Sadly, Abraham turned and headed to the cabin behind the sleeping shelters. As he approached, he saw Isaac and Jacob wrestling each other in the sand in front of the cabin. They were too embroiled in their contest to notice him as he passed. Then he looked up and saw Caleb standing on the porch. Caleb was watching him intently. As their eyes met, Caleb cocked his head and gave him a shy smile, then he ran up and wrapped his arms around him.

Abraham patted Caleb's back.

"I love you!" Caleb said.

"I love you too," Abraham smiled down at his little brother and mussed the boy's hair affectionately. Somehow, Caleb could always tell how he was feeling.

Together they walked inside. The room smelled of fish and warm bread. Mum was sitting at her loom by the fire. She looked up from her weaving as they entered.

"There is soup in the pot and bread on the table if you are hungry," she said.

"Hungry!" Caleb said and looked up at Abraham.

Abraham nodded and went to fetch two wooden bowls. He filled one for Caleb and set it down on the table in front of him along with a thick slice of buttered bread. Then he went to fill his own bowl. His hands began to warm as he held the bowl cradled between them and bent to sniff the soup. Aromas of rich whale meat, onion, and garlic made his mouth water and his stomach rumble. He took a seat beside Caleb, picked up a slice of bread, and dipped it into the broth. Hmmm. It was good and warmed him from the inside out. Whale watching was cold business.

Several hours later, the men returned from the hunt. When they did, Abraham could tell from the sounds they were making as they hurried toward the cabin, that something was wrong. Suddenly, the door burst open and Japhet came in carrying a cot from one of the shelters on the beach. He set it up along the back wall, near the fireplace and turned to give Abraham an anxious look. Before he could say anything, Da and Ralph entered with Sam supported between them.

Sam was dripping wet and moaning. They directed him to the cot, stripped off his wet clothes, wrapped him in a wool blanket, and lay him down. Japhet picked up the discarded clothing and hung it by the fire to dry.

"Damned beast got away," Da said, angrily, "and nearly took Sam with him."

"The rope got wrapped around his arm when he threw the harpoon," Ralph explained. "It stuck in well enough, but as the beast dove, he carried Sam with him. He managed to free himself, but he broke his arm going over the side of the boat. It is a miracle he survived at all."

The doorway darkened and Abraham turned to see Uncle Ahanu standing there with his medicine kit in hand. He came in, closed the door behind him, and walked over to look at Sam. He looked in his eyes, felt his head, and then carefully lifted the injured arm out of the blankets. Sam moaned as his arm was exposed.

The arm was purple and hung unnaturally. Strange lumps protruded from his forearm. Uncle Ahanu shook his head slowly and made a strange clucking sound in the back of his throat. Then he took a wooden mug and added bark from the willow and dogwood trees. He crushed them with a pestle and then walked to the hearth to add boiling water from the kettle that hung there. He swirled the tea around with a small bone spoon and let the mixture steep for several minutes. Then he helped Sam to drink it down.

After a few minutes, Uncle Ahanu gently lifted Sam's injured arm and held it at the wrist. He spoke softly to Sam, but Abraham could not hear what he said. Then suddenly, Uncle Ahanu pulled the wrist toward him in one quick motion. Sam screamed, and Abraham saw that the bones had been pulled back into place. Uncle Ahanu splinted and wrapped the arm and then set it gently on the cot as Sam fell into an uneasy sleep.

Chapter 19

Hunting

Alsoomse, December 15, 1663

Alsoomse rose early in the morning and trekked a short way into to woods outside their winter home. She stood on a low rise overlooking the village, obscured from sight beneath the cover of an old oak tree. Snow had fallen the previous night and lay over the landscape like a soft fur blanket. It was a clear day, but cold. She drew her bear skin cloak closer around her as she watched the villagers beginning their morning rituals.

Women prepared food while the men gathered their provisions and weapons for the impending hunting trip. They would stalk deer, elk, and moose and be away from the village for several days, perhaps even weeks. Alsoomse had readied her own pack with food, a sharpened knife, bow and arrows, and a bear skin blanket. Her mother's words still echoed in her ears. *You are a woman now. You are no longer free to roam the woods and do as you please.*

Alsoomse set her jaw with determination, turned her back on the village, and headed into the woods. The snow crunched softly beneath her fur-lined moccasins. The air smelled crisp with the scent of pine and frosted with each breath she exhaled. It was a beautiful morning!

"Hello, Sister." Kitchi stepped out from behind a large tree in front of her and made her jump in surprise. She had not heard him approach.

"Why aren't you with the other men?" She threw her words at him like a spear. Her eyes darkened beneath furrowed brows.

Kitchi raised his eyebrows and then smiled broadly. "Were you thinking of sneaking out on your own?"

She sighed.

"When *Noshi* found you missing, he thought that might be your plan." He laughed. "Come. *Ókas* has another use for you."

Alsoomse turned and followed her brother back to the village with heavy steps.

Their father was waiting for them at the entrance to their *nush wetu*. He looked at Kitchi with a raised eyebrow. Alsoomse glanced at her brother just in time to see the small nod. She huffed softly and approached her father.

"You wished to see me, *Noshi*?"

"Yes, Daughter. Your mother wishes to make a trip north to visit the Mohawk tribe. She has business with their medicine woman. I do not want to send her alone, so you and Kitchi will go with her." He paused and looked her over. "I see you have already prepared for a trip. How fortunate." He gave her a wry smile.

Kitchi chuckled and entered the *nush wetu*. He returned shortly carrying his own pack and weapons. *Ókas* followed him out.

"There you are Daughter. I was wondering where you had

gone." Her mother looked her up and down. "Have you eaten?"

Alsoomse shook her head, and her mother handed her a chunk of corn bread and a piece of dried venison.

"Let's get started," *Ókas* said and started off down the path. "We have a long way to go."

"Are you sure you do not want me to send two warriors with you?" *Noshi* called after them.

"I will be safe enough with Kitchi and Alsoomse," *Ókas* replied.

It took them four days to reach the Mohawk village. As they approached, a man stepped out of the forest. He was tall, broad-shouldered, and moved with the grace of an elk. He approached them slowly and sized them up. *Ókas* stepped forward and greeted him. He made the traditional greeting in return and then smiled broadly as his eyes drifted over Alsoomse.

He turned back to her mother. "I am Okwaho," he said. "You must be here to meet with my mother?"

"I am, but how did you know we were coming?" *Ókas* replied.

"My mother had a vision of you on the path."

Ókas nodded. "This is my son, Kitchi, and my daughter, Alsoomse."

"I have met your son and daughter before," Okwaho replied and nodded to Kitchi. "It is good to see you again, Kitchi. I see your sister is still as wayward as ever?"

Kitchi laughed. "You will find she is not changed. She tried to go hunting alone on the very day we left to come here."

Both men laughed. Alsoomse scowled, and cheeks burned. She

huffed. *What does it matter what this man thinks!*

"Kitchi, do not speak badly of your sister," her mother scolded as they followed Okwaho through the gateway in the palisade.

Alsoomse followed slowly, anger building, as her brother continued to tease and humiliate her as he chatted with Okwaho. The Mohawk led them to a longhouse in the center of the village and asked them to wait as he went to summon his mother. A few minutes later, an older woman preceded Okwaho out of the *nush wetu*. Alsoomse remembered her name was Matoaka.

The women greeted each other warmly, talking in low tones. Alsoomse thought of Etienne. Where was he now? She hoped he was safe. Then she scowled at her brother. She should have left for the hunt earlier. Then she would not have been forced to come on this useless journey!

"Do not be too angry with your brother," a voice said in her ear. Startled, she looked up into Okwaho's fawn-colored eyes, which smiled warmly down at her.

Her anger melted instantly, and her face flushed.

"Alsoomse, come!" She looked past Okwaho to see her mother beckoning her from the doorway.

As she pushed past the young wolf, he caught her shoulder gently, leaned in, and whispered, "Meet me by the great river after the meal tonight. Follow it north for a few paces past the canoe landing. There is an old willow tree bending over the water. I will be waiting there."

Then he released her and joined Kitchi a few paces away. The two walked off together talking and laughing. Alsoomse ducked her head as she entered the longhouse and paused to let her eyes adjust to the darkness. She found her mother sitting near the fire talking with Matoaka, who was weaving a large basket. They both looked up as she approached and sat down beside her mother. Matoaka's sharp eyes examined her for a moment and then softened. She smiled.

"Have you considered my offer, Child?"

"What offer?" Alsoomse frowned and thought back to the last time she had been in the village. They had talked of women's work and Matoaka had recognized her independent spirit. She had told Alsoomse of her own desire for independence when she'd been a girl and how she had then married and settled into her new role. But Alsoomse was determined she would not be broken.

"Do you wish to be trained as a medicine woman or not?" Matoaka asked after a few moments of silence.

Alsoomse looked at her in surprise. Was that what her dream was trying to tell her? Being a medicine woman would allow her freedom to wander and explore the woods as she gathered medicinal plants. It was an accepted role for both men and women. She suddenly felt like an eagle, as if she could soar into the air. A smile lit up her face. "Yes," she said. "I would like that."

The evening meal dragged on long past dark. Alsoomse was anxious to get away, but her mother kept a close watch on her. The men had drifted off to the large fire in the center of the village to smoke and tell stories. She scanned the faces of the men gathered there but could not find Okwaho or her brother.

She felt like a cornered rabbit. She shifted her weight and tried not to look impatient.

Finally, her mother rose to join the other women around the fire in the back of the sachem's longhouse. Her mother took a few steps and then turned to look at her. "Are you coming, Daughter?"

Alsoomse rose quickly and then paused. "I will come in a

moment, *Ókas*. I must first go make water," Alsoomse replied.

"Be quick," her mother said and ducked into the *nush wetu*.

Alsoomse walked slowly toward the edge of the village, and as she reached the extent of the firelight, she ducked around a small house. Keeping to the shadows, she made her way to the palisade and out into the woods. She found the trail that led west to the great river and followed it until she saw the canoes lined up along the shore. Then she slipped into the woods and turned north. She had no intention of walking along the shore where Okwaho could see her coming. She would keep to the safety of the trees until she could assess his intentions.

She moved as quietly as possible through the underbrush, being careful to avoid snapping twigs as she passed. The few inches of snow covering the fallen leaves aided in keeping her footfalls quiet. The snow was powdery and so did not crunch as an icy snow would. She could see the willow tree up ahead. It was immense in height and breath. She approached it cautiously and saw a man standing beneath its canopy. The man's back was toward her. She approached the tree cautiously.

Suddenly, another man stepped out of the bushes to her left. Instinctually, her hand went for her knife and she raised her arm in defense. But the man was ready and easily grabbed her wrist and then her other as she tried to swing at him.

"I mean you no harm," he said and held her arms over her head.

She blinked and pulled her arms free as she looked up into Okwaho's golden eyes. "You startled me!" she said and scowled.

He smiled broadly. "As you had intended to do to me."

The man under the tree alerted to the commotion, now joined them. "Kitich! What are you doing here?"

Kitchi laughed and smacked Okwaho on the shoulder. "I win!" he said.

Okwaho reached into his pouch and handed something to Kitchi.

Alsoomse frowned and looked from her brother to Okwaho and back again.

"I told him you wouldn't come the way he'd instructed, but that you would try to sneak up out of the woods and surprise us."

"So, we decided to lay our own trap for you instead," Okwaho and chuckled. "The bet was just a bit of fun." Then he held out his hand. She looked at it and then at her brother, still scowling.

Alsoomse refused to take the proffered hand and stood rigid where she was.

"I am glad you decided to come," Okwaho said, nonplussed. "I worried you wouldn't, or that you might think I had ulterior motives" he said. "I asked Kitchi to come also so that I would not dishonor you."

Kitchi was still grinning broadly and looked very well pleased with himself.

"Am I so predictable?" Alsoomse muttered to herself.

Kitchi chuckled. "I am going to stretch my legs, but I will not go far." He looked pointedly at Okwaho and then walked toward the river and disappeared through the canopy of hanging boughs.

Okwaho parted the curtain of willow boughs with a hand to let Alsoomse pass through and then followed her under the canopy. He led her to the blanket he'd spread out on the hill overlooking the great North River. He extended a hand to help her sit, but she ignored it and plopped down onto the blanket. He gracefully lowered himself down beside her and spoke. "Kitchi said you rescued a white woman from the Esopus last summer. Is that true?"

"Yes, but I didn't do it alone. Kitchi was there and …" She hesitated, "and another friend of mine."

Okwaho watched her. His eyes seemed to read her thoughts. She looked away.

"Kitchi also told me about the French boy," Okwaho said quietly.

She looked up and found his eyes still watching her. "He did?"

Okwaho smiled with his whole face and leaned back on his arms. He looked up at the moon as it shimmered through the gaps in the hanging boughs. Alsoomse leaned back too and looked up. She relaxed and felt a calmness envelop her. What was it about this man that made her feel like this?

After several long moments, Okwaho asked, "So, you like to hunt?"

"What?" she asked, startled.

"Kitchi said you like hunting. What do you like to hunt?"

"Mostly beaver, rabbit, and fox," she replied. "I sell the pelts in the town of New Amsterdam." And then after a pause, added, "And the meat is good in stews."

"Have you ever shot a deer?"

"No. But I would have if Kitchi had not stopped me!" she said defensively.

"They are such beautiful animals! I have shot many, but it always pains me to do it," Okwaho said and continued to stare up at the moon.

Alsoomse blew out her breath slowly and relaxed. They were silent for a long time. Finally, she asked, "Do you like to hunt?"

Okwaho looked at her thoughtfully. "I do not enjoy hunting as some do, though I am often successful. My father says I have skill in tracking and my aim is true. I hunt because I must. I hunt because it provides food, clothing, shelter, and other necessities we need to live. By hunting, I will be able to support a family someday. But, no,

I do not love hunting."

Alsoomse watched him, curiously. "Do you like fishing?"

He smiled. "I like fishing more. They are not so familiar. One quick blow and they are dead instantly. But a doe. She watches and fears. An arrow or two will bring her down, but then you must get close and cut her throat. She dies slowly, knowing what is happening to her. She is warm and you can feel her heart beating as she bleeds out."

He fell silent. Alsoomse could hear a rustle in the trees and looked up to see a squirrel dart away. Somewhere in the distance an owl hooted.

"I suppose I have really only hunted birds then," Alsoomse said, thoughtfully. "I have laid traps for beaver, rabbit, and foxes. They were already dead with I arrived to retrieve them. Though once I had to finish off a squirrel with a sharp blow to the head. I have never had to actually watch them die. I have shot quail and pheasant with my arrows."

"When I must kill an animal, I always thank her for her sacrifice and stroke her head to comfort her…." he continued. "And when she dies, I pray to the Great Spirit for the gift of life and thank him for the animal's sacrifice. It helps me feel better, but it is not easy to take a life."

Okwaho turned to look at her. "Do you think me less of a man now?"

"No," she said and smiled shyly up at him.

He returned her smile, grunted, and then suddenly stood up. He held out a hand to help her up too. This time she took it. "We should get you back before your mother sends out a search party. I shall leave you with your brother." And then he was gone.

Kitchi popped his head through the boughs. "Come on, Alsoomse. I'll make up an excuse for you." She sighed and followed him back along the shore to the path leading to the village.

"Where have you been?" *Ókas* asked when they arrived back at the longhouse. Fire burned in her mother's eyes.

"I found her wandering around in the forest," Kitchi replied for his sister. "I think she must have gotten herself lost."

Her mother eyed her suspiciously.

"I did not want anyone to come upon me, so I went farther into the woods than I should have. I had trouble finding my way back in the dark."

Their mother studied each of them with furrowed brows.

"Don't worry, mother," Kitchi said. "She was not doing anything inappropriate."

Their mother narrowed her eyes and said, "Next time you will stay closer to the village." Then she turned away without waiting for a reply.

Alsoomse, Kitchi, and their mother were given beds at the opposite end of the long house from Matoaka and her family. Okwaho didn't return until long after they'd settled down for the night. He entered silently and paused briefly as he passed her. Alsoomse pretended to sleep, though it was a long time before sleep finally found her.

Darkness surrounded her. She was cold, and wet, and alone. She felt around trying to discover where she was. She opened her mouth to yell, but only a screech came out. In the distance a small light approached. She looked down at herself in the darkness. Her body was like that of an eagle. She looked around her and discovered that she was inside a large iron cage. Then she felt cold, wetness around her feet. Water was rising around her. What was happening? The light

continued to approach slowly. She could now see that the cage was inside a wooden room, like those made by the white men, but there were no windows. Boxes and crates lined the walls. It was so cold. Where was she? The ceiling was low so that the approaching man had to duck his head. He carried a lantern in one hand and a rope in the other. Then suddenly she knew ... Etienne!

Chapter 20

Medicine Woman

Winter was not the time for gathering medicinal herbs and other plant materials, and so Alsoomse had to content herself with learning to recognize by sight and smell the dried plant materials Matoaka had already gathered. She sat and listened for hours to her mentor as she described how to heal various types of wounds or how to make the antidotes for the different types of snake bites. It was hard to remember it all without watching it being done. She quickly grew bored, her legs were restless, and she looked for any excuse to leave the longhouse on some pretext.

On one such occasion, she became frustrated with the progress of the medicine basket she was weaving and left to get some air before starting it over again. Matoaka sighed and watched her go.

"That girl needs to learn patience." Alsoomse heard the old woman tell her mother as she left.

It is so much easier to be patient looking for rabbit tracks or beaver dens than sitting in the house monotonously weaving! She didn't know where she was going, just that she had to move. She headed off toward the river. It felt good to walk. The wind was cold, and she wrapped her bearskin tighter around her. Here in the open she could breathe! She saw something dart into the underbrush and looked to see what it was…. Suddenly, she ran headlong into someone and would have fallen, had not strong hands grabbed her arms to steady her. She looked up into the soft fawn-colored eyes of Okwaho.

"Where are you going in such a hurry?" he asked. Humor played at the corners of his eyes.

"I don't know."

He raised an eyebrow in question.

"The smoke from the fire was trying to smother me, and I couldn't get the reeds woven tightly enough on the medicine bag I am supposed to make, and …" She sighed. "I had to get out."

A smile flicked across Okwaho's face as he watched her.

"What are you laughing at?" she asked, suddenly angry.

His smile only broadened.

Her face burned in humiliation. "Get out of my way!" she said and tried to push past him. But he stood his ground and would not let her pass. She pulled her hand back to strike him, but he caught it easily and held onto it.

"I am not laughing at you," he said, his voice low and warm. "You surprise me. I have never known a woman like you."

She stared at him. "Is that good or bad?"

He smiled again. "It just is. Wait here. I have something to show you."

He watched her until she gave a slight nod, and then he turned and ran off toward the village. Even in his heavy winter clothing, he looked both strong and graceful. When he returned, he had something in his hand. He held it out to her, and she took it. It was a small pouch. She admired the tight weaving and the black pattern of an eagle woven on the front.

"It's beautiful!"

He smiled.

"Whose is it?" she asked.

"Mine, but you may have it if you want."

"But who made it?" Alsoomse studied the weaving again. It looked a lot like the bags Matoaka made, though it didn't look like her work.

"I made it," Okwaho said softly. "But don't tell your brother."

"You? When?" She looked up into his golden-brown eyes. "Why would you?"

He laughed. "I made it when I was a boy. I was bored and had injured my leg, and I couldn't play with the others. My mother showed me how to weave, so I would not make her crazy. I found I enjoyed it. Sometimes, in the downtime between hunts, after all my arrows are finished and my axe has been sharpened … sometimes I still find time to weave. It is peaceful."

Alsoomse stared at him in surprise. She recovered quickly though, and nodded, smiling, as she examined the pouch again.

"It is very nice work."

"Please keep it," Okwaho said.

She looked up at him again. He looked so earnest. Finally, she smiled and slipped the strap over her head and arm, so that it hung against her right hip.

"Thank you. I must get back to the village now, or your mother will accuse me of slacking." Then she turned and left to the sound of Okwaho chuckling.

Later that evening when her mother was distracted and laughing with the other women, Alsoomse rose and slipped away from the settlement. Her feet moved quickly over the path to the edge of the great river. She turned north and picked her way along the shoreline until she reached the great willow bending over the water. She looked around. No one was there.

She listened. The water seemed to laugh at her as it tumbled over rocks, washed past fallen trees, and swirled in the small eddies along the shore. The waxing crescent moon was barely visible above the trees and made the night all the darker. Stars stood out like thousands of tiny campfires scattered across a great plain.

"I'm glad you've come," a deep melodic voice said behind her.

Alsoomse startled and turned to see Okwaho. She'd not heard him arrive and frowned up at him, but when she saw the humor in his eyes at seeing her surprise, she made an annoyed sound in her throat.

Okwaho laughed out loud, a rich, infectious laugh. Alsoomse couldn't keep from smiling.

"Do you ever think about the future?" Okwaho asked.

She looked at him curiously. "What do you mean?"

"Your father and mine are both are leaders of our people. Do you ever think about what it would be like to take their places someday?"

"No," Alsoomse said. "I don't think about the future much."

"It is a lot of responsibility to lead people. I hope someday, I will do as well as my father," Okwaho said quietly and stared up at the stars.

Alsoomse watched him, and then she too looked up at the stars. "I resent the freedom my brothers have to roam the forest hunting and fishing, while I will be forced to stay in and around the village doing all the tedious jobs women must do."

Out of the corner of her eye she saw Okwaho cock his head to study her. "You think men have freedom? We have responsibilities and obligations. We must go out and hunt and fish so that we can provide meat and skins for our families. If we are not successful, our families may starve or freeze in the winter. Yes, women must grow the corn and vegetables, gather herbs, tan the skins and make clothing, but women also can express their creativity in weaving, beadwork, and pottery."

Alsoomse looked at him in surprise. "Men make things too."

"Yes, we make arrow heads, fishing nets, bows, weapons, and other tools." He paused and smiled at her. "Men and women serve different roles, but both are needed for families and societies to thrive. Only women can birth children, but they cannot do it without men's seed. Men provide meat and hides, but women provide clothing, blankets, cornmeal, and fruit. Just because our roles are different does not mean that all men must be the same. Some men like to hunt, others prefer to fish. Some are warriors at heart, while others are peacemakers, shaman, or medicine men." He paused again. "You are not like other women, and I like that very much."

They stood in silence for a few moments until Alsoomse heard her mother calling for her.

"I must go!" she said and bolted toward the sound of her mother's voice.

The next day, one of the elders came in search of Matoaka. He presented her with a pair of slain rabbits and said his wife's hands were crippled with pain. Matoaka collected three different roots and put them in her medicine bag. Then she and Alsoomse followed the elder to his house. When they arrived, Alsoomse saw that the woman's hands were knotted and deformed so that she could not use them. Matoaka examined the woman and then sent Alsoomse to prepare the smoke house. Matoaka helped the woman to stand and led her there. After a time, Alsoomse placed the red-hot stones in the fire pit and the women undressed and entered the smoke house.

Together they bathed the old woman in water scented with herbs. They poured more water over the hot stones. The steam filled the house and the old woman sighed as slowly her hands began to relax. Matoaka said some words over her. After several long moments, the three women left the smoke house, rinsed off in the cold water of the great river, and dressed. Matoaka and Alsoomse wrapped the old woman in blankets and helped her back to her *nush wetu*. They gently lay her down on her bed and Matoaka instructed Alsoomse to place the roots they'd brought into the mortar and crush them with the pestle until they were a fine mush. Matoaka then added bear fat and a little honey and mixed it into a supple cream, which she gently rubbed into the woman's hands.

Matoaka rose to leave and said, "Either Alsoomse or I will return tonight and again tomorrow to reapply the cream. Your hands should improve in a few days."

The woman nodded and thanked them. Then they left.

As they turned toward home, Okwaho came running. His face looked worried as he caught Alsoomse's eye. A child had come down with a high fever and they were needed at once. They hurried after him and paused at the doorway to catch their breath before they entered. The child was moaning softly and writhing on his bed. He looked to be about ten summers old. Beads of sweat stood out on his forehead. Matoaka approached him and wiped the hair from his face. She motioned for Alsoomse to touch him too. His head was burning with fever.

Alsoomse was sent to fetch cold water from the river. Okwaho was waiting for her outside.

"Will he be alright?" he asked.

"I don't know, but I must get cold water from the river."

"Let me go," Okwaho said. He took the clay pot from her, and she watched him run off for a moment before she returned to the sick bed.

Alsoomse helped Matoaka make the *Beson*, the medicine, in a large kettle. She pounded dried herbs and dogwood bark into a fine powder and added them to the water boiling over the fire. While it simmered, Matoaka preformed a ritual over the boy. Alsoomse listened carefully to the words and tried to memorize them. Okwaho returned and Alsoomse accepted the pot from him, and paused for a moment.

"Thank you," she said.

He smiled and brushed a strand of hair out of her face. Then he turned and left.

Alsoomse brought the water to Matoaka and helped her strip the child down to his breach-cloth. The medicine woman dipped old cloths into the water and lay them on the child's forehead and over his body. Then she bid Alsoomse to fetch a dipper full of the *beson*. Alsoomse handed it to her and lifted the boy to a sitting position. Matoaka coaxed the child to swallow the medicine. They watched throughout the day, refreshed the cool cloths, and fed him more medicine several times.

As evening approached, Matoaka told Alsoomse to return to the old woman to reapply the cream to her hands. Alsoomse nodded and left quickly. When she arrived, she was surprised at how much better the woman's hands already looked. The old woman greeted her with a smile and held out her hands. Alsoomse gently rubbed the cream into her wrinkled skin and rewrapped them. Before she could return to the child's home, the old woman pressed a small loaf of cornbread into her hands. Alsoomse thanked her and hurried away.

Matoaka and Alsoomse continued their vigil through the night, and by morning, the boy's fever had finally broken. The medicine woman told the boy's mother to continue to feed him the rest of the *beson* throughout the day until it was gone, along with some watered-down corn soup.

"Do not feed him any meat until he is well enough to stand on his own," Matoaka said.

The mother thanked her and offered three large pumpkins as payment. Before they returned home, Alsoomse and Matoaka stopped by the old woman's home and reapplied the cream. The swelling was gone, and woman happily showed them how she could use her hands again.

Matoaka offered the woman the remaining ointment and told her to use it twice a day.

Alsoomse smiled. As they walked home, she suddenly felt exhausted and longed for her bed. Still, it felt good to help others.

Ókas and Kitchi were waiting for them when they returned to the longhouse.

"A snowstorm is coming soon," *Ókas* said. "It is time to return home."

"But we have been up all night! I am so tired. Can't we wait a bit longer?" Alsoomse frowned. "What about my training?"

"You have no proposal yet, and I do not wish to spend the entire winter here. We must go home now, but perhaps we can return in the spring." *Ókas* looked to Matoaka, who smiled and nodded.

"Can't we wait a little longer?" Alsoomse asked. She felt her throat catch.

"We will go now," *Ókas* replied.

"But …" Alsoomse looked around, but there was no sight of Okwaho.

"He has gone hunting," Kitchi whispered.

Alsoomse was filled with a strange feeling of loss. It surprised her. Then she realized she hadn't thought about Etienne since she first met Okwaho under the willow tree. Guilt replaced the feeling of loss. Her mother put a hand on her arm.

"We must go if we are to get home before the storm arrives."

Reluctantly, Alsoomse took the pack her mother offered and waved to Matoaka. The she turned to follow her mother and brother out of the village. As they walked, Alsoomse scanned the woods and looked for signs of the handsome third son of the Mohawk leader. Her mother and Kitchi pushed ahead, and as Alsoomse took up the rear, she allowed the distance between herself and her mother and brother to lengthen.

She heard a stone bounced off a tree trunk and turned quickly, just as Okwaho stepped onto the path.

"You are leaving?"

Alsoomse nodded. "My mother wants to get home before the snow gets too deep."

He nodded sadly, his smiled a weak imitation. "I will miss your company."

"I will miss you too …" Alsoomse's voice caught in her throat. She swallowed hard and tried to smile.

"Alsoomse! Hurry, Daughter."

Alsoomse looked back up the trail, but her mother was out-of-sight. "I must go," she said.

Okwaho caught her hand and pressed something into it. Then he smiled and disappeared into the forest. Alsoomse opened her hand and saw a necklace of beautiful blue-green stone beads coiled there. She slipped it over her head and ran to catch up with her mother and brother.

Chapter 21

Christmas

Abraham, December 25, 1663

The rolling drum beat from the church in Southampton was heard softly in the distance calling the townsfolk there to service. Abraham grabbed Caleb by the arm, straightened his collar, and tucked his shirt back into his breeches. He shoved one of his brother's arms into the soft velvet jacket, and then the other. He put the cap on his head, placed the cape over his shoulders, and clasped it snuggly at his neck.

"There, now you look presentable," Abraham said. "Try not to get dirty before we get to church." He turned to see how Jacob was faring and saw him wrestling with his jacket buttons. His brother had missed a buttonhole and his jacket bunched up funny in the middle. Abraham went over to help.

He was just finishing up with Jacob when his mother emerged from the bedroom she shared with Da. She was carrying his new baby sister, Sarah, wrapped in a wool blanket. Mum was wearing a new dark green velvet skirt and jacket over a white linen blouse. She had done up her hair in a bun at the back of her head, like the English women did, and donned a bonnet garnished with a wide satin ribbon. She looked more like the elegant wife of a well-to-do Englishman than the traditional Montauk woman she was the rest of the week.

At that moment Da came inside. He stopped in the doorway when he saw his wife, smiled, and crossed the floor quickly to kiss her and his new daughter. Then he offered his arm and led her toward the door.

"Hurry boys and get into the wagon," he said as he passed them.

Abraham grabbed his brothers' hands, led them outside, lifted them up into the wagon, and then climbed in himself. He took a seat next to his younger brothers and across from Ralph and Sam. Da took the baby and helped Mum up onto the bench. Then he handed her the baby and wrapped a large bear hide around them. He laid another across Mum's knees, and then took the seat beside her.

Da clicked his tongue to signal the horses, and the wagon pulled out onto the narrow dirt road that would take them to Southampton. The small settlement of North Sea, which was located on the southern bank of the Great Peconic Bay, which split the east end of the island into two parts, was too small to have its own church. As a result, the family traveled to Southampton for services. The town was situated in Shinnecock land toward the southwest. His grandfather had been one of the founding settlers many years ago and served as an interpreter to the Shinnecock and later to the Montauketts until his death when Abraham was only two years old. Abraham didn't remember his grandfather, but everyone spoke of him reverently as a man of noble character and a leader in the community.

The wagon bumped along the narrow dirt road as they headed

west past the bay to the north, and then followed the road as it bent south toward the town of Southampton on the southern coast of Long Island. Clouds hung heavily above them and a cold, sharp wind blew from across the bay. Caleb and Jacob snuggled closer to Abraham, and he pulled the wool blanket tighter around the three of them. Abraham looked across at Ralph and Sam. As they were older, they sat on crates rather than being jostled along on the bed of the wagon.

"What are you going to do with your share of the oil proceeds?" Sam asked Ralph.

"The last time I was in New Amsterdam I saw a new type of musket. It had a flintlock mechanism, instead of the matchlock Da has. I want one."

"I'm gonna buy a better hunting knife," Sam said.

Abraham scowled. "Why would you get any of the oil money, Sam?" he asked. "You've been laid up in bed for weeks!"

"Because I was out there in the boats with the other men before I got injured," Sam said and grinned. "Not like the babies on lookout."

"I'm not a baby!"

"Don't mind Sam," Ralph said. "I only getting a half share and Sam a quarter share anyway."

"And Sam's the back end of a horse," Abraham muttered.

"Abraham, watch your mouth!" Da said from the front seat.

Sam stifled a laugh and Ralph shrugged. Abraham felt his face burn. Ralph leaned forward to pat his knee.

"You'll get your turn in the boat."

Abraham grunted. One day he'd show them. He'd be the best whaler anywhere!

As the wagon rumbled on, Abraham could see the outskirts of

the town with the church steeple rising in the distance. Houses lined both sides of the main road through town. The small wooden church stood in the center of town next to the assembly hall and the mayor's grand house. All the people from the town and the surrounding regions had turned out for the service. Everyone was wearing their finest clothing and looked like brightly colored candies spilled out over the barren ground.

Da pulled the wagon up to the railing and got out to tie it up. Then he helped Mum down, while Abraham and his brothers jumped down off the back. He could feel Mum stiffen as they made their way up the aisle to sit with Da's siblings and their families in the benches midway up. Abraham heard whispers as they walked to their seats and watched his mother as she walked resolutely, chin thrust out, and shoulders squared.

Men and women were divided and sat on opposite sides of the aisle. Da, Abraham, and his brothers slipped into the row with Uncle Thomas and his son, Nathaniel, while Mum, holding Sarah, squeezed in next to Aunt Alice. His aunt smiled down at baby Sarah, cooed to her, and ran her gloved hand over her gently.

The deacons sat in the row at the front of the church behind the altar, facing the congregation. The altar was a small table covered in a white cloth embroidered in gold thread. A large, gilded Bible lay open on a raised book stand in the center of the table.

The church quieted as a shout came from the back of the room.

"Please stand!"

Abraham stood with everyone else and the voice continued.

"Blessed be God: The Father, the Son, and the Holy Spirit!"

Two altar boys walked down the aisle carrying ornate candelabras, followed by the minister, the honorable Reverend Robert Fordham, carrying a large golden cross. Abraham dutifully bowed his head with everyone else in his row as the cross passed, then lifted his eyes to watch the altar boys place the candelabras on either side of the table in front. Then Rev. Fordham placed the cross in the center of the table in front of the open Bible and walked around the table to stand behind it.

The congregation remained standing as they sang from the psalm book. The minister led them in a prayer that seemed to go on forever. Abraham tried not to fidget. Finally, it ended, and everyone sang the doxology.

Da took up a book, called the lectionary, and opened it to the appropriate page. Abraham let his mind wander as the congregation recited the readings from the Old Testament predicting the birth of the Messiah. The recitation droned on shifting to the familiar Gospel reading on the Advent of Christ. When they reached the part that spoke about how Jesus, the promised Messiah, was born in a stable, Abraham looked down at the words in the lectionary. Both his brother Caleb and baby Sarah had been born in a barn. When his mum's time had come, she'd gone out to have the baby on her own, as her people did, only she'd given birth in the barn because they didn't have a separate women's house like they did in her village. Abraham glanced over at Mum and saw her smiling down at Sarah.

The recitation finally ended, and the congregation was allowed to sit as Reverend Fordham climbed the stairs to the pulpit and began the sermon. Abraham tried to listen to what he was saying, but he kept thinking about the image of God as a baby in a barn, surrounded by smelly animals and soiled hay. Why would God choose that way to come into the world?

Abraham looked over at Sarah. God could have chosen to have his son born in a palace, to an important royal family. But instead, he had chosen for Jesus to be born to a poor family, like his. Caleb was squirming in his seat and playing with his cap. Abraham leaned over, took the boy's hat, and scolded him to sit still. Then he wondered if Jesus had fidgeted during a sermon, too?

Sarah began to whimper, and Abraham glanced toward Mum again. His mother rocked her and tried to hush her, but the baby only cried louder. The minister looked down at her with disapproval. Others in the church were staring at her too, shaking their heads. Da leaned into the aisle and urged her to quiet the child. Suddenly, Mum stood up, turned, and walked down the aisle. Da watched her as she brushed past him and quickly exited the church.

Reverend Fordham cleared his throat loudly and glared around the room. Da turned back around to face the minister and everyone else settled back to respectful silence. Abraham turned to look for Mum, but Da grabbed his leg firmly and held him in place as the sermon resumed.

The minister finally stopped talking, and the congregation stood to recite the Nicene Creed. Reverend Fordham prayed again and then asked everyone to kneel and confess their sins to God in their own personal prayers. Abraham knelt and thought of Pannoowau and his anger toward him. Uncle Ahanu had also told him to give up his anger and forgive him. Why was it so hard to forgive him? Abraham sighed and dropped to the kneeling bench. *I don't know if you are the same as the Great Spirit Uncle Ahanu worships or not, but I am not ready to forgive Pannoowau.* A pang of guilt clutched at him. *I'm sorry. Amen,* he added.

Then Rev. Fordham walked to the altar and said, "The passing of the peace is a renewal of our obedience to our Lord. In Matthew 5:24 it says, 'First be reconciled to your brother, and then come and offer your gift,' and then in the admonition of Paul to the Corinthians he says, 'Aim for restoration, comfort one another, live in peace; and the God of love and peace will be with you.'"

Pannoowau had tried to reconcile with him, even if he hadn't meant it, but Abraham had refused to accept the apology. He hung his head as a wave of shame swept over him.

The congregation rose to sing, but Abraham just stood there grimacing as the music filled the room. Reverend Fordham prayed again and led them in communion.

Abraham awaited his turn impatiently, eager for the service to end. When it was his turn, he hesitated … *You must be reconciled* … The minister cleared his throat, and he felt a nudge from behind him. Slowly, he extended his hands and accepted the bread, but he palmed it and only pretended to eat it. Likewise, he let the wine touch his lips, but he did not drink any of it. He stuffed the piece of bread into his pocket as he returned to his seat.

When everyone had taken communion, the minister said, "In second Corinthians 5:18 it says, 'All this is from God, who reconciled us to himself through Christ and gave us the ministry of reconciliation. …'" The minister then opened his hands toward the congregation and recited the last few verses from Numbers, chapter 6, "The LORD bless you and keep you; the LORD make his face shine on you and be gracious to you; the LORD turn his face toward you and give you peace."

The service finally ended, and people began to file out of the church to shake hands with the minister. Abraham and his family were the last to leave. Reverend Fordham was standing by the doors shaking hands with the men and greeting the women warmly as they passed. As Da approach the minister, he held out his hand and the minister took it and smiled broadly.

"Samuel, it is so good to see you! How is your family?"

"We are well, Reverend," Da replied. Then he motioned to Mum who was standing just outside the door.

"Medlen, it is so good to see you again," Reverend Fordham said. "We will need to get the child christened soon."

Mum smiled and nodded.

Rev. Fordham gave her an awkward smile. Then he turned back to Da and asked, "Is it true that you are starting a whaling venture?"

"It is, though I'd be grateful to you for not spreading the word. Like to keep competition down, you understand?"

"Word spreads of its own accord, Samuel, but I shall do what is in my power to do. And Merry Christmas to you all!"

"Merry Christmas to you too, Reverend," Da said, and ushered us all back to the wagon. The drive to Aunt Alice's house was cold and silent; everyone feared to say anything that might set Da off. Only Mum sat humming softly to herself, as if everything was as it should be.

Chapter 22

Aunt Alice

The Backer house was large, double the size of the house Abraham shared with his family of nine, but it felt small filled as it was with all Da's extended family. Uncle Thomas greeted Da and Mum at the door and ushered them inside. As Abraham followed his brothers, Aunt Alice stopped him and took his chin in her hand, directing his eyes to meet hers.

"Merry Christmas, Abraham. Today is a day to celebrate, not to be grumpy! Whatever is bothering you can wait until tomorrow." She smiled down at him, and he tried to smile back as she released him.

The distinct smell of cinnamon and nutmeg mingled with those of roasted turkey, plum pudding, minced meat pies, and mulled wine. Uncle Ralph and Uncle Robert were already partaking of the wine. Mum went to join the other wives at the hearth.

As Mum approached the women, Uncle Ralph's wife gave her a cursory look and turned away.

Then Uncle Robert's wife peaked at Sarah, turned toward the hearth, and muttered, "Well, at least the baby is fair-skinned."

Mum's face hardened and then quickly softened. "It is good to see you both too." Then she pushed past them to join Aunt Alice.

"Medlen, dear!" Aunt Alice said and embraced her. "It is so good to see you. I am surprised to see you out so soon after giving birth?"

"I am well," Mum said. "And Sarah is strong."

"I think your people must be so much better at birthing than ours. My brother's wives lay about for months after each birth!" Aunt Alice gave Mum a knowing look and glanced at her sisters-in-law.

Mum smiled. "Some of our women have a harder time too, but Sarah is my seventh. Each one gets easier."

"Has your family been well? I hear several in the village have come down with a fever."

"Thank you for asking," Mum said. "We are all well."

"I am so happy to hear it," Alice said. "We women are going out caroling. Would you like to come with us?"

His mother's face brightened. "I am happy to join you." Mum tucked Sarah into the basket she'd brought for her and set her near the hearth. She tucked a blanket around her and turned to Abraham.

"She's just eaten and should sleep for a while, but keep an ear out for her, would you?"

"I will, Mum," he said.

Abraham watched the women fasten their cloaks around their shoulders and leave the house. He then turned to see the men setting up a game of cards at the table. Mugs of mead were passed out as the men sat down to play a card game called Spoil Five. He knew it involved bidding and trick-taking, but he still didn't understand all the rules.

"Come on, Abraham, we're going out back to play hoodman-blind," Ralph said. He grabbed him by the shoulder and ushered him outside. Their boots thumped across the wooden porch and down the steps into the frost-crusted lawn. "And you're it!"

Ralph pulled the hood over his eyes and spun him around several times until he was completely disoriented and swaying on his feet. Abraham could hear his brothers and his cousins taunting him as he held out his arms and groped for them. Someone smacked him on the back. Another tried to trip him as he lunged toward a voice that sounded like Ralph's. He steadied himself and lunged again, then spun around quickly and grabbed a hold of someone's coat. He pulled the hood off and saw his cousin Nathaniel trying to wriggle out of his coat.

"You're it!" he said. He released him and popped the hood over Nathaniel's head. As the game continued, Abraham was soon laughing with the others as each boy in turn taunted, was eventually captured, and served their turn as "it."

After a half hour or more, snow started to fall, and the boys scrambled inside for hot cider and warm bread, butter, and blackberry preserves. Abraham peeked into the basket by the hearth and saw that Sarah was still sleeping contentedly. Then he looked toward the grouping of men gathered around the table. A pile of coins had accumulated in the center of the table and the men were flushed and raucously goading each other to play their hands. Da stood up to pour another round of mead. The boys took their mugs of cider and slices of bread and sat in a circle on the floor near the hearth. Ralph produced a deck of cards, removed the twos and threes, and shuffled the rest, while the boys fished in their pockets for copper coins, brass buttons, glass beads, and other treasures to support their bets. The cards were shuffled and dealt.

As Da returned to his seat, Uncle Ralph said, "I'm glad to see you've finally civilized that Indian wife of yours, Samuel."

Before he could speak, Uncle Robert laughed and said, "But not too tamed, judging from the number of children she's given you!"

Abraham felt his face burn and turned to scowl at the men.

Da grunted and looked up from his hand of cards. "Are you going to play your card, Robert? Spades are trump."

Robert laid down a card and Da chuckled as he scooped up the trick and laid it down in front of him. "That makes three tricks for me," he said and pulled the pile of coins toward him.

"Maybe if you paid more attention to the cards and less on the condition of my household, you would be winning more and losing less," Da said and led out the fourth trick.

"We didn't agree on jinking!" Robert said and banged the table with his fist.

Da looked up at him calmly. "We always allow jinking. You jinked last time and cleaned us all out. Now you refuse to allow it?"

"Samuel's right," Ralph said and placed more coins in the center of the table.

Robert mumbled something and tossed his coins into the pile.

"Hey, Abraham, are you going to play or not?" Nathaniel asked, but Abraham barely heard him.

His anger had been building to boiling over through the men's discussion. His face burned, and he clenched his teeth. Resolutely, Abraham stood to face his father and his uncles. "Mum is *NOT* a savage and never has been! She has always been more civilized than any of you! And if you really loved her, Da, you'd know that too!"

Da stood abruptly, moved toward him, and smacked him hard across the face, nearly knocking him over. Abraham's eyes stung and he tasted blood; he realized he'd bit down on his tongue. Da grabbed his neck to steady him and leaned in to speak softly, but firmly into his ear. "You will *not* speak to me that way again, do you hear? Neither will you address your uncles, or any other adults, in that manner. Do you understand?"

The room had become completely silent. Abraham could only nod his agreement.

With that Da released him and returned to his game.

Abraham slumped back to the floor and struggled to focus on their game. Nathaniel tried to put a hand on his shoulder, but he shrugged it off. He scowled through a blur of tears at his cards and finally threw down his hand. Then he stood, grabbed his coat, and went outside, banging the door a bit too hard behind him.

Abraham sat down on the steps and stared out at the street without really seeing anything. He had no sense of how long he sat there. After a while, he started to feel cold and looked up to see his mother and aunts returning. They were laughing and chatting as they approached. Mum looked happier than he'd seen her in a long time. She smiled at him, and he stood to greet her.

"What is wrong?" Mum asked, a worried expression darkening her face.

"It's nothing," he said, and tried to smile.

Mum studied him for a moment. The worry did not leave her eyes, but her lips smiled, and she gave him a quick hug. "Well, then, let's go inside for dinner, shall we?"

He nodded and followed her through the doorway. His aunts were already removing their bonnets and cloaks.

"You men are going to have to put away those cards so that we can eat," Aunt Alice said. "And you boys, go wash up and tell the girls to come and help set the table."

"Yes, Mum," Nathaniel said and jumped up. Abraham joined Nathaniel and followed the boys to wash for dinner.

Mum followed the other women into the kitchen to lay out the supper. Alice called up to the girls in the loft. The girls climbed down the ladder, giggling and conspiring, and went over to the bucket of water Alice had placed by the hearth and washed their faces and hands. The table was filled with mince-meat pies, roasted turkeys, spiced pumpkin, and plum pudding, and everyone crowded around to find the place at the table. Spiced cider and mulled wine were poured out and Uncle Thomas rose to say grace.

"Thank you, God, for the gift of your son, this blessed day and for the sacrifice he made for us all. Thank you for the family gathered here today and for the blessings you have bestowed upon us. Amen." Then he lifted his mug and said, "Merry Christmas to one and all!"

A cheer when up as everyone raised their mugs and repeated Merry Christmas. After dinner there were sweet rhubarb and apple pies and gingerbread. Abraham ate so much he thought his stomach might burst. Then the table and benches were pushed back, and Uncle Ralph brought out his fiddle. Everyone danced until late into the evening until Robert and Ralph finally gathered up their families and took them home.

"See you at our home tomorrow afternoon," Uncle Ralph said as they left.

"You boys can sleep up in the loft with Nathaniel. I've put extra mattresses down for you. Medlen and Samuel, you can sleep in our room. Thomas and I will sleep out here."

"We can't do that, Alice," Da said. "We will sleep here."

"You are our guests, and Medlen needs a comfortable bed. She's only recently given birth after all. T'is no trouble to us," Alice replied.

"Have you seen the beds her people sleep in?" Da asked. "Believe me when I say, we will be perfectly comfortable out here."

"Nonsense, Brother! Don't argue with me. You know I will

have my way!"

Da looked at Uncle Thomas, who just smiled and shrugged.

"Boys, get up to bed! It's late and there will be more celebrating tomorrow at Uncle Ralph's house," Mum said.

"And if you're fooling around, we'll hear it!" Aunt Alice said with a grin as Abraham followed his brothers and Nathaniel up the ladder.

Abraham lay on his mattress and listened to the wind howling through the rafters until eventually, sleep found him.

Chapter 23

La Rochelle

Etienne, December 25, 1663

The worst of the storm had passed, but the ship was taking on water. I had patched the tear in the hull the best I could, but water still seeped in all along the mended seam. Captain Janssen had ordered the ship to put in at La Rochelle for repairs. He had then ordered me locked in the brig. It was no more than an iron cage in the lower hold with a wooden crate to sit on and a small bucket to use as a latrine.

The two seamen who had locked me in had left a single candle burning. The small wavering light provided some comfort but did not keep my imagination from inventing indescribable terrors lurking in the corners. And to add to my unease, I could hear numerous rats scurrying back and forth along the walls, their claws scratching over the wooden floorboards, though I could not see them. I felt a chill run up my spine. *I must get ahold of myself and think what to do.*

We were going to La Rochelle. I remembered the last time I was in that city. It was four years since my family had fled in the middle of the night to avoid my father's arrest for heresy. I remembered the wagon ride bumping and jostling us over the uneven cobblestones and the soft pools of light, like dragon eyes, staring at us from the arched shop entrances lining the road. I remembered being rowed out across the inky water of the inner harbor, and the ominous feeling I'd had as we'd slipped beneath the ever-vigilant towers guarding the mouth to the larger outer harbor. The king's navy had nearly caught us that night.

I was going home. If I could find a way to get out of this cage, make it onto the deck unseen, and slip into the water, I could swim ashore and find Nicolas. He would shelter me. Then once the *Zeelandia* left, I could find work on another ship heading back to New Amsterdam. It would be good to see my cousin again. What stories we had to tell one another! I smiled as I thought of it.

The light grew as a lantern was placed at the top of the ladder leading down to my prison. A sailor carefully made his way down the rungs laden with a small platter.

"Merry Christmas," he said as he reached the bottom and turned toward me. It was the sailor who had given me Magdalena's note. He walked over, placed the tray on a large crate, and unlocked my cell door. Then he moved another crate inside the cell to serve as a table and placed the tray on top of it. "I saved you some food from our dinner."

"Thank you," I said as he relocked my cell and turned to go. "Wait!"

The sailor turned around and stared at me. I felt around in my pockets and found the letter I'd written to Nicolas and a stub of charcoal I'd last used in measuring planks of wood for patching the larger holes in the hull.

"When will we reach La Rochelle?"

"I dunno," he said and shrugged. "I'm not a navigator. We haven't spotted land yet, and it's still pretty foggy."

I scribbled a quick note on the back side of the letter and refolded it. Then I wrote a name and address on the top and handed it through the bars to the sailor.

"When we reach the port, could you please find my cousin, Nicolas Mestereau, and give him this?"

The sailor took the note and looked at it. "I can't! This is aiding a prisoner. I'm not even supposed to be here. I am disobeying a direct order by just bringing you food. If I get caught, he'll know I came to see you. No! I can't." He tried to shove the note back at me, but I wouldn't take it.

"You're already involved. You gave me the letter from his daughter in Texel. I will tell him you've been aiding me all along! You've already disobeyed orders. I'll scream it to the whole ship. You must do this for me!"

The sailor hesitated and shifted on his feet. He looked down at the note again. "I can't read."

"His name is Nicolas Mestereau," I said again. Then I read the address slowly, so he could memorize it. He lives in a large house with a walled back garden, just up the hill from the docks, past the cathedral. Look for this number on the front of the house." I pointed to the number I'd written on the note. "If you get lost, ask around. They are well-known in the area."

The young man hesitated again and started backing away. "I'll be noticed if I'm gone from my duties too long. What if I get caught? I can't help you. I'm sorry." He turned and started climbing up.

"Please! Please help me," I urged. But he had picked up the lantern and disappeared.

I sat down on the crate and looked at the food he'd brought in amazement. He'd brought me a roasted chicken leg, a chunk of bread with butter, boiled plums, a bowl of watery stew, and a mug of beer. He'd gone to a lot of trouble to get these for me. A wave of guilt swept over me.

My stomach rumbled; I hadn't eaten much since being locked up. I pushed the guilt away, leaned over, picked up the chicken leg, and took a bite. It wasn't as good as the Christmas dinners *Maman* made, but it was still warm and filled my empty stomach. He had been my last hope of getting a message back to my family. I was so close to La Rochelle and to Nicolas, but there was no way to get out of this accursed cell!

I leaned back against the wall and water soaked into my shirt. I jolted upright and looked around. The feel of the ship was different, more sluggish. In the dim light I could see the open hatch leading down to the very bottom of the ship where the blast was. There was a flickering of light reflecting from the candle. I looked down at my feet. The floorboards were wet. The water was rising! How high would the water climb? Would the ship make it into port? And if it did, would I be able to make it out, or would I be drowned in a cold, watery cage?

I scanned the room again and looked for something, anything, I could use to pick or break the lock. On one wall, there were large coils of rope and a pile of wood planks, and on the other side, crates and barrels were stacked haphazardly. I glanced at the candle. It was down to a stub now, as melted wax pooled around it on the small crate. I couldn't see anything that could help me, even if I'd been able to reach it. Then candle the went out.

Part 3, Darkness Descends

1664

Long Island and Benin, the Slave Coast, West Africa

The first object which saluted my eyes when I arrived on the coast was the sea, and a slave ship, which was then riding at anchor, and waiting for its cargo. ⇒ Olaudah Equiano

Houses of Benin, with their executions and their way of mounting a horse.
M. De La Harpe, Abrége de l'histoire générale desvoyages (Paris, 1780), vol. 3, facing p. 295. (Copy in Library Company of Philadelphia) Public Domain.

Chapter 24

A Harbinger

Abraham, February 20, 1664

braham was on watch again, only this time Isaac had been sent up to the platform with him. The sun was well up now, but it was not yet at its apex. It was still cold, and the boys huddled under a shared wool blanket for warmth. Abraham was carving on the piece of driftwood he was shaping into a whale. It was hard to find time to work on it, so he'd started carrying it around with him all the time, so when time allowed, he could whittle away at it here and there.

"Remember, Isaac, you are looking for spouts with two plumes," he said and looked up from his work. "Those are the right whales. They are slower and easier to catch."

"I know! You've already told me," Isaac said a sullen pout. "It's cold up here, and boring, and I'm hungry!"

Abraham sighed. "Someone else will come and take our place soon."

"When?"

"I don't know. Soon." Abraham was tired and hungry too, but there was nothing he could do. Abraham's eyes drifted to the beach, and he saw a movement. He looked harder and spotted a man hurrying along toward the encampment.

"Stay here and keep looking for whales. I'll go and see what he wants," Abraham said. He slipped out from under the blanket and moved to the ladder.

"Why do I have to stay up here?" Isaac whined.

"Just do it! I'll be back soon." With that Abraham slid down the ladder and went to meet the visitor.

As he approached, Abraham could see that the messenger was Pannoowau. *What does he want?* Anger flared inside him as he moved to intercept him, but his anger vanished just as quickly when he saw the boy's face.

"Where is the medicine man?" Pannoowau's tone was urgent.

"Come, this way," Abraham said and led him toward the cooking hut.

When he opening the door, a wave of warmth enveloped them along with the comforting smell of warm cornbread. Uncle Ahanu was sitting by the fire with his father, while Mum chopped squash, onion, and garlic to add to the pot of water simmering over the fire.

The men looked up as they entered.

"Why have you left your post?" Da asked. "Isaac cannot yet be trusted …."

Uncle Ahanu cut him off with a hand and stood to meet them. "What has happened?"

"Many in the village are sick with fever." Pannoowau paused

and then turned to Mum. "Your mother is one of them."

After a pause, Mum gathered up the vegetables she'd chopped, carried them over to the iron pot, and dumped them in. Then wiped her hands on her apron and began to pack a small satchel. She strapped Sarah into her cradleboard and pulled her onto her back. While she was doing this Uncle Ahanu gathered up his supplies and took up his medicine bag.

Uncle Ahanu and Mum started to follow Pannoowau to the door when Da stopped Mum. "You are not going!"

"I must help care for my mother," Mum said.

"It's too dangerous. I forbid it."

Mum looked at Da quietly, but Da stood his ground. Mum's face softened and she put a hand on his arm. "I must go, Samuel. Do not fear. I will be back as soon as I can."

Mum turned and hurried after Uncle Ahanu and Pannoowau. Da visibly shrank as he watched her go. Then he turned to Sam, who was still unable to go out in the boats because of his broken arm, and said, "Keep an eye on Jacob and Caleb until your Mum gets back." Then he put a hand on Abraham's shoulder and ushered him outside.

"Keep a sharp eye out for the whales, Son. We really need to catch another before the season ends."

"I will, Da!" Abraham said and squared his shoulders.

"I am afraid for your mother," Da continued softly. "Many have died or been left scarred from smallpox in Southampton. I fear the disease is spreading."

Abraham was startled by the sudden cawing of a crow and looked around to see it flapping off over the barren grassland behind them. As they reached the beach, Ralph came out of one of the huts to join them.

"Where are Mum and Uncle Ahanu going?" he asked.

Da quickly explained while Abraham went to check on Isaac. As he reached the top of the ladder, Isaac suddenly called out, "Look!"

Abraham looked in the direction he pointed and shuddered. Dark ominous clouds were gathering on the horizon and the waves were churning, white with rage, as they rushed toward them to crash forcibly onto the shore.

Chapter 25

The Sickness

Abraham's mother was gone for two weeks. Whaling season ended and Abraham, Da, and his brothers returned to their house at North Sea. A severe storm had prevented the boats from going out for several days. After that, there were a couple of near misses, but they hadn't caught any more whales. Da was frustrated and angry much of the time and had taken to pacing and brooding in Mum's absence. Abraham tried to keep up with the cooking and cleaning. Ralph made sure they had wood for the fire and meat or fish for the stew. Sam just sat by the fire and sometimes kept the fire stoked.

"Sam! The fire is dying. Add another log or two."

"Come and do it yourself!"

"I am cleaning the kitchen. You're sitting right there!"

"My arm ..." he said and held up the slinged arm.

"Nothing's wrong with your other arm."

"They're heavy ... fine!" Sam stood up scowling, picked up a log from the pile, and dropped it onto the embers. Sparks flew in all directions. "Happy?"

"No! You could help with more of the chores," Abraham glared at his brother.

Just then, the door opened and Mum appeared in the doorway. She hung her cloak on the peg near the front door and walked to the hearth to place Sarah in the basinet. She looked around the room and acknowledged that everything was in order. But she looked haggard, like she hadn't slept in days, and she barely acknowledged the younger boys when they ran up to hug her. Abraham offered her a bowl of stew, but she waved him away. Then she stretched and without a word, went into the bedroom she shared with Da and closed the door.

Later, when Da came in from bedding the animals in the barn, he noticed Mum's cloak by the door, and asked, "Is your mother here? Where is she?"

"Yes, she just returned, but she went straight to bed," Abraham replied. "I tried to give her soup to eat, but she shook me off."

Da stopped to check on Sarah and then hurried to look in on Mum. He did not leave her side for the rest of the night. Ralph and Abraham were left to get the younger brothers ready for bed and settled in the loft. Then they joined Sam by the fire.

"Your stew was good, Abraham," Sam said. "As good as Mum's."

Abraham looked over at him in surprise. "Thank you," he replied, almost like a question. He waited for some snide remark to follow.

"Sam's right," Ralph confirmed. "I don't know what we'd have done without you when Mum was gone. You've done well keeping the house running and the little boys in hand."

Abraham felt his cheeks get hot and turned to watch the fire. "Thank you," he repeated, softly. "That means a lot."

Early the next morning, Da took Ralph and Isaac with him to carry out the morning chores, while Abraham set about making oatmeal for breakfast. Sarah woke up crying and Abraham was startled to see that she had slept in her basinet all night. No one had taken her into the bedroom. He picked her up and gently knocked on the door to his mother's room. When there was no answer, he opened the door.

Mum was lying still on the bed. He carried the baby over to her. "Mum, Sarah is hungry. Will you feed her?"

His mother moaned softly but didn't say anything, so he walked over and placed his free hand on her head. She was burning with fever. Abraham folded back two of the quilts, leaving only a thin sheet. He lay Sarah down on the bed and walked to the washstand. He poured water from the pitcher into the basin and dipped a washcloth into the cool water. He wrung it out and placed it on her forehead.

His mother stirred and whispered, "Thank you, *Aranck*. Don't worry about me. I will be better tomorrow."

Sarah was still crying, and Mum slowly shifted her weight to prepare to nurse the child. Abraham placed Sarah in his mother's arms.

"How is grandmother?" he asked.

A look of sadness crossed Mum's face. She closed her eyes and drew a deep breath before she opened her eyes again. She spoke softly, but calmly.

"She has passed on to join the Creator God. She and many others in the village."

Abraham was stunned. He didn't know what to say and could only stand there in shocked silence. His mother closed her eyes. Abraham was just about to leave the room when she spoke again. He walked back to bed to better hear what she was saying.

"It was terrible. So many died. They had boils filled with puss all over their faces, arms, and torsos. And sores in their mouths and throats kept them from eating. I did all I could to help them, but … many are still sick."

"How is Uncle Ahanu?"

"Your uncle and the men returned from whaling buried the dead in a mass grave. I placed shells over the mound …."

Abraham looked at his mother, but her eyes had closed even as she nursed the baby. He refreshed the cool rag on her head. When Sarah pulled away from Mum and started to cry again, Abraham picked her up and put her up to his shoulder to burp. He pulled the sheet over his mother and left the room.

Sarah still acted like she was hungry, so Abraham tried to give her a spoonful of cow milk, but it ran down her face or choked her. Finally, Da wrapped the baby in a warm blanket, stuck her in a basket and left the house with her.

Abraham ran out after him. "Da, where are you taking her?"

"I am going to town to find a woman who can feed her," he said and walked to the barn.

Ralph was already there, leading the horses out of their stalls. He and Abraham harnessed them and hooked them to the wagon. Da placed the basket with Sarah in the bed of the wagon just behind him and urged the horses to trot. Ralph went back to milk the cow, but Abraham stood and watched the wagon disappear down the road. What would Mum think when she awoke to find Sarah gone?

Da didn't return until late that evening. No one could be found to nurse Sarah and Mum was unable to nurse her as she drifted in and out of fevered sleep. Abraham did the best he could to feed her cow's milk with a rag soaked in the milk, but it was not enough. Sarah too, became feverish and stopped eating. By the end of the week, her tiny body had given up.

Da wrapped her in sackcloth and laid her in a hole he'd dug in the backyard. The boys gathered around the small grave while Da read Psalms 23. *The Lord is my Shepherd, I shall not want …*

Abraham looked down at the small bundle wrapped in linen. She was so small, so innocent.

Ye though I walk through the valley of the shadow of death, I will fear no evil, For thou art with me …

Mum didn't even know she was gone.

Surely goodness and mercy will follow me All the days of my life, And I will dwell in the house of the Lord forever.

Abraham felt tears sting the backs of his eyes. He scowled, blinked them away, and clenched his fists at his sides. *It's not fair!*

The boys each bent and picked up a handful of soil and sprinkled it over the baby's body, then Ralph picked up the shovel and started to bury her as they all watched in silence.

They were all cold when they finally returned to the house. Da immediately went into the bedroom to check on Mum. Abraham started to heat cider to warm them up. As he worked, he thought he heard sounds like crying coming from the bedroom. He poured some of the warmed cider into wooden mugs and passed them out to his younger brothers first, then to Ralph and Sam, and finally he took one for himself. A few minutes later, Da came out of the bedroom, strode across the room, and donned his winter coat and hat.

"I am going to find a doctor," he said and walked out of the house.

It had been three days since Da had gone in search of a doctor. Mum's fever continued to burn, and she grew weaker by the day. Abraham carried a bowl of broth into her bedroom and set it down on a side table. She had lost a lot of weight and looked old and frail. She was sleeping fitfully.

"Mum, wake up. You must eat something."

She let out a soft moan and tried to roll over.

"Mum, please try to eat something. You are so weak," Abraham said. He tried to gently prop her up on pillows.

She opened her eyes and tried to focus on his face.

He sat down beside her and took up a spoonful of broth to feed her. She opened her mouth and Abraham could see sores had broken out on her tongue and throat. He blew on the broth to cool it and proceeded to feed it to her. Her brows furrowed and her eyes closed as she struggled to swallow. He tried to feed her another spoonful, but she shook her head.

"Let me sleep. I am so tired."

"Just one more bite, Mum."

She opened her mouth, and he slipped in the spoonful.

"I'll let you sleep, but I'll come back a little later to give you some more."

That evening, when Abraham went in to check on his mother, he noticed flat, red spots had appeared on her face, hands, and forearms. She wouldn't open her eyes or even try to eat. He dribbled broth into her partially opened mouth and watched to see that she swallowed it. Then he took cool damp rags and cleaned her face and arms. She was shivering with cold, and he drew another blanket over her.

Suddenly, he heard the front door bang open. Abraham got up to see what was going on. As he exited her room and closed the door behind him, he looked up and saw that Da had returned. He looked angry as he paced before the fireplace and pulled at his hair. He turned as Abraham approached.

"Da, what is it?"

"There are no doctors anywhere who will come!" he said. Anger had transformed his face into a rigid mask. "None at North Sea, East Hampton, or Southampton! I rode all the way to Brookhaven and there was none there either."

"What about Uncle Ahanu? You could send Sam to fetch him," Abraham said. He dished up a bowl of stew and handed it to his father.

"What will he know about curing this illness?" Da asked as he took a bite of the stew.

"He's a medicine man," Abraham said.

"Foolish superstition and poppy cock!"

Abraham watched his father finish the stew and then he handed the bowl back to Abraham and went into the bedroom. Abraham set the bowl in the kitchen and went outside to find his older brothers. Ralph was brushing the horse their father had ridden and Sam was hanging up the harness with his one good arm.

"Did Da tell you he couldn't find a doctor?" Abraham asked.

Ralph nodded.

"Do you think we should send for Uncle Ahanu?" Abraham asked.

"Da doesn't think he can do anything," Sam said.

"But we have to do something!" Abraham said.

Ralph took a deep breath and looked thoughtful. "I don't know if he can do anything either, but then maybe he can. Take the other horse, Abraham, and go find him."

Abraham nodded with relief as Ralph helped him saddle the horse. He led her out of the barn and Sam helped him up. He kicked her into a gallop and took off down the road. He rode her hard all the way to the Montauk village. He slowed as he approached. The village looked abandoned. The cooking fires were all out. Where was everyone?

Abraham dismounted, tied the horse to a lean-to, and slowly walked through the village calling out to anyone who might hear him.

"Hello? Is anyone here?"

He heard a movement and turned to see Japhet come out of his house. Abraham asked, "Where is everyone?"

"Those who have survived are still weak. Those of us who did not get sick, or have recovered, do what we can for the rest," Japhet said. "Why are you here?"

"I've come to fetch Uncle Ahanu. My mum is ill now too."

"He can't go with you. There are too many sick here. Come, I will show you."

Abraham followed his cousin into his *wetu* and found Uncle Ahanu sitting by the fire stirring a pot of herbal tea, singing softly as he stirred. He looked tired and years older than he had just weeks before.

"How's your mother?" Abraham asked his cousin.

"She's in the back. Go and see for yourself," Japhet said.

Abraham walked to the back of the bark hut and found his aunt lying in bed. She had fluid-filled boils all over her face and arms. She was sleeping. Japhet's sister was lying in the next bed, though her boils had burst and puss oozed out of them.

When Uncle Ahanu was finished with the tea, Abraham and Japhet helped him feed it to the family. The boys lifted each person up by the shoulders while Uncle Ahanu spooned the tea into their mouths. Then they made the rounds to the other homes, checked on the families, and fed the tea to those who remained.

In one house, they found that a young girl had just died. They carefully wrapped her body, and then Uncle Ahanu gently lifted her into his arms. The girl's father sat on the floor crying.

"Where's her mother?" Abraham whispered, but Japhet just shook his head sadly. Abraham watched his uncle carry the girl away. Gently, he laid a hand on the man's shoulder. "Come, we must bury your daughter."

The man looked up at him and nodded. Abraham offered a hand up, and they followed the others outside. A second pit had been dug outside the village, next to the first shell-covered mound. A roof had been erected over the pit, and crude walls built around it to keep the animals away. They entered the small doorway and stood a moment to adjust their eyes to the dim light. Several others had already been laid in the pit. Slowly, Uncle Ahanu climbed down into the shallow pit and gently laid the girl next to her mother. Her father buried his face in his hands and sobbed.

Abraham stood by silently and watched as Uncle Ahanu said a few words over the girl and then climbed out of the pit. They all turned to follow him out of the death house. No one spoke.

Abraham and Japhet followed Uncle Ahanu to the next house and entered. Abraham saw Pannoowau lying on his bed. Sweat beaded on his forehead and he was moaning in his sleep. Uncle Ahanu handed Abraham a ladleful of the medicine and Japhet went over to the bed to lift Pannoowau by his shoulders so he could drink the medicine. Uncle Ahanu motioned to Abraham to administer the medicine as he began to sing softly over the sick boy. Abraham looked at Pannoowau, but he couldn't move. Images of their past confrontations flooded his mind. Then without thinking, he tipped the ladle and poured the medicine onto the ground. Uncle Ahanu stopped singing and looked up at Abraham. Abraham suddenly realized what he'd done. He dropped the ladle into the bucket, turned, and ran from the *wetu*.

When Japhet and Uncle Ahanu left the house several long moments later, they didn't say anything. Japhet wouldn't look at Abraham directly, but Uncle Ahanu did, and that was far worse. His uncle's eyes held his own and had such sadness and disappointment in them that Abraham wanted to melt away into the ground. He had to look away.

"It's his fault my mum is sick. If he hadn't told Mum, she wouldn't have come here and gotten sick." His halting voice broke between sobs.

"Would you have the whole village die then?" Uncle Ahanu asked. He lifted Abraham's chin so could look him directly in the eyes.

Abraham closed his eyes. Tears leaked out of the corners. "No," he whispered.

"Abraham, you must let this anger go, or it will destroy you," his uncle said softly. He released his face and dropped a hand onto his shoulder. Then he patted his gently and continued, "Come. We have many homes yet to visit."

Abraham looked up and watched his uncle take the pot of medicine from Japhet and limp off toward the next house. Abraham sucked in a deep breath, and with determination, hurried up to his uncle and took the pot from him. Japhet studied him silently as they followed the medicine man to the next home.

Before they finished their rounds, three more bodies had been found and brought to the communal grave. It was nearly dark by the time they finished. Only one-third of the villagers still survived. Those who had nearly recovered were marked with scabs or deep pits where the scabs had been. The disease did not discriminate between the old or young, males or females, and no household was unaffected.

After everyone had been attended to, they returned to Japhet's home. His uncle took the pot from him and set it down on the rocks in the fire.

"Uncle, you need to come back with me now. Mum is sick and needs your help."

His uncle was sitting by the fire filling a large gourd, used for carrying water, with the remaining medicine. He plugged the end and held it out to Abraham. He took it and slipped the rope straps over his head and arm so that it hung across his chest. Uncle Ahanu instructed Japhet to fetch more water and then added herbs, roots, and bark to a stone bowl. He picked up a pestle and began to crush the ingredients into a powder.

"We must hurry, Uncle. Mum is very sick. She needs your help," Abraham said.

Uncle Ahanu looked up at Abraham. "I have many to tend to here. I cannot leave for just one." Uncle Ahanu looked at Abraham. There was sadness in his eyes. "Take the medicine to you mother. Feed it to her, just as we did here."

"But I can't do this by myself!" Abraham felt tears welling in his eyes. He blinked them away, but a couple escaped and snaked down his cheeks.

"If your mother had stayed, I could have cared for her here, but when she started to feel ill, she insisted on leaving. She said she wanted to see her children again before she died," Uncle Ahanu said gently. "I warned her it was unwise …."

"She isn't going to die! She can't …" Abraham couldn't stop the tears now. They rolled down his face in great waves. "She just … can't!"

Uncle Ahanu stood and took hold of Abraham's shoulders. He lifted Abraham's face to his and looked at him sternly. "You must master your feelings. Do not let them control you. You are strong." His uncle lifted the dolphin pendant from his chest and looked at it. "You are strong, just like the dolphins that hunt the great sharks. Believe in yourself. Have courage. Now hurry back to your mother. Feed it to her slowly, as much as she will take, several times each day."

Abraham nodded and left, just as Japhet returned with the water. He acknowledged the look of concern in his cousin's eyes and hurried away.

Chapter 26

The Berlingues

Etienne, March 20. 1664

I had tried to keep track of the days by scratching lines into the wall of my cell each time a seamen brought me a meal, which seemed to be twice a day. Near as I could tell from my markings, we had stayed in the port of La Rochelle for over two months during the worst of the winter storms and while repairs were made to the ship. I could hear the men working on the decks above me and longed to help, even if it meant filling cracks with hot oakum. I had not been released from my cell, nor had I seen the sailor to whom I'd given my note, until today. He came to collect me but he did not speak a word to me or look me in the eye. I supposed that meant he had betrayed me and given the note to Janssen. Now I'd likely be executed, and no one would ever know what happened to me.

I stood on wobbly legs in front of Captain Janssen's desk. He had not yet acknowledged my presence. I looked around the stateroom. It was sparsely but comfortably furnished. His bed was covered in fine linens and blankets, the chairs padded and covered in silk fabrics. What a contrast to the utilitarian furnishing I remembered from his house in Amsterdam.

I thought of *Maman*, Papa, Lidie, and the little ones. How would my father run the farm alone? How could he possibly come up with the remaining sum owed for our trip to the New World? I didn't think they had debtor's prison in New Amsterdam, but they were within their rights to make my father work for them directly as an indentured servant. Then what would happen to *Maman* and my siblings?

Then, I thought of Kitchi and Alsoomse. They too would never know what happened to me. What were they doing now? I ran my fingers over the wampum belt Alsoomse had given me. How angry she will be when *Le Dauphin* returns to New Amsterdam, and I am not on it. Of everyone I'd left behind, I missed her the most.

Janssen finally finished what he was writing and looked up at me.

"We have left France and are nearing the shores of Portugal and the rocky coast of the Berlingues." He studied me for a moment before he continued. "Are you ready to obey me now?"

I couldn't take any more of isolation and darkness or that shadows that haunted my dreams. I didn't trust my voice to speak, so I nodded, and brought my hand to grasp my forelock in salute.

Janssen looked over his desk and lifted a map out from under a scattering of papers. He lay it down on top and placed weights on the corners to prevent it from rolling up. I watched him trace our course with a finger. We were headed to Africa. There was only one cargo we could be obtaining there … slaves.

Janssen looked up at me again. "Now that there is no longer a chance of your escape …" He paused and glared at me. "You have two choices. I will give you the opportunity to officially sign on as a member of my crew. If you do, you will receive a share of the profits. If not, you will be thrown overboard. I cannot afford to feed you without receiving your labor in return, nor will I allow you freedom if I cannot trust you."

Janssen leaned back in his chair and studied me. He'd made no mention of the note. Had he not seen it? I glanced at the seaman standing beside me. He still refused to look at me. Perhaps he had not betrayed me, but that didn't mean he had delivered the note either.

"So, what will it be, Etienne? Will you sign the roster or not?"

I took a deep breath. If I signed on, I would receive a share of the money we earned. I could help my father repay his debt and save my family. There was no other choice.

"I will sign," I said.

Janssen took a large book out of one of drawers of his desk and set it down heavily on the desk. Then he opened it to a page with a list of names. I watched as he dipped his quill into the ink pot and wrote my name neatly at the bottom of the list. Then he spun the book around and handed me the quill.

"Make your mark here."

I signed my name.

"You are now free to return to your duties. But understand," he paused and looked directly into my eyes, "this is your last chance to prove yourself useful."

I nodded and turned to leave. The seaman accompanied me out. As the door closed behind us, I turned to confront him, but he was already gone.

The sea was rough, and the sky was an ominous grey. I was grateful for the wool sweater to keep me warm and the oiled jacket over it to keep out the cold wind that whipped through my hair. I dug my wool cap out of my pocket, pulled it down over my ears, and went to find the quartermaster.

It was approaching evening as we neared the Berlingues reef. All hands were called to watch for rocks that could damage the hull as we passed. I stood in the bow and searched the black water for any hint of white that might indicate hidden danger. I was determined to succeed in my task this time. No one spoke. As I watched, a fin surfaced off to port. It was a shark. I knew they hunted sholes of fish that fed off the bounty of the reef. I watched it as it wound its way farther ahead, and then I saw … white caps. I spun around and yelled the warning to the navigator. Then other seamen confirmed my warning, and the ship began to turn. I could see the white caps growing and worried we would not make the turn fast enough. Timbers creaked and men shouted. I held my breath as the ship slipped by mere feet from the jagged coral reefs.

Hours later, the dark shoreline slipped away as the ship moved into deeper water. A cheer erupted across the deck. We had made it! Darkness had engulfed us, but we had made it past the reef without injury.

"Etienne!"

I heard the captain's voice booming out over the celebrating men and turned to face him. His face was stern, and I wondered what I had done wrong now. I squared my shoulders and walked to meet whatever fate awaited me. As I approached, the captain held out a hand and I took it. He pulled me in and clapped me hard on the back.

"Congratulations! You saved the ship and earned a place among us. I am proud of you!"

I felt my chest swell. The men were cheering for *me*. I smiled. It felt good to be accepted and praised for doing good work, but I felt a sinking feeling too, in the pit of my stomach. I looked at the seamen clapping for me. They were pirates. I was now a crewman on a pirate ship sailing for Africa, to enslave other men. I thought of my father. I could see the disappointment that would show in his eyes when he learned of this. Would he even accept the money I'd earn from this endeavor? Probably not, no matter how much it was needed.

Janssen turned toward the remaining seamen and held up his hands for silence. "Are there any here who have never passed the Berlingues before now?"

No one spoke up. Finally, Janssen turned to me. "What about you, Boy? Was this your first time passing the reef?"

I thought of the story of the Baptisms, Janssen had described years before, and looked up to the main yardarm. If I didn't do it, I would have to pay a shilling. Years before I had jumped off a yardarm similar to this one and escaped capture and impressment. I supposed I could do it again. I took a deep breath and nodded.

"Yes, Sir. This is my first time passing the Berlingues."

The ship erupted with shouts and laughter. I was quickly led to the main mast, where the quartermaster tied one end of a long rope securely to my waist and the other end to the ship's railing. Then everyone watched as I climbed the rat rope and, reaching the yardarm, walked out along its length. I looked down. It was a long way down. I thought of the last time I had jumped from this height and the pain I'd felt as my body hit the water. Would it be better to jump feet-first or to dive in? I heard jeers and encouragements from the seamen below. I examined the rope at my waist. The knot was secure. At least the men would be able to pull me back on deck. I only hoped they would.

I took a deep breath and dove. I felt invincible as cold water washed over my body.

Chapter 27

Despair

Two days after Abraham returned home, the red spots on his mother's face and arms had become puss-filled boils, just like those on many of the people in the Montauk village. Abraham administered the medicine just as his uncle had instructed him. And for a while it seemed to be working. His mother even opened her eyes and smiled at him. But before the week was over, she took a turn for the worse.

The house felt different now, empty. Even his younger brothers were subdued. Whaling season was over. It was time to plow the fields and plant the corn, beans, and squash. He tried to work the fields as he had with his mother, but the ground fought him. Three days passed, but he had made little progress. He sat in the dirt and stared at nothing. Tired. Numb. Empty. Lost.

Then he felt a hand on his shoulder. Ralph had come out to help him. His brother's face was grim. He looked into Abraham's eyes and they shared a moment of sadness and loss. Ralph extended his hand and Abraham took it. He was able to stand only by relying on his brother's strength. They didn't say anything as they worked, but somehow it helped to have his brother there.

Abraham surveyed the fields. Jacob and Isaac made small mounds every couple of feet, as he'd instructed them. The rows weren't perfect, but they were close enough. Mum would have been pleased. He felt tears sting his eyes and blinked them away. He sighed and picked up the basket of corn kernels and walked to the first mound. He stooped to place two seeds on the top of the mound and pushed them gently into the soil. As he moved to the next mound, he felt a tug on his shirt. Looking down, he saw Caleb standing there, sucking his thumb. He'd stopped sucking his thumb months ago. Abraham sighed softly. "What do you want, Caleb?"

"Want to help you," he said with a whine in his voice and eyes squinted pleadingly.

Abraham hesitated. Then he nodded. "Take two seeds and press them into the top of the mound, like this."

Caleb watched him carefully and hopped up and down in his eagerness.

They moved to the third mound, and Abraham handed two kernels to Caleb.

Caleb's tongue stuck out of the corner of his mouth, and he furrowed his brow in concentration, as he teetered over the mound and placed the seeds on the top. Then he shoved them deep into the soil.

"Not so deep," Abraham said. He dug the kernels out and replaced them on top of the mound.

Caleb frowned.

"Gently," Abraham said. "Try it again."

Caleb poked gingerly at the seeds until they were just barely beneath the soil.

"That's right!" Abraham said. Caleb smiled broadly, clapped his hands, and then ran to the next mound. Abraham handed him two more seeds. After a few more mounds, Jacob and Isaac came out to help them. The work went much faster until Caleb lost his balance, fell on top of a mound, and squashed it.

"Caleb! Look what you've done," Abraham said scowling and stopping his foot.

Caleb started to cry. Jacob and Isaac looked over at Abraham with disapproval. Abraham closed his eyes for a moment, took a deep breath, held it, and then let it out slowly. He took another as Caleb continued to wail.

"It's okay," Abraham said. He opened his eyes and helped his youngest brother to stand up. Caleb's bottom lip quivered as Abraham brushed the dirt off him. "Come help me fix the mound." Together they rebuild the mound and planted the seeds, while Jacob and Isaac continued down the field.

They were all tired and dirty by the time the sun was setting. They hadn't finished planting the corn, but at least they'd made a good start. Abraham took his brothers over to the well to wash up. As Abraham finished scrubbing the last brother, Isaac came over and patted him on the back. Then he walked up to the house and Abraham followed his brothers inside.

Da was still sitting in the chair by the fire in the same place he'd been in the morning before Abraham had left for the fields. Da was staring into the fire, his eyes unfocused. He held a mug of beer in one fist. It looked like this was far from his first.

Food's ready if you're hungry," Sam said.

Abraham looked over toward the table to see Sam dishing a watery soup into wooden bowls. "Da, are you coming to eat?"

His father didn't respond; he just stared into the fire.

"He's been like that all day," Sam said. "There isn't much smoked meat left."

"I'll go fishing tomorrow," Ralph said as he slid onto the bench.

Abraham took a seat at the table and dipped his spoon into the soup. It was mostly broth. He looked up at Sam. "Thank you for this."

"There aren't many carrots or onions left either. Part of the roof of the root cellar collapsed and snow and rain got in, so a lot of them rotted."

"What about the corn? We could make *sappen* tomorrow."

Samuel scowled. "I don't think so. Anyway, I don't know how to make it. I barely knew to add vegetables and meat to water for the stew."

Abraham lifted a spoonful of soup to his mouth. No, it was clear that Sam had no idea how to cook. He'd not thought to add salt, garlic, or molasses to the broth.

"It's okay," Abraham said. "I'll check tomorrow. Is there any bread left?"

"No," Sam replied. "There's still mead though." He stood up to fetch it.

"If you'll help the boys with the planting tomorrow, I will sort through the vegetable cellars and see what we have left. Then I'll make bread."

Sam nodded and sat down to eat.

They passed the rest of the evening in relative silence. Ralph mended his fishing nets by the fire, Sam played with the little boys on the hearth rug, and Abraham cleaned the kitchen. Da only left his chair to go to the outhouse or to refill his mug. The younger brothers were so tired they didn't even argue about going to bed. Later, as Abraham lay in bed and stared up at the ceiling beams, barely visible in the growing darkness, he let the tears he'd held back all day, escape to roll down the sides of his face and into his ears unhindered.

Chapter 28

Benin

Etienne, April 7, 1664

We had sailed around the northwestern bulge of Africa and entered the Bight of Benin. We were now approaching the coast and the canal of Lagoa. The mouth of the canal was dotted with several sand bars and islands which left only a small channel deep enough for the larger vessels to navigate. It was slow-going and tensions were high.

The shoreline was edged in golden-yellow sand and skirted with strange looking trees with a single tall trunk, no branches, and topped with large feather-like leaves that stuck out of the top in all directions like a fluffy ball. In the distance, groves of lush, normal-looking trees accentuated the skinny, pale trunks of the funny-looking trees on the shoreline. I later learned they were called palm trees. As we crept up the channel, small huts of dried grass and reeds were just visible among the foliage.

One of the more experienced sailors confided to me that most

Dutch ships didn't venture into this channel for the danger of the sandbars but preferred to trade in one of the large towns along the coast. I wondered why Janssen would risk his ship like this.

We rounded a bend and came out into a large lake surrounded by tropical forest. Slowly a large village came into view. Small one-room houses were crowded together in a clearing dotted with a few branching trees and more palm trees. Behind the houses a stone wall surrounded a small citadel. Janssen ordered the anchor dropped and the boats readied. I watched the row boats being lowered into the water.

"Etienne!" Captain Janssen yelled from the quarterdeck. "You're with me!"

I quickly followed him down to the waiting rowboat and took my place at one of the oars. Nearly the entire crew and all the rowboats were now heading to shore, though all I could see was the *Zeelandia* rocking back and forth as she pulled gently against her anchor. I could feel a tug in my heart as I rowed. I too was anchored to her, to the crew I rowed beside, and to Janssen. Even if escape were possible here, where would I go? I was half a world away from everyone I knew and cared about.

We arrived on shore and pulled the boats up out of the water. It was already warm, and I felt sweat rolling down my back. Insects were buzzing around my ears. It was only early April, but it felt like early summer.

"Etienne, stay with the boat," Janssen said briskly as he headed into the village with the other officers.

I watched the people in the village as they went about their business. Dark skinned people with short cropped hair were dressed in beautiful, brightly-dyed clothing made from a light-weight fabric. It didn't look like linen, though, and the fabric was woven into exotic patterns of green, blue, black, red, and yellow. The women wore only skirts, or dresses pinned over one shoulder and the men wore only short loin cloths. I couldn't help staring at the spectacle, though I knew I should turn away.

Stalls had been erected along the shore where women sold brilliant bolts of cloth, pottery, oils, and soaps, while men displayed magnificent artifacts carved from ivory and wood or cast from bronze. The market was busy. As I watched, I noticed people using strings of cowrie shells to pay for the wares. The shells were rounded on one side and had what looked like a large partially open mouth on the other side. It was remarkable that here, halfway around the world, people used shells for currency, just like the native peoples back home used the shell beads they called *wampum*.

I heard a commotion and looked up to see Janssen and the officers returning. They were leading a long row of darkly skinned men and women, dressed in plain spun cloth. The line of people snaked out from the citadel. The men and women were chained to one another from shackles fixed around their necks. They were guarded by other dark-skinned men holding spears or swords and wearing bronze helmets, brightly colored loin cloths, and sword sheaths strapped across their chests.

Janssen arrived and ordered us to take the slaves to the ships. We pushed the boats into the water, and I held the stern as other seamen helped the men and women into the boats. When filled, they started back to the *Zeelandia*. I could only stand there in shocked silence. Back and forth the boats rowed to shore and ferried the frightened people to the ship.

The last boat returned for the few remaining people. Janssen climbed into the boat and motioned me to follow. I stood there rooted to the ground. How could Africans sell other Africans? How could we think to buy them? And where were we taking them? I should say something, but what could I say? And who would listen?

"Etienne! Get in the boat!"

I jerked to attention, climbed into the boat, and took the last seat in the stern.

Chapter 29

A Proposal

Alsoomse, April 15, 1664

Alsoomse stood looking out over the rolling waves of Long Island Sound. The fishing boats were returning though the sun was still high in the sky. She searched the distant horizon for the sails of the white men's ships.

She sat on the rise of a hill and sorted through the cracked clam shells looking for those with the deepest purple and brightest white. She had finished the belt she would someday give to her future husband, but now she needed to make more beads to decorate the garments she would one day wear on her wedding day, though she still didn't know who that future husband would be. She thought of Okwaho and his golden eyes smiling down at her. He had a warm, gentle way about him, and he understood her. He had liked that she was not like the other girls. He was a good hunter and fisher. She also knew that one day he would be a leader for his people. Still, he hadn't made a proposal, and then there was still Etienne to worry about.

She scanned the horizon again. She missed their adventures in the woods. She remembered when she'd helped him make his dugout canoe and smiled. He had so much to learn! He was always getting himself into trouble, but now she wasn't there to help him out of it. He should have stayed on *Manahatta*! What foolishness had taken him out onto the Great Sea away from her where he would be helpless to save himself?

She knew her parents would never accept a marriage with Etienne. It would mean abandoning her tribe, but then that did happen sometimes when girls were traded to other tribes or kidnapped by them. But the white men's ways were not like their ways. White women did not have as much authority as Indian women, nor did they seem to have much influence with their husbands. Etienne was different though. He respected her. He accepted her for who she was.

She picked up her chisel and hammer and started gently chipping away at the shells, separating the colorful inside from the plain outside shell. It was delicate and tedious work, but it helped keep her mind from ruminating on things she could not control.

By the time Kitchi and Hasun had returned from fishing with baskets full of sea bass, Alsoomse had created a large pile of broken shell castings and had made a small handful of wampum beads. She watched her brothers haul their catch toward their *wetu* where their mother waited to receive them. She sighed and quickly finished the bead in her hand. Then she stood and went to help her mother clean the fish.

Alsoomse and her mother draped many of the cleaned fish over poles they'd hung over a small fire. Then they covered the fire with wet, green seaweed to create smoke. Finally, they laid wet reed mats over the poles to cover the whole assemblage. The smoked fish would keep for many days. Some of the fish they added to large clay pots with water and corn, which they set over low fires to simmer for the next day. The rest they roasted over the fire for the evening meal. Alsoomse took a bite. The flesh was moist and savory. This was her favorite way to eat fish. A little grease ran down her chin and she quickly wiped it away.

The sun had set and the fire cast a comforting warmth against the cool breeze that blew off the water. The stars were bright against the moonless sky. She could see the path in the sky that her ancestors traveled on their way to meet Manitou. Etienne had called it the Milky Way. Again, she wondered what he was doing. Maybe he was looking up at the stars too.

Suddenly, her father stood up and turned to greet someone, and Alsoomse looked to see who had arrived. Two people were approaching with arms heavily laden. As they neared, she recognized Matoaka and Okwaho! His fawn-colored eyes acknowledged her and he smiled before turning to address her father. He lay his bundles down on the ground in front of him. Then he took the burden from his mother and added her bundles to the pile. There were several finely woven blankets, new bear coats, beaver skins, and soft buckskins. Then Okwaho offered a basket filled with many strands of wampum beads. He pulled a particularly beautiful strand out of the basket and held it out for her. She felt the warmth of his hand as she took it and examined it. The purples were deep and vibrant. The whites were bright and seemed to nearly glow in the firelight.

"Whom are you representing?" her father asked.

"I am here to ask Alsoomse to be my wife," Okwaho said and

turned to look at her.

Her father looked at him quizzically. "It is unusual for the petitioner to come himself," her father stated.

"Your daughter is an unusual woman," Okwaho said and smiled. "I wanted her to know how much I honor and respect her by coming myself." Then he took two more beaded stands from the basket and walked up to Alsoomse. He stooped and placed them around her neck. She could smell his musk and her breath caught in her throat. She looked up into his eyes and felt a jolt of excitement run through her. He had the eyes of a wolf, cunning, knowing, dangerous, and yet there was humor and warmth too. Her heart was beating fast, and she opened her mouth to respond, but was unable to find her voice and closed it again.

Okwaho smiled warmly and turned back to address her father.

"With your permission, my mother and I will stay and wait for her answer."

"We are honored by your presence," her father replied and offered him a seat beside him.

Her mother quickly stood and went to fetch food for Okwaho and his mother as they settled down by the fire.

Chapter 30

Vision

Alsoomse awoke early to accompany Matoaka into the woods. She had still not given Okwaho an answer to his proposal. She enjoyed his company, but she still worried about Etienne. Okwaho and his mother had agreed to give her more time. She had heard her mother discussing the situation with Matoaka. In the meantime, Matoaka had agreed to continue Alsoomse's training.

The air was still chilly, and dew sparkled over the grass like hundreds of the glass beads the white men had brought with them from across the sea. Birds were just beginning to awaken and search for food, leaving their young to cry forlornly in their absence.

They were following a narrow path that led down to a rocky stream. Alsoomse could hear the water burbling as it trickled through the rocks. As they reached the bank, Matoaka stopped and pointed to a young tree growing near the water's edge.

"Today I will introduce you to the alder tree," Matoaka said. "It is a powerful sacred plant with many medicinal uses. You must learn to recognize it. See the long catkins hanging from its branches like icicles? They come out in the spring just as the leaves begin to bud."

Alsoomse studied the tree. Clusters of the slender catkins hung from the delicate branches like fringe on a buckskin dress, while bright green leaf buds swelled ready to burst out along the top and tips of the branches.

"You may collect the bark during spring, after the tree has awakened from its slumber. You may not take the bark in the summer, for that time is reserved so the alder can grow stronger. You may, however, collect the bark in the fall after the leaves have fallen, but not in the winter, for then it sleeps and has no strength."

Alsoomse nodded.

The medicine woman continued. "Every sacred plant has its own song. You must learn each of these songs to give the medicine power. But first you must establish a relationship with the plant. Wild plants have more power than those we domesticate. When we grow the plants in our gardens, we tame them and control them, so they lose part of their natures. They lose some of their power, as they bend to our will. But when they are wild, we cannot just take from them as we wish. We must come as supplicants."

"How do we do that?" Alsoomse asked.

Matoaka smiled. "We must make a sacred relationship with the plant. We must treat it with respect, and gently, as we would wish to be treated. Because all things are made from the fabric of the Great Spirit, all things have awareness. Because we were all created by the Great Spirit, we can communicate with each other."

Alsoomse nodded thoughtfully and waited for Matoaka to continue. When she did not, she asked, "And how does one do this?"

Matoaka chuckled. "With patience. Let us sit and meditate on the alder a while."

Matoaka spread a blanket on the ground beneath the alder and Alsoomse sat down beside her. Now you must remember what I am going to tell you."

Alsoomse inclined her head. "I will remember."

"The bark of this tree contains healing properties. If it is drunk as a tea, it can treat diarrhea and sores of the mouth and throat. If used as a wash externally, it can heal cuts, hives, poison ivy, swellings, and sprains."

Alsoomse repeated what Matoaka had said to herself so she would remember it.

Then the medicine woman offered up a prayer to the spirit of the tree, closed her eyes, and waited. Alsoomse closed her eyes and tried to listen for the alder's voice. Before long she felt herself drifting to sleep. She stretched and tried to focus. She listened to the trickling of the stream and the sound of the wind in the tree. A bird called out for his mate somewhere in the distance. She shifted her weight and stretched her neck. She heard a rustle in a nearby bush and opened her eyes. Matoaka made a disapproving noise beside her, so Alsoomse tried once again to relax and concentrate on the alder. After a few minutes, her head nodded onto her chest, and she jerked awake. She shifted her position, but no matter how hard she tried, she was unable to keep the drowsiness from creeping over her.

Alsoomse's eyes fluttered open, and she looked up into the canopy of the alder. The catkins hung in many layered tiers over her head. As she watched them swaying in the breeze, a butterfly fluttered down from the pinnacle, bouncing erratically from one cluster of catkins to the next, circling the trunk. Its wings were black, but as it danced in and out of the sunlight, dark spots of midnight blue flashed alluringly from each wing tip.

A song drifted in on the wind, softly at first, and then growing in strength. She listened as the words repeated themselves over and over. "Father, send a voice. Father, send a voice. A hard task I am having. Father, send a voice. A hard task I am having."

As the song repeated, Alsoomse noticed the butterfly coming closer and closer. It fluttered across her face and then over to the edge of the water where, suddenly, a frog flicked out its tongue and ate it. Alsoomse watched as the frog slid back into the water, just as a large fish leapt out, caught it in its mouth, and disappeared back under the rippling surface.

Alsoomse awoke with a start and turned to see Matoaka's eyes still closed in meditation. The old woman shook herself and looked at Alsoomse contemplatively.

"You saw something. It is plain on your face. Tell me what you saw and heard."

Alsoomse thought for a moment and then began. "There was a black butterfly in the tree. It fluttered down and moved from one cluster to the next. It moved across my face and then over to the water where it was eaten by a frog. But then a fish leapt up and ate the frog. It was strange because the fish was a sea cod and was much too large to live in this stream."

"Did you see or hear anything else?" Matoaka asked and her eyes narrowed slightly as she studied me.

"There was also a song. It kept repeating over and over on the wind."

Matoaka looked thoughtful and then smiled. "You must remember that song, the words and the melody. It is a sacred song of healing. You must sing it whenever you use the medicine you make with the alder bark.

Alsoomse asked, "Should I sing it for you?"

Matoaka shook her head. "The alder has already given me a song, child. And merely repeating a song given to someone else will not work. To make a song work, you must have a direct experience with it. Some can teach it, but only very thoughtfully and over a long time of working together with the plant."

"I will remember it," Alsoomse promised.

"The black butterfly represents death. It means that death is coming. The fish represents the sea. And the frog represents the people who live along the coast. Death is coming to the people who live by the sea." Matoaka paused before continuing. "Do you know anyone who is still living near the sea? It will likely be someone you know personally."

"My friend, Etienne, lives with his family on *Manahatta*, but he isn't there now. He is on a white man's great ship somewhere on the ocean, but perhaps his family is in danger." She thought for a moment. "There is also a boy I met recently. His name is Abraham. He lives on the tip of the long island we call, *Wamponomon*."

Matoaka thought for a while before she spoke. "The vision was given to you along with the song for a reason. I think we should make our way south to see your friends. If they are sick, then you have been given the power to heal them. First, we must go back to the village to make preparations."

Alsoomse leapt to her feet and bent to help Matoaka up. The medicine woman moved slowly and stiffly. She seemed suddenly older and frailer than she'd been even a week before.

As they headed back, one thing still bothered Alsoomse ... *the fish swallowed the frog. If the frog was dying, did that mean the fish would too?* She thought of Etienne again and frowned.

Chapter 31

Sails

Abraham, April 30, 1664

As the days passed, Da had taken to going out at night only to return early in the morning or not at all. If he did return, he would stumble in smelling strongly of ale. He would then head off to bed and sleep away the day. Abraham tried to keep up with the chores around the house and in the garden, while his older brothers cared for the animals, hunted, and fished. Isaac was somewhat faithful in watching over Jacob and Caleb, though Abraham still had to check on them frequently.

Abraham was just finishing planting the last of the squash and pumpkin seeds, when he looked up toward the sea and caught a glimpse of white glinting off the water. He dropped the basket and ran toward the coast. It was past noon, and the sun was warm. It felt good to run. He hadn't run since when? The harvest festival when he'd broken his ankle in the games. He'd had a birthday since then too. He felt older and stronger. A lot had happened since those games. Pain stabbed at his chest. A *lot* had happened since then. He frowned, but he wouldn't think of it now. It felt good to finally move, not from duty or necessity, but by his own will.

He darted across a pasture, leaped over the fence, and turned toward the beach. He crested a low hillock and charged down to the beach. The lookout tower was still standing, and he darted over to it and climbed the rungs easily. At the top, he panted as he held his hands over his eyes and scanned the horizon. Maybe he had imagined it. No, there it was! The first ship of the season. Was it the *Dolphin*? Was Etienne coming back?

When Abraham arrived back home, his father was awake and getting dressed to go out for the evening.

"Da, I saw a ship heading for New Amsterdam today."

"Seems early," Da said. "Are you sure?"

Abraham nodded. "I ran to the lookout tower and made sure. It was still too far away to see the flag, but it was a ship, sure enough. Should we take the oil in to sell? Then if it is the *Dolphin*, we can pick up the harpoons and other supplies. I could go if you want?"

Da stretched and scratched the top of his head. "It'll be a few days before it arrives. That should give us enough time to load up the rowboat and get there. Prepare food to take with us. We'll load the boats tomorrow."

Da reached out for his hat, but then paused and dropped his hand to his side as he turned to face his boys. "That was good thinking, Abraham."

The next morning, Da was up early. Abraham served bowls of oat porridge around the table. A sense of anticipation hung over them as they ate. Then suddenly, Da stood and stretched.

"Abraham, take Sam and Ralph with you to start loading the boats. You'll need help with the barrels. I'll be along directly, after I drop your younger brothers off at Aunt Alice's house."

Abraham nodded and went to fetch the bundle of food he'd prepared the night before. Then he left with his older brothers for the storage house they'd built along the coast.

It was a beautiful day, sunny with a light breeze, and not too hot. He could almost forget the darkness that enveloped him even now. Abraham stared out over the blue-grey water. It would be good to have something important to do, a distraction from the constant reminders that Mum was not there.

They reached the storage house and Ralph removed an iron key from his pocket and fitted it into the door lock. The door opened into the darkened room. Since whaling season was over now, the boats had been brought inside and piled up in the back of the room. They would need two of the boats for the trip to New Amsterdam. The boats were heavy. They'd been designed to hold six to eight men, so they would be strong enough to hold the precious barrels of oil.

They dragged two boats and four oars down to the edge of water, just out of the tide's reach and returned to the storage house. The oil had been hidden in a cellar beneath the house. It was accessible only through a trap door hidden beneath the rug in the kitchen. A heavy table stood on top of it. That was where Mum had stood for hours and prepared food for all the whalers. Tears started to blur Abraham's eyesight and he blinked them away quickly.

As he started toward the table, Abraham noticed it had been moved. It was not sitting squarely on the rug. And the corner of the rug was flipped up. Someone had been in the cellar during their absence. Abraham's stomach clenched in fear. Just then, Da trudged heavily into the kitchen.

"Da, look! The table's been moved." Abraham said.

"Don't be silly. How could anyone get in here?" Da replied harshly as he shoved the table away and flipped up the rug. The cellar door also had a lock and Da stooped over to fit his key into the keyhole. The key clicked and Da swung open the large, heavy door.

"Ralph, light a lantern and bring it here," Da said.

Ralph did as he was told and handed it to their father. Da descended first, followed by Ralph and Sam. Abraham came last and reached the bottom stair as Da hung the lantern from a hook in the ceiling. Abraham looked around. The barrels of oil stood along the back wall. They had only gotten sixteen barrels of oil from the whale. A full-grown whale might produce twenty barrels or more. The whale they'd killed had seemed huge, though it had only been a yearling. Other attempts had failed utterly. Either the men had been unable to catch the whales, or as Ralph had told him, the harpoons had shattered and ripped away from the animals as they had dived deeper into the sea. By the time the boats had regrouped, the remaining whales were too far away for any hope of catching up to them.

Four barrels had been given to the Shinnecock and four to the Montaukett in payment to the whalers and tribute to the village leaders. That left them with eight barrels to sell. But Abraham saw that there were only seven barrels left in the cellar.

"Da, one of the barrels is missing!" Abraham said.

Da looked around. "They're all here," he said.

Abraham started to protest, but Da held up a hand and Abraham closed his mouth.

What had happened to the missing barrel?

It was noon by the time six barrels had been removed from the cellar, rolled down to the water, and loaded into the boats. Abraham was already tired from their exertions.

Three barrels were loaded into one rowboat. As the sixth barrel was loaded into the second boat, Da said, "Ralph and Abraham will take that boat. Sam and I will take this one."

"But what about the last barrel?" Abraham asked.

"That one stays," he answered. As Abraham opened his mouth to ask why, Da continued, "I owe money to Frank at the tavern. I told him I'd give him some of the oil to settle my tab."

"But a whole barrel?"

"We may need some of it too for lights, since ..." His voice caught and he paused to master himself. "Since your Mum's not here to make candles."

No one spoke as they pushed the boat out into the sea and took their places at the oars. It took Abraham several strokes before he was able to row in time with Ralph, but soon they were keeping pace and the boat slid out into the deep water.

As Abraham rowed, he let his eyes wander out to the horizon. He thought of his mother lying on her bed, covered in boils, moaning through her fevered dreams, and felt his anger rising again. Uncle Ahanu talks about *Manitou*, the Great Creator Spirit who cared for his people so much he gave them sacred healing plants. Reverend Fordham said God the Father sent his Son to die for the sins of all people because he loved everyone so much. Did his uncle and the minister describe the same god or different gods? And why didn't

Manitou, or God, heal his mother? She had prayed every morning and every evening. She had loved Creator God and had believed they were two expressions of the same God. But if he cares so much for people, why did he let her die?

Chapter 32

Inquiries

The pier was busy with activity as they approached and found a place to tie up the rowboat. A large ship was anchored off the end of the dock and men were swarming on and off like ants as they carried boxes, crates, and barrels from the ship to stack them up in the storehouses. The men were laughing and joking with each other as they worked.

"Sam and Abraham, stay with the boat," Da said. "Ralph and I will go in search of a buyer."

"Why can't I go too?" Abraham asked.

"I need you and Sam to stay and guard the barrels," Da replied.

"Let Sam stay by himself," Abraham replied.

"It is safer if you both stay," Da said sternly. He hurried off with Ralph before Abraham could protest more.

As soon as they disappeared from view, Sam lept out of his boat and said, "Stay with the boat."

"Where are you going? Da said to stay with me!" Abraham said. The spark of anger Abraham kept hidden inside flared to life.

"I have an errand to make. I'll be back before Da knows I'm gone." He paused and gave Abraham a stern look. "And if you tell Da I left, I'll beat you senseless!"

Abraham watched Sam hurry down the pier and disappear into a nearby tavern.

It was midday, but the activity on the docks were slow since the transatlantic ships hadn't started arriving in numbers yet. There was still some local trade coming from the mainland, Long Island, and Staten Island, along with a few colonial ships plying up and down the coast, but it was no comparison to the busy months of June to October. Still, warmer days had arrived, and people were coming outside to enjoy it. Men and women in fancy clothing strolled along the streets arm-in-arm, while fishermen sat around on barrels and crates mending their nets. Shopkeepers stood in their doorways and greeted passing townsfolk.

It seemed to be taking Da and his brothers a long time. Abraham massaged the sore muscles of his arms and shoulders as he waited. It had taken three days to row along the southeastern coast of Long Island and around the western tip to reach the port of New Amsterdam. Each evening, they had to haul the boats onto the beach as far as they could above the high-water mark and anchor it so the tides would not take them away while they slept.

Abraham looked up to see a well-dressed French man approaching. As he neared, Abraham recognized him as the owner of the ship he and Da had taken to Boston last September. He appeared to have recognized someone, and Abraham turned to see who it was. Captain Jolls had just stepped onto the deck farther down the pier and was heading this way.

"Master Carteret!" the captain called as he approached.

The men stopped a few paces away to talk.

"Captain Jolls! It is good to see you. How was your trip?"

"Successful, sir. We encountered a storm in the North Atlantic, but we still made good speed to London, and then to Texel harbor. The Baltic Sea was still open, and so we were able to deliver the pelts to Muscovy and get back to London before the ice closed in. As it was a mild winter, we were able to get an early start back with a full hull."

"Excellent! Take your ship's log to my bookkeeper and he will give you the ship's wages," Carteret said.

"Thank you, sir!" Jolls doffed his hat and started to turn away.

"Captain Jolls, before you go …."

"Yes, sir?"

"Where is Etienne Gayneau, the new seaman I assigned to you? I am anxious to speak with him," Master Carteret said.

At the mention of Etienne's name, Abraham began to listen more intently. He noticed the captain's face darken with anger.

The captain paused a moment. Then he said, "I am sorry to tell you, sir, Etienne deserted the ship in Texel. We waited an extra day for him to return, only because I knew he meant something to you, sir. The boy didn't even have the decency to inform me of his departure!"

"I would not have expected that from Etienne," Carteret said. A worried expression crossed his face. "Well, thank you for the information. You should stop by my house tonight for dinner. Shall we say 7:00?"

Captain Jolls doffed his hat again and headed toward the shops, while Carteret continued down the end of the pier where seamen were unloading cargo from the *Dolphin*. Abraham didn't have long to think about what he'd just heard because at that moment his father and Ralph returned with a tall, blond man in an expensive-looking gold jacket with a wide lace collar and gold cape over dark breeches.

Da looked around for Sam, frowned, and then took the merchant to examine the oil. Abraham watched as they haggled over the price. Finally, the merchant smiled broadly and he and Da shook hands. Then the merchant handed Da a small leather purse.

As the merchant started to leave, he said, "You may unload the barrels here and I will send my men to come and take possession of them. They should be here before you finish."

Da nodded, and as soon as the man's back was turned, an angry scowl spread across his face.

"Where is Sam?"

Abraham shrugged. "He said he had to run an errand."

Da shook his head and motioned Ralph and Abraham to help him unload the barrels.

"We will have enough money to pay the balance on the harpoons and to purchase supplies for the coming season." Da grumbled as he jumped down into one of the boats. "We did not, however, bring in enough to repay the loan to Mr. King. I hope these new harpoons will improve our haul this winter. We need to see greater success if we are to save the house."

"Come on," Ralph said and slapped Abraham on the back. "Let's get to it!"

Abraham grunted and jumped into the boat to begin the process of unloading.

Sam returned after one barrel had been unloaded.

"Where have you been?" Da asked.

"I had to see a friend," Sam replied.

"You've been drinking," Da said.

Sam gave a sheepish smile. "Mattie works as a barmaid."

"It seems Abraham is more trustworthy than you are, Sam. Next time I will leave you at home to watch the little boys."

Abraham felt a swell of pride fill his chest and a surge of energy as he helped Ralph with the next barrel. Finally, the oil was unloaded, and the merchant's men came to take possession of them.

"This time, Sam, you will come with Ralph and me to collect the harpoons we ordered and purchase more supplies. Abraham, do you want to come too?" Da paused and stared off along the pier. Abraham looked up to see what had caught his father's attention. Alsoomse was walking toward them with an old medicine woman with stooped shoulders. Alsoomse was looking directly at him. Da smiled, nodded to the girl, and patted Abraham's shoulder. "You have earned a rest, Abraham."

Alsoomse waited as the men left, her head cocked to one side. She was grinning.

"Are you embarrassed to see me?" she asked.

"No!" he said. He felt his face flush. Then he shrugged and laughed. "What are you doing here?"

A strange look crossed her face for a moment. Then she gestured toward the old woman with her. "I had a vision concerning you while Matoaka and I were gathering herbs in the woods. We thought we should come and see if you were well, but it took us a few weeks to convince our sachem to agree to let us travel here."

Alsoomse paused and studied Abraham. "You look pale. Are you well?"

Abraham shrugged and looked down. "Well enough."

"I had a vision that death was coming here."

Abraham nodded slowing and seemed to study something on the deck. When he finally looked up, his eyes were moist and red.

"My mum died of smallpox with over half her village."

Matoaka stepped forward and placed a hand on his forehead. Then she looked into each of his eyes. She felt his neck, looked down his throat, and finally put her ear to his chest. She found the pendant he wore around his neck and lifted it out of his shirt. She gazed at it thoughtfully. Then she let it fall back onto his chest, nodded, and stepped back. She turned to Alsoomse, who stepped forward and gazed intently into his eyes. Then her eyes dropped to the pendant hanging around his neck.

"What?" Abraham asked. "It has been several weeks since she died. I can't have gotten it! Could I?"

Alsoomse reached out a hand and lifted the pendant of the dolphin he'd won at the ball game and traced the lines with a finger. "Is this your spirit animal?"

"No. I mean, I don't know. I haven't …"

Alsoomse nodded with understanding. "You have many trials ahead of you yet, but you are not ready for them."

"What do you mean, 'I am not ready for them'? I *am* ready!"

Matoaka held up a hand to silence him. "Your soul is sick." Then she reached into her medicine bag and pulled out a small leather pouch. She handed it to Alsoomse and nodded.

Alsoomse opened the pouch and pulled out a piece of woven cloth. She unfolded it. A small cross had been wrapped in it. A long thong had been tied to the cross, and this she placed over his head. "Wear this. It will help you remember who you are."

Abraham picked up the cloth and saw the image of a broken arrow painted on it. Then he fingered the cross. It was made of oiled wood of a rich medium dark color. In the center was imbedded a round stone of translucent pink. A thin strip of lighter wood wound around the vertical trunk of the cross. He thought of the cross that hung in the church they attended every Sunday. That cross was meant to remind people of the sacrifice God had made by sending his son to Earth to take the punishment for the sins of mankind. He ran his finger over the strip of lighter wood up to the pale pink stone and traced it several times. He looked up at Alsoomse. Her eyes were closed, and her hands were lifted palms up. She was singing something so quietly he could barely make it out.

"The broken arrow symbolizes peace," Alsoomse said after she finished her song. "The cross represents Earth's forces, their origins, and the ways of the Earth. The wood is from the alder tree and the pale strip is from the willow. The stone is rose quartz. All these materials have healing properties. It is meant to reconnect you to the land, to show you who you are, and who you are meant to be. It will help to heal your broken spirit."

Abraham fought back tears as he carefully folded the cloth, tucked it into the pouch, and slipped it into his pocket.

Then Matoaka whispered something into Alsoomse's ear, turned, and walked away.

"She is going to the market to shop and will wait for me there," Alsoomse explained. "I saw a ship had returned from across the great waters. Do you know if Etienne is back?"

Abraham quickly told her what he had overheard. When he finished, she was scowling.

"Etienne would not have left Captain Joll's ship by his own will," she said.

At that moment Abraham noticed a small man strutting toward them like a cock. He was wearing a leather apron and carrying a wooden toolbox. His small beady eyes looked them over and a malicious smile played about his mouth.

"Looking for your friend, are you? Don't look for him here," he said, smiling broadly. "In fact, I doubt very much whether you will ever see him again."

As the man continued down the pier, Alsoomse huffed angrily. "I am sure he is to blame for Etienne's disappearance!"

"Who is he?" Abraham asked.

"He is a vindictive and petty man! When Etienne first arrived here, that man wrongfully accused Etienne of stealing his cherries, though the fruit trees didn't even belong to him. They belonged to Master Carteret, and he had given Etienne permission to pick them."

"Who's this?"

Abraham recognized the voice and looked up to see Sam standing there. "Just a friend," he said.

Sam grunted and placed an armful of harpoons into the boat.

"I should go. Matoaka is waiting for me," Alsoomse said. "Be well and send me word if you hear anything about what has happened to Etienne."

"I will." Abraham assured her.

Chapter 33

Slaves

Etienne, May 5, 1664

I filled a bucket with fresh water from the storage hold, found a ladle, and dropped it into the bucket. Then I reached into my pouch and pulled out a small jar of mint infused grease the ship's doctor had given me. I smeared a generous quantity under my nose and replaced the jar in my pouch. Then I pulled my handkerchief over my nose, picked up the bucket, and started for the ladder. I had put on my boots for this task, not wanting to step into the muck that awaited me with my bare feet.

As I reached the bottom of the ladder, I set the bucket down and relit the lantern that swung from the low beam above. The whites of hundreds of eyes glowed in the dim light watching me. I closed my eyes and struggled to steady my nerves. Then I took a deep breath and stepped into forward. Janssen's men had led three hundred twenty-six men and two hundred thirty women and two dozen children down to the cargo hold where they had chained them to rings attached to posts, walls and floorboards by collars fitted around their necks. Their feet were also shackled.

Men were contained in the larger hold and women and children in the smaller one. The slaves were crowded in with barely enough room for each to lay down next to each other to sleep at night. I carried the bucket of water and gingerly stepped over legs and around bodies to give each prisoner a drink in turn. The number of bodies and lack of ventilation made the hold unbearably hot, and sweat was soon soaked through my linen shirt. The mint grease did little to cover the fetid smell of body odor, feces, urine, and vomit that covered the floorboards and made them treacherously slick.

After I'd given each a drink, Janssen ordered me to bring them up to the deck in groups of twenty to get some air and exercise. I started with the men. They covered their eyes as they reached the deck, blinded by the sun after having been in the dark hold for over three weeks. As their eyes adjusted, sailors dumped buckets of sea water over their nearly nude bodies and loin cloths to wash away the grime and stench. Then they were forced to dance to the quartermaster's whip. My hands clenched into fists at my sides. Rage burned in my chest. Before I could think what to do, I was sent to swab the hold where they had been moments earlier.

After the men had all been brought up and returned to their temporarily clean hold, I brought up the women and children. The women too, wore only loin cloths and I tried not to stare at their bare chests. The children were completely naked. I heard sobbing and turned to see a skinny boy clinging to his mother's arm. Po!

I lurched over to the railing and emptied my stomach into the rolling sea. I wiped my mouth and turned back to look at the child. The boy was staring at me with large, frightened eyes. I could see that he wasn't really Po, the boy who had hidden me in Amsterdam and later rescued me when I had escaped the pirate ship, but he might have been. I reached into my pocket and found a hard candy I'd bought in Amsterdam and forgotten about. I handed it to him and motioned putting it in my mouth. The boy did as I instructed him, and his eyes widened in surprise as the sweetness began to melt in his mouth.

Was there some way I could save these people? We were in the middle of the Atlantic Ocean far from land. I couldn't take over the ship alone. I would only be killed. I vowed to watch for an opportunity. If one surfaced, I would be ready.

The women and children were also bathed in seawater, but they were not forced to dance, though they were subject to lewd stares and comments from the seamen. I cursed Janssen silently as I returned below decks to swab out their holding cell grateful the women could not understand our language. Five men and three women had died from dysentery. Five seamen helped me carry their bodies up to the deck and toss them into the sea.

I was exhausted when I finally crawled into my hammock. As I lay there in the dark, I couldn't get the images of Po out of my head. Tears welled behind my eyes until I could bear it no longer. I softly wept until I had no more tears to cry.

Chapter 34

A New Mother

Abraham, May 10, 1664

Abraham had taken Jacob, Isaac, and Caleb to work in the fields with him, while Ralph and Sam went fishing in Peconic Bay. The morning had been chilly and cloudy, but the sun had come out after noon and its warmth was comforting as they stooped to pluck the weeds from between the young crops. It hadn't rained in several days, so Abraham had sent Isaac to fetch water from the well. He took the bucket and ladle and drizzled water over the seedlings, while his brothers continued with the weeding. Finally, as the sun began to reach the horizon, they headed home exhausted and sore.

Ralph and Sam were cleaning their catch on an old wooden table outside the back door as they approached. Abraham pulled water from the well and washed his hands and face. Then he ordered Isaac to clean himself up and to wash the younger boys for dinner. He went to the root cellar and collected some of the corn and root vegetable he'd salvaged from the collapsed root cellar for the evening meal. Food supplies were nearly gone. Soon he would have to start foraging for dandelions, seaweed, and other wild plants to supplement the fish and clams Ralph and Sam brought back until the beans were ready to harvest.

The house was dark when he entered. The lamps had not been lit and the fire had been left to go out. Abraham sighed heavily and set the produce down on the table. He found the tinderbox and went to the hearth to rebuild and light the fire. As he squatted there, he heard a soft noise that sounded like crying, coming from the main bedroom. He rose quietly and went to peak into the room. Da was sitting in Mum's rocking chair with his face buried in Mum's buckskin dress. She'd been buried in her Sunday dress, despite Abraham's protests. Da's chest was heaving as he sobbed into the worn leather garment. Abraham's own heart ached as he backed out and closed the door quietly behind him. There was no time for mourning now. He needed to prepare dinner. His brothers would be hungry.

When his brothers returned, Abraham added the fish they had caught to the thin hominy he'd put to simmering over the fire. When it was finished, he called his brothers into supper. Abraham was about to take a bowl to his father when Da opened the bedroom door with a bang and came to the table. They ate in silence for a while.

After dinner, Abraham cleared the dishes, put the leftover food away, and wiped down the table, while Ralph and Sam sat by the fire. Da was sitting in his chair watching Jacob and Caleb playing with the wooden toys Da had made them years before. Isaac just sat staring into the fire.

Abraham walked into his father's bedroom, retrieved the Bible, and then joined his family at the hearth. "Da, would you read to us?"

he asked and held out the Bible.

Da looked up at him with glassy eyes and slowly shook his head. "I'm tired. I'm going to bed."

The next afternoon, Aunt Alice and Uncle Thomas arrived with their cousin, Nathaniel.

Aunt Alice scanned the house as she removed her bonnet and cape. Da was again sitting sullenly by the fire. Abraham was preparing the evening meal and Aunt Alice came over to help. "Nathaniel, why don't you take the boys out to play?" Aunt Alice suggested.

The younger boys eagerly jumped up to follow Nathaniel outside.

"What are you making?" his aunt asked and peeked into the pot.

"*Sappen*," Abraham replied. "It is a type of corn chowder with garlic and onion for flavoring. Hopefully, Ralph and Sam will get home soon with some fish we can add to it."

Aunt Alice wrinkled her nose but then tried to smile. "This was one of your mother's dishes, I suppose."

Abraham nodded.

As the afternoon progressed, Abraham went outside to help Nathaniel, who was playing with his younger brothers. Aunt Alice and Uncle Thomas sat by the fire to talk to Da. The sun was setting when Ralph and Sam came home from fishing. Abraham added the cleaned and skinned fish to the pot to cook. It was dark when they all sat down to eat, so Aunt Alice lit some candles.

Dinner was a lively affair with laughter and amiable discussions. Abraham thought it almost felt like a normal dinner, like it was before Mum died. Afterwards, Alice cleaned up and shooed Abraham out of the kitchen to sit with the men. Uncle Thomas read the story about how David, the shepherd boy, stepped up to kill the giant, Goliath, when the other warriors were too afraid. Caleb clapped his hands at the end.

"More, more! Read another one, *please.*"

"That's enough for now," Aunt Alice said. "You boys go on to bed. Your uncle and I have something to discuss with your father."

Nathaniel, Isaac, Jacob, and Caleb hurried up the stairs.

"You too, Abraham," Aunt Alice said sternly.

"But, Ralph and Sam …"

"They will be along too as soon as they see to the animals," she said, cutting him off.

Abraham reluctantly followed the boys upstairs and lay down on his bed. He listened to the gentle breathing of the other boys, but he couldn't sleep, so he lay still and tried to hear the conversation taking place around the fire.

"Samuel," Aunt Alice said. "Thomas and I haven't seen you or your family at church for months now. We are worried about you."

Abraham could not hear Da's reply.

"You have a lot of responsibilities with the farming, the animals, your whaling venture, and the boys. You need help." Uncle Thomas said.

There was some discussion Abraham couldn't quite hear. He rolled out of bed as quietly as he could and crept to the top of the ladder to hear better.

Aunt Alice was sitting in Mum's rocking chair. She was leaning forward with a worried look on her face. Uncle Thomas was standing behind her with his hands on the back of the chair. He couldn't see Da's expression because his back was toward him.

Aunt Alice took a deep breath and said, "I think you should take another wife. You could use someone to help you with the house and the boys …"

"No!" Abraham blurted. "Mum's only just died. You can't replace her just like that!"

Caleb started crying and Jacob and Isaac sat up and looked at each other, eyes wide, as if expecting terrible retribution to reign down upon them.

"Abraham!" Da said angrily. "Get yourself down here this instant!"

Abraham quickly pulled on his trousers, slunk down the ladder, and went to stand in front of his father.

"Abraham, it is rude to listen in to other people's conversations, especially when you don't understand the situation."

"But I *do* understand!" He looked over at his aunt and frowned. "I thought you were different. I thought you respected Mum. But you're the same as the rest of my aunts and uncles who think she was an uncivilized *savage!* And you, Da, you were ashamed of her!"

Da's hand landed on Abraham's check with such unexpected force that Abraham nearly lost his balance. "What have I told you about speaking out-of-turn?"

Abraham opened him mouth to answer, but Da waved him off. "Now get out to the barn. You can sleep there tonight!"

Abraham trudged off to the barn. He found a place on the clean hay and lay down, but he couldn't sleep. He lay there fuming. *It wasn't fair! Why did Mum have to die? She was the only one who understood him. She was the only one who loved him for what he was. She was so good, and she loved God too! So why would God let her die like that? Why didn't he heal her like he had so many others in the Bible? It wasn't fair ….*

Tears burned his eyes. He rolled over and beat his fists into the straw until his energy was spent. Then he lay his head on his aching arms and cried like a baby until he had no more tears left.

The house had quieted down and the candles had been blown out, but it was still far from dawn when Abraham got up and crept from the barn. He found an old hatchet used to split wood for the fire and stuck it through a length of rope he'd tied around his waist. He was barefooted but couldn't risk going into the house to retrieve his shoes. So, he slipped past the house and headed toward the bay where his family kept a small dugout for fishing in the surrounding bays. He pushed it out into the deeper water and jumped in as it slid silently from the shore.

Chapter 35

Curaçao

Etienne, May 28, 1664

We reached the small Dutch island of Curaçao in the late morning. From the crow's nest I could see the island was largely rocky and barren. Strange plants dotted the sun-scorched hills. Some looked like clumps of pipes for an organ, while others looked like someone had joined together dozens of small oval canoe paddles. Dangerous cliff faces and wide, rocky beaches skirted the shoreline. A volcano rose from the center of the island surrounded by rocky hills, low scrub, and spindly, multi-trunked trees with large leaves. The weather was already hot and humid; only the strong ocean breeze brought relief from the blinding sun.

The ship slipped into the narrow straight that quickly emptied into a large, protected harbor. The banks of the harbor were flanked by both Spanish-style buildings with their white-plastered walls, arched windows, and columned verandas, and Dutch-styled buildings with steeply peaked roofs and narrow multi-storied façades. A defensive wall encircled the busy trading town, protecting it from land invasions. The docks and piers were busy with ships flying Dutch or Portuguese flags and people moving cargo around.

The *Zeelandia* found an empty mooring on the south end of the bay and gently slid up to the dock. Men hurried to secure her and tie down the remaining sails. I quickly climbed down the rat line to assist in securing the ship. As my feet hit the deck, I heard Captain Janssen calling me, so I hurried over to him.

"Etienne, ready the Africans for unloading. Check them over and clean them up so they look presentable. We will bring out the healthiest-looking ones first, as they will fetch the best prices."

I nodded and headed for the cargo hold. After being above deck for the last few hours, the stench and oppressive heat of the hold made me dizzy, and I took a moment to steady myself. Grimly, I walked among them and looked for those with good color, those who had retained some muscle mass. I avoided looking into their eyes. How could I do this, knowing what came next? But what could I do? Even if I freed them, where could they go? Where could I go? We were thousands of miles away from our homes.

I chose several strong-looking men and unchained them from the floor. Then I linked every two slaves together by their leg manacles and attached their neck collars to a long rope. When I had assembled a double line of about thirty men, I led them onto the deck. There I washed them off with seawater as their eyes adjusted to the bright sunlight. The African men were led away, and I returned below deck to bring up more of them.

Slowly, with the emptying of the hold, the suffocating congestion below deck lessened. As I returned with another group of men, I saw Captain Janssen speaking to the first mate. "Stay on board and be ready. If I am spotted or confronted by the GWC, then sail out with anyone left on board and run. I will try to reach the

Piscadera Bay and meet you there."

The first mate nodded and returned to the upper deck to speak to the navigator.

"Etienne, join me on the dock," Janssen said as he walked past.

I nodded and fell in beside him. Rows of slaves were being led toward a wooden platform at the end of the pier. There they were separated by gender and displayed in small pens on either side of the platform while European men and women examined them. As we approached, I could see that some were made to show their teeth. Men looked into their eyes and felt their arms and legs. Women were made to turn around. I felt sick. It was like when Papa bought our horse, how he examined its teeth and felt its legs to assess its age and strength. It felt wrong. And then I caught sight of the boy who reminded me of Po. He was trying to hide in a corner of the pen. He looked scared and alone.

Captain Janssen walked up to a finely dressed man and they spoke quietly, as he pointed out each slave one by one. The man nodded and then climbed up onto the platform. He held up his hands and a crowd of European men and women, dressed for a festival, gathered in front of the platform.

One by one the men were brought up onto the deck and the bidding began. Captain Janssen stood in front of the platform and collected the money as it was offered and then each slave was led away. Some looked terrified, one or two pulled at their chains with furrowed brows, and still others looked defeated and barely aware of their surroundings. Sweat ran in rivulets down my back and spread into large lakes under my armpits. I wiped my face with my kerchief and I wished the auction would end.

The event seemed to last hours, though the sun stubbornly refused to move. I tried not to look into the eyes of slaves as they were led away by a vibrant Spanish rooster, a flamboyant Portuguese peacock, a somber Dutch crow, or occasionally, a haughty English cock. The slaves were nearly all sold when they brought up the boy who looked like Po. He was crying and trying to hide his face, but the auctioneer roughly yanked him forward and held him still. I felt a pain in my gut, as if I'd been stabbed. I couldn't breathe and looked around for some place to escape, to hide myself. The crowds were thinning, but still there was nowhere to go. I felt dizzy, like I might vomit.

A wolf of a man stepped forward, licked his maw, handed a purse to Janssen without taking his eyes from the boy. Then he took the slave boy and led him away. The auction finally ended, and the auctioneer handed a document to Captain Janssen. Just then an official looking man approached with a ledger.

"Captain, sir, I need to see your permit from the West India Company. It is needed for the sales to be finalized and we'll collect the tax for the GWC."

"Absolutely! Give me a moment to retrieve it," Janssen said. He turned toward me and pulled me after him. We rounded the platform and broke into a run.

"Stop that man!" the official called out as we darted down narrow street and sprinted toward the city wall. We heard footfalls following us as we skirted along the wall and rounded a corner. We reached a small lookout tower, and I glanced back. Our pursuers hadn't rounded the corner yet, but I could hear their raised voices. We were met by a shifty-looking man and ushered inside the tower. Janssen palmed him a coin and the man showed us through a back passage and a door that brought us outside the wall. We made our way down the rocky cliff face and into a small cave overlooking the ocean, where a small rowboat had been hidden. There we waited until dark and then rowed out into the surf.

Part 4, Road to Recovery

1665

Caribbean Sea and Long Island Sound

Out of the belly of Sheol I cried, and you heard my voice. For you caste me into the deep, into the heart of the seas. And the floods surrounded me; all your billows and your waves passed over me. Then I said, "I have been cast out of your sight; yet I will look again toward your temple." – Jonah 2:2b-4, NKJV

The Fall of New Amsterdam in 1664, by Jean Leon Gerome Ferris (1836-1930).
Library of Congress, Prints and Photographs Div.. Public Domain

Chapter 36

Vision Quest

Abraham, May 15, 1664

Abraham wasn't sure where he was headed, specifically, just that he wanted to get away from everything. If he stayed on Long Island, he knew he would be found. Because of his father's family, he was known from North Sea to Southampton and East Hampton. Because of his mother he was known by the Montauk and the Shinnecock. As soon as it was discovered that he was gone, word would spread quickly among the white people and the Indians. There would be no place to hide on Long Island.

Before the sun rose, he'd rowed across the Little Peconic Bay and through the straight between Shelter Island and North Haven. Now the sun was peaking over the horizon. He was hungry and thirsty. He'd not thought to bring any provisions with him, for fear of waking his family. But he had his hand axe.

He rowed over to one of the smaller islands in Gardiners Bay and found a secluded spot to land. There were grasses on the island,

and he hoped he might make a fishing line. He tried braiding the grasses, but it made the line too thick, and he couldn't find a way to make it long enough. He tried twisting the grasses together, but as soon as he let go, they unfurled and fell apart in his hands. Then he decided to make a net. He tried tying the grasses together, but they simply snapped into pieces.

Then he remembered making harpoon tips with Uncle Ahanu. Maybe he could use the same technique to make a spear head. He searched the entire island, but it was small, and he couldn't find anything suitable. He took a quick dip in the water to cool down, and then he pushed the canoe back into the water and headed out into Gardiners Bay. It was a large bay, and the currents were strong. He was exhausted by evening and decided to spend the night on Gardiners Island, though he knew he wouldn't be able to stay here for a long time, since it was only a short canoe ride across the water from the Montauk village. He'd had nothing to eat all day, and his stomach complained bitterly.

He decided to see what he could forage. It was too early for berries. He might find some dandelions or mushrooms. It was getting dark and clouds covered the moon, so it was hard to tell one plant from another. He hadn't thought to bring a tinderbox either. He stumbled across a patch of mushrooms growing along a fallen tree. He picked a few and smelled them. They looked like the ones he had picked with his mother. He tasted one. It tasted a little different, but not bitter or foul.

His stomach rumbled again. So, he gathered what he could and took it back to his campsite. He ate one of the mushrooms and waited a few minutes. Nothing happened. His mouth watered and his stomach begged for more, so he ate the rest. He found a small stream and leaned down to drink from it. Again, he cursed himself for not thinking to bring anything to hold water. He would have to look for something suitable in the morning. He knew that wild gourds grew in the area, though they wouldn't come ripe until late fall.

Still, his hunger was sated, and his thirst abated. Abraham lay on his back in the sand and stared up at the stars. If he had been raised in the Montauk village, he would have participated in the *Huscanaw*, or Vision Quest, with the other boys. He'd heard all about it from his cousin, Japhet, who had already had his two years ago. The ceremony would have taken three days. For the first two days the men and boys would dance while the boys' mothers would mourn as if their sons had died. Then on the last day, the mothers would say goodbye to their sons and the boys would venture alone into the wilderness without food or water. The boys would have to survive for days, weeks, or sometimes months, until they became delirious. It was then that they would find their spirit creatures, which would tell them their life calling as shaman, hunter, fisher, councilman, warrior, or leader. When they returned to the village, the boys would be given new names to signify their transition into adulthood. Abraham had looked forward to his own vision quest, until he realized that his father would never allow it. As he drifted off to sleep, he wondered what his spirit creature would have been.

The night had not passed well. Abraham had only just fallen asleep when he awoke to retch up everything he'd eaten and drank. Even after his stomach was empty, he continued to vomit bile until he could only dry heave. He was exhausted and weak as the dawn rose with pitiless humor. He dragged himself to the stream and took a tentative sip to cleanse his mouth. He debated staying on the island longer but reconsidered it. Surely, someone would be out looking for him by now. So, he continued his journey around Gardner's Island and out into Block Island Sound.

He was weak, but the tide was working with him this time, so he let the current pull him as he surveyed his options. He could head over to Block Island, where there were protected bays for shelter and fishing. Or he could make for the mainland where there would be more resources for food and shelter, but potentially more dangers too. Many more people inhabited the mainland, both native tribes and European settlers, and while he knew there were friends there, like Alsoomse and her Lenape tribe, he also knew there would also be foes, like the Narragansetts and Pequots who had been long-time rivals of the Montauk. He decided to head for Block Island. The tide changed, though, and in his weakened state, it became nearly impossible to make any headway. He rowed all morning, but all he could hope for was to maintain his position, if not to make small gains, until the tide turned again in his favor.

The noon sun was hot, but what little sweat he produced quickly dried and left his skin cracked and burned. His mouth felt dry as if he'd eaten sand, and he wished again that he had brought something to store fresh water in. He knew enough, though, to not drink from the salty water of the Sound. It might appear to help at first, but the salt would only make his dehydration worse. His arms strained at the paddle, and he felt light-headed, even as his vision blurred. He was tired, so very tired. He felt the current catch hold of his boat as it rushed out of the mouth of Long Island Sound to join the ocean on the outgoing tide. He let the flow carry him east and rested his arms. He fought to keep his eyes open but lost the battle.

Suddenly, he was jolted awake by a sharp thump as something struck his boat. He looked around and saw a dolphin leap out of the water, inches from his boat, blowing mist into the air. He watched as it circled his small craft and again bumped into the boat. The dolphin then balanced on its tail with its head out of the water and chattered at him urgently.

Abraham looked around. His boat was well past Block Island now and was rushing out to sea. He picked up the oar and paddled toward the closer and larger of two approaching islands. The current was strong. He pushed the paddle into the water and pulled hard. He had to reach the island. It was his last hope of safety before being swept out into the Atlantic Ocean. Sweat poured down his face. No matter how hard his rowed, he seemed to make little headway against the strong pull of the current.

The dolphin chattered at him again, more urgently.

"I am trying!" he replied. "The current is too strong."

Then the dolphin leapt into the air and disappeared beneath the water.

"Thanks for the help," Abraham grumbled as he fought to push the boat toward shore.

Just then, the dolphin returned with several others. Slowly the dolphins took turns shoving the boat toward the sandy shore on the south side of the island. Several feet beyond the beach, sandstone cliffs rose into the air. To the east towering pillars of sandstone seemed to walk down to the water's edge to cool their feet in the foaming surf.

With the dolphins' help, the boat crept ever closer to the shore. As the hull brushed against sand, Abraham leapt out and turned to thank the dolphins, but they had already disappeared beneath the waves. He dragged his boat onto the beach and collapsed onto the sand.

Abraham awoke to the taste and smell of saltwater splashing into his face. He looked around. The sun was setting. He sat up stiffly, shivering in his wet clothes, and brushed the sand from his face. Where was he? As he stared out to sea, memories of rowing, poisoned mushrooms, and dolphins drifted back into his mind. His stomach rumbled and his mouth was dry. A seagull squawked overhead.

He briefly wondered if it had been a mistake to run away from home. He sighed deeply. "No, I must prove to Da that I'm as much a man as Ralph or Sam!" he said to a passing gull.

His shirt was damp and cold in places and stiff with dried salt in other spots, so he stripped it off, along with his wet trousers and laid them out on a large outcropping to dry. He noticed the tide was coming in, so he looked for a suitable place to secure his boat against the surf. He walked between the stony sentries guarding the beach and found a secluded inlet shielded from the ocean by a natural rock wall. He tied his boat to a bolder and assessed his situation.

He saw another island farther out in the distance to the southeast. *That must be Nantucket, so this island must be Martha's Vineyard*, he thought. It was getting late now, so he found a place to make camp above the high tide line and set about gathering driftwood for a small fire. He hadn't eaten in two days and was ravenous. He walked out along the beach and looked for the tell-tale siphons, or small holes, in the sand that indicated the presence of soft-shell clams. He found several and used a large shell to dig them out. It was surprisingly difficult to retrieve the clams, and after several failed attempts, was finally able to recover a small handful.

He returned to his campsite and dropped them down beside the pile of driftwood he'd collected. He wished again that he'd gathered supplies from the house before he left. A tinderbox would have very useful now. Japhet had shown him once how to start a fire with a stick and a piece of wood, but he still needed tinder. On the beaches at home, wild grasses grew along the shore, making for perfect fuel. He looked around. This beach was all sand and rock. He walked to the cliff face and felt around with his hands for moss or grasses, anything he might use. But the rocks were bare. Slowly, he moved along the edge, until finally, his hands fell upon some clumps of grass. He pulled out large handfuls and brought the grass back to his campsite.

Then he sat cross-legged on the sand and used his hatchet to make a pointy end on the stick. He cut a shallow notch out of a small log, broke up a small bit of grass, and placed it in the groove of the log. He hoped the grass was dry enough. It was hard to tell in the dark. Then kneeling over the wood, he rubbed the stick back-and-forth in the groove as fast as he could to try to generate enough heat to catch the grass on fire.

He heard the waves lapping against the shore and felt the breeze chill his skin. *Should have brought a blanket.* ... The stick caught and jabbed into his hand. He yelped and sucked on the injury. His stomach complained again, and so he picked up the stick and started again. His arms ached, and his hands were rubbed raw, when finally, he saw a tiny spark. He bent down and blew ever so gently on the ember to coax it into a flame. Then he quickly added more grass, little by little. He set the small fire into the pit he'd dug and continued to add grass and then small pieces of driftwood, then larger pieces, until finally he had a steady flame. He retrieved his clothing and brought it near the fire to finish drying as he warmed himself in the comforting glow.

He placed several large stones in the fire to heat up. When the stones were ready, he used his hatchet to roll them out to the edge of the fire and he set the clams among the stones to cook. When they burst open, he used his fingers to pry the bits of meat from the shells. The clams tasted good! They were salty and chewy, but too soon they were gone. He wished he had found more. He cleaned out the shells and set them at the base of the cliffs, where he found evidence of erosion, in the hope of collecting fresh water.

His clothes were dry now, so he put them back on and settled down next to the small fire to watch the stars.

Chapter 37

Susannah

The next morning, Abraham went to check the shells he'd placed the night before. Small drops of water had collected in the bottom. It was enough to wet his mouth, but not enough to quench his thirst. He had to find fresh water and a more plentiful source of food. So, he looked for a place where the cliff face was less steep and gingerly made his way to the top. Why hadn't he thought to bring shoes?

At the top, Abraham found a broad grassy plateau overlooking the sea. Early spring flowers scattered across the field greeted him. Several different types of birds hunted for their breakfast among the low grasses, but he had no way of catching them. He picked some dandelions, ate the flowers, and saved the stems, leaves, and roots for later. In the distance, he saw a line of trees. He hoped he might find a stream there and maybe something more substantial to eat.

Hours later, he finally reached a forested area in the center of the island. Abraham did not recognize many of the plants that grew wild along the wooded animal trail he now traveled, though he did find some blackberry bushes along the edge of the forest and plucked the immature fruit from the brambles by the handful, heedless of the sharp thorns that scraped and cut his palms and fingers. The berries were tart, but added to the dandelion flowers, they filled his stomach and gave him strength.

He'd been unsuccessful in his attempts to catch any of the ducks, ground mice, or skunks that he'd seen during his walk and lamented not spending more time hunting with his older brothers. He'd seen deer venture out into the clearings to graze but had no bow or arrows with which to hunt them. He watched them and admired their beauty, until they had spotted him and ran away.

As he followed the deer path that wound through the trees and underbrush, he heard what sounded like young children playing. He slowed his pace and was careful where he placed his feet so as not to make much noise. He reached a small clearing and stopped in the shelter of the trees to survey the scene warily. His eyes widened in surprise as they fell upon four white children in the center of the glade.

The oldest child, a plump girl of eight or nine, had the most remarkable hair Abraham had ever seen. It was the color of boiled crab or ripe pumpkin and glinted with gold in the sunlight. It fell down her back in long, lazy curls. She was sitting on a log entertaining a small blond boy of maybe two or three with a crudely carved wooden horse. The boy giggled as she bopped him on the nose with it and then jerked it out of his reach as he tried to grab a hold of it. There was an older gangly boy of maybe seven or eight. His hair was a light brown, and he was sitting on the ground carving the top of a long stick. His angular face was frowning in concentration and his tongue moved in and out of the corner of his mouth as he worked. The last child was a girl of maybe six or seven. She was barefooted and picking flowers to add to her growing bouquet. Her straw-colored hair was parted down the middle and plaited into two tight braids that snaked behind her ears to drape over her shoulders. She looked up and stared at him. Her eyes were the most piercing blue he'd ever seen, and he recoiled in surprise. Abraham backed away quickly, but the girl walked straight toward him.

"Don't run away. We won't hurt you," the girl said in a strangely accented English that was thick and hard to decipher. She stared at him. Then to Abraham's great surprise, she switched to Algonquian and repeated what she'd just said.

Abraham stopped and stood open mouthed as the girl approached. She cocked her head and looked him up and down, studying him.

"Who are you?" she finally said in the native tongue.

"My name is Abraham," he responded in English and held out his hand.

She took it timidly, smiled, and answered in her funny English. "I'm Susannah. These are my brothers and sister." She gestured at her siblings. "Come." She led him by the hand into the clearing. Her siblings looked up and stared at him as they approached. "This is my sister, Mary, my brother, John, and the baby is Benjamin."

"What are you doing here?" Abraham asked.

Susannah giggled. "I was going to ask you the same thing!"

Abraham just stared at her.

"Daddy bought land from the Indians here. We have a small farm over there…." She pointed toward the east. "But we had to get out of the way because Mama is trying to get our new brother or sister out of her tummy."

"Are there any other white people here?" Abraham asked.

"No, we are the only ones," Susannah replied. "We have some Wampanoag friends living here. I thought you might be one of them, but I didn't recognize you, so I wasn't sure."

Abraham nodded and smiled.

"Who are you then?" John asked and eyed him suspiciously.

"I am from Long Island. My mum was Montauk, but Da's English. You don't sound like him though."

"Our Daddy's English too, but Mama's Scottish." Mary said. She picked Benjamin up and set him on her lap.

"What are you doing here?" John asked.

Abraham squared his shoulders. "I left home. I … I'm on a vision quest."

John studied him skeptically. "You look pretty unprepared to be out on your own," he said and shook his head. "I'd say you ran away from home and are now lost."

"What would you know about it?" Abraham said angrily. Then he paused, took a big breath, and let it out slowly. "I guess you're not wrong," he said finally.

Susannah smiled and said, "Are you hungry? We have some bread and cheese we can share with you."

Abraham nodded and his mouth watered. "Do you have any water?"

John picked up a large gourd canteen and handed it to him. Abraham took a long drink and handed it back, while Mary reached into a basket she'd placed behind the log and passed out slices of bread and cheese to each of them. Baby Benjamin smashed the bread and cheese in each chubby hand and stuffed them into his mouth.

Mary shook her head and said, "Careful or you'll choke."

Benjamin just stuffed more into his still full mouth and chewed contentedly.

Abraham sat down on the log beside John and Mary. Susannah sat down on his other side. She twisted to face him.

"Why did you have to leave your home, Abraham?"

Abraham looked up and startled to see her blue eyes studying him. The silence grew awkward as she waited for his response.

He sighed. "Mum died a few months back …" He paused to regain his voice. Susannah's eyes softened, reflecting his own pain. He quickly looked down at the ground. "We were getting along fine, Da, my brothers and I, but my aunt and uncle came to convince Da to take another wife…."

Abraham glanced up at Susannah. She looked like she might cry, and he quickly looked down again. He felt her hand come to rest on his knee.

"I'm sorry," she whispered. "I haven't lost my mama, but I lost my favorite aunt. I mean, she didn't die, but we had to leave the town where she lives, because Daddy got in trouble…."

"We used to live in Wenham, on the mainland, in Massachusetts Bay Colony," John said to clarify. "But Dad got into some trouble with our neighbors. Our neighbor's wife, Mrs. Pease. She accused Dad of selling them a milking cow that could no longer give milk. Mother said she came with her husband and asked for their money back, but Dad wouldn't give it to them. He said the cow had given us plenty of milk up until the day he sold her and so Mrs. Pease was lying. Her husband apologized and took her away, but she must have complained to her brother, Mr. Jones, because he started spreading rumors about Dad being a swindler and a cheat."

"Daddy didn't like that," Susannah added and shook her head.

"So, Dad sued Mr. Jones for something called 'defamation of character,'" John added.

"What does that mean?" Abraham asked.

"It means," Mary answered, "that Mr. Jones was spreading lies about Daddy that made people think poorly about him for something he didn't do!"

"Well," John continued, "Mr. Jones told everyone about the milking cow as proof that he had only told the truth."

"The cow *had* stopped giving milk," Mary said softly.

Startled, Abraham looked up at Mary. She shrugged.

John continued, "But Dad then said Mrs. Pease was lying because she wanted to get her money back and keep the cow. He went on and called her worse names too. Mama tried to tell Dad to give them the money, but he wouldn't. So, Mr. Pease sued Dad."

Mary frowned and said, "By the end of it the whole community was so against Daddy we had to leave and were told not to come back."

"I miss Auntie Rebecca," Susannah said with a sigh. "She gave us cookies when we came to visit and made dolls for Mary and me and let us play with her tea set. She told great stories too!"

"They were good cookies," Mary affirmed.

"So, we came here," John said, "the only white people on the Island!"

Shadows crept over the dell as the sun slipped behind the trees.

"We should see if it's safe to go home. Mama's been at it since before dawn. She must be finished by now," Mary said. She stood up, gathered their things into the basket, and handed it to Susannah. Then she hoisted Benjamin onto her hip and started down a well-worn path.

"I hope it's a girl," Susannah said.

"I hope it's another boy," John said and followed Mary down the footpath.

Susannah stood and held out her hand to Abraham. "You can stay with us tonight."

"Thank you, Susannah," Abraham said. He took her hand and following her down the narrow path.

Chapter 38

Comprehension

Abraham followed Susannah and her siblings as they wound their way along the deer path. Dappled light filtered in among the trees. Occasionally, he heard a rustle from beneath a nearby bush or a squirrel chattering from somewhere above. As they turned a bend, the light grew brighter, and they stepped out into a small clearing. The ground looked as if it had been plowed recently but did not appear to have been planted yet. A small one-room log cabin stood on the far side of the clearing. A whisp of smoke curled up from its chimney.

John sent a pebble skittering across the uneven ground as they made their way toward the little house. An upended log with a hatchet stuck in the top stood by the front steps and next to that was a large pile of logs waiting to be split.

As they approached, the front door opened and a short squat man stepped out. Abraham stifled a smile as he watched the man who looked more like a small brown bear wearing clothing than a man. His auburn hair was long and unkept, as was his beard. The man walked toward them; his shockingly blue eyes scrutinizing

Abraham from beneath his bushy eyebrows.

"Hi, Daddy!" Susannah said and ran up to hug the bear-man. "Did Mama have the baby?"

The man nodded slowly. "Mary, go and help your mother," he said gruffly. "And John, go and tend to the animals." Mary, still carrying Benjamin, hurried inside, while John scuttled around the house and disappeared. All the while the bear-man's eyes never left Abraham, who stood stiffly waiting to see if he would be welcomed or assaulted.

Susannah then turned toward Abraham and said, "This is my new friend, Abraham. We found him in the woods."

"Where have you come from, Boy?" the man asked.

"My family lives on Long Island, near Southampton."

"You are a long way from home. What are you doing here?"

"I ... needed to get ..."

"Ran away, eh?" the man said. His eyes narrowed as he studied Abraham.

Abraham nodded.

"I told him he could stay here tonight, Daddy," Susannah said. "He can, can't he?"

"I already have a lot of mouths to feed. You'd have to earn your keep," the man said sternly. "What can you do?"

"I can chop wood," Abraham said. He looked around at the plowed earth and added, "and I can plant your fields for you."

"Can you now?" the man said, half to himself. His face softened a little, and he stepped forward and extended his right hand. "Name's Francis. Francis Usselton. You can start by chopping the wood. Tomorrow, I'll show you where I keep the seed and you can help me plant the fields." Then he turned on his heel, took Susannah's hand, walked back inside, and left Abraham standing alone in the yard.

It was dark by the time Abraham finished chopping all the wood. He wiped the sweat from his forehead and stuck the axe back in the log. He was trying to decide whether he should knock on the door when Susannah came out holding a candle.

"Supper's ready," she said and led him into the house.

A small table stood by the front window to the left of the door. John stood on one side of it and Susannah took her place next to him. Benjamin was strapped into one of the two chairs the family possessed. Francis sat in the other chair. The fire burned low in the hearth centered on the left-hand wall. A bed stood along the back wall. A small woman with long brown hair cascading over her thin shoulders lay propped up. She smiled at him warmly as she patted the baby's bottom held up on one shoulder.

"Abraham, bring in some of that wood for the fire," Mr. Usselton said without looking up from his food.

Abraham quickly retreated outside and returned with an armful of wood. He stoked the fire and lay the remaining split logs on the hearth. As he stood, Mary dished out a bowl of soup for him and set it on the table. He followed her and stood at the table to eat. He paused, but when it was clear there would be no prayer, he bent down, picked up his bowl, and ate with the rest of them.

That night, Abraham was given an old blanket. He lay down on the floor near the hearth, while the other children climbed the ladder to the loft. His muscles ached from the exertion of chopping wood, but his belly was full and his thirst slaked. He listened contentedly as Mrs. Usselton sang softly to the new baby, who it turned out, was another girl. He was soon asleep.

Abraham spent the next week chopping wood and helping Mr. Usselton with the planting. They stripped the bark from the base of trees Mr. Usselton wanted cleared to create new fields for the coming year. He then accompanied him into the forest to set traps for rabbits, possums, and squirrels. Mr. Usselton took him fishing and showed him how to use a three-pronged spear to catch fish and frogs. He showed him how to make a net and where to place it to catch the trout and catfish inhabiting the nearby streams. This strange bear-like man even took him hunting, taught him to use the musket, and smiled when Abraham shot his first deer.

Several weeks went by, and though Abraham and Mr. Usselton never spoke much beyond what was needed to further his wilderness instruction, they slowly developed a mutual understanding. Each evening they returned to the cabin with whatever they'd managed to catch that day. Mrs. Usselton took it and prepared the evening meal. She always smiled at him and thanked him for his help.

Then after dinner, they all sat by the fire while Mrs. Usselton read a story from the Bible. Mr. Usselton took his pipe outside to smoke while she did this. Then sometimes Abraham told Mary, John, and Susannah stories about whaling, or about making the spearheads with his uncle, or about games he'd played with his brothers.

"Abraham, how come you have a limp?" Susannah asked one night.

He sighed. "Last harvest season, we went to my mother's village for the harvest celebration. Every year the Shinnecock and

Montauks play a ball game to celebrate the earth's bounty. My cousin gave me his old stick and feathered belt, so I could play with them. It was a great game, and I made an amazing save, caught the ball in the netting on my stick, and hurtled it back to our offensive teammates. But one of my teammates tripped me. I fell and broke my ankle. My uncle, the medicine man, splinted it and applied ointments, but it has never healed quite like it'd been before I broke it."

"Does it still hurt?" Susannah asked and placed a hand on his knee.

"No. And I can walk on it okay, but my uncle says I might always have a limp."

"I'm sorry," Susannah whispered.

"It's pretty great that you could play in the ballgame," John said. "It must have been exciting."

"It was," Abraham said and smiled.

"Abraham," Mrs. Usselton said. She held up a new shirt. "I've made this for you. Put it on and see how it fits."

Abraham took the garment and quickly slipped it over his shoulders. He pulled on one sleeve and then the other. It fit perfectly. "Thank you, ma'am. It is very nice!"

Mrs. Usselton smiled and continued to darn the sock in her hand. After a while she spoke again. "Where is your mother? You have been gone a long time. Don't you think she is missing you?"

"My mother is dead," Abraham said and looked at the floorboards. "She died of the smallpox epidemic last spring, along with my baby sister."

"I am very sorry," Mrs. Usselton said. "What about your father and your brothers? Do they even know where you are?"

Abraham shook his head. "My aunt and uncle came over to

convince Da to remarry, and … and I got angry. They were trying to replace Mum, but we were doing just fine as we were! Mum was Montauk and Da's whole family was ashamed of her! They wanted to pretend she'd never existed …," he paused to regain control of his voice. "No one can replace her." He hung his head and blinked back the tears that threatened to leak from his eyes.

Silence filled the room and grew into an uneasy standoff. Finally, Mrs. Usselton broke the tension. "Abraham," she said gently. "It is true that great misunderstandings exist between the native peoples and the European colonists. We come from vastly different cultural backgrounds and experiences. And those misunderstandings have led to horrific tragedies.

"When I was a baby, my father witnessed the war with the Pequots. The Pequots were a powerful and an aggressive tribe. They wanted to control all the fur trade in New England and fought against the Narragansett and Mohegan tribes for control. At first, they were friendly and traded with the Dutch and English colonies. But tensions developed between the Dutch and Pequot and then when a hurricane destroyed much of the fall crops, competition for food led to increased tensions between the Pequot and the English. The Narragansett saw this as an opportunity to gain more power by making an alliance with the English and then turning them against the Pequot. The Pequot started raiding our colonies and became a threat to our survival. So, our leaders decided to attack them to remove that threat. The Narragansett and Mohegans joined with our militia. They surrounded the largest Pequot fort. But instead of fighting them in outright combat, the captains ordered the fort be burned in the predawn hours when everyone was asleep. A few warriors escaped, but most of the Pequot in the village were killed, including the elderly, woman, and children.

"My father was horrified, as were many others from our colony and our Indian allies too. It showed us all that evil still lives in the hearts of men. But there is good in men also. A man named John Elliot, with the help of his interpreter, is learning the Algonquian language so that he can better communicate with them. He has developed a written language for the natives and is teaching them to read and write in their own tongue. He has even translated the Bible into Algonquian.

"There have been many men who have built an understanding between the colonist and the native peoples. My father was one of them. He traded with all the local tribes in New England. My husband, too, is one of them. He can speak Algonquian and has often negotiated with them. That is why we are here. He brokered a land purchase from the Indians who live here on behalf of three English investors. We are now living here to hold the land for them."

"My grandfather was an interpreter to the Montauketts," Abraham said quietly. "That was how my mother learned English. She even learned to read and write it. She too was asked to negotiate land deals between her people and the English."

Mrs. Usselton smiled at Abraham. "It seems clear to me that your father loved your mother, and I am sure he respected her too. It is always difficult in marriage when two people bring different traditions into the family, but that does not mean there is no love. This new marriage proposal your aunt suggested is for practical purposes. Men and women serve different roles in the family, and both are needed for the family to thrive. Other family members can fill in the duties of a missing member, true. But the family is still harmed by the lack."

Mrs. Usselton finished darning the sock and put it away. Then she hurried Mary, John, and Susannah off to bed. Abraham pulled the carving he'd been working on out of his pocket and studied it. Then he took a piece of cloth and a small tin of oiled sand and began to smooth the surface of the wood. He smiled. It really looked like the whale his father and brothers had beached.

He heard Mrs. Usselton climb the ladder to the loft and listened as she said prayers with her children. She fed the baby and tucked her into the bassinet before returning to her chair by the fire. She watched Abraham as he worked for a moment and then picked up her knitting.

"If you have been as useful to your father as you have been to us, then I am sure your father misses you terribly. Perhaps it is time for you to go home?"

Abraham was silent for a long time. He hadn't felt so appreciated and needed since … since Mum died. He thought of the possibility of having a new mum. His heart ached and he blinked away a tear. He thought of Jacob, Isaac, and Caleb … especially Caleb. He stared at the small wooden whale in his hands and sighed. Finally, he looked up at Mrs. Usselton. She was watching him closely. He gave her a weak smile but didn't trust his voice and simply nodded.

"I will prepare a traveling pack for you tomorrow," she said softly. Then after a long pause, she continued, "We will miss you, Abraham."

"I will miss you too."

Chapter 39

A Letter

Alsoomse, June 12, 1664

Okwaho stood ridged and stared at Alsoomse, waiting.

The sun was setting behind them as Alsoomse looked out across Long Island Sound. The water was grey and ominous in the failing light and wisps of clouds floated overhead and added to the apprehensive feeling of hopelessness growing inside her chest. Her hand fingered the blue-green beads and wampum that hung around her neck. Okwaho would make a good husband. He would be loyal and kind. He would fight alongside her and do his share to protect and provide for their family.

Then her hand drifted to the crude wooden Musketeer that also lay against her chest suspended from a narrow length of pink ribbon. Etienne had given it to her when they first met. Ever since that day she'd worn it secretly beneath her dress, but since he'd left, she'd worn it openly. Where was he? Was he well? Would she ever see him again?

The sky had turned the color of maple syrup as one-by-one the stars glinted into view. A cool breeze drifted off the water and rustled the grasses at her feet. It had never been hard for her to make decisions before this one. She'd always acted with her heart, but now it betrayed her.

"I have waited two full cycles of the moon for your answer, Alsoomse. If you will not give one, then I will assume your answer is *no* and I will leave in the morning." His tone was firm but not unkind.

Alsoomse turned to face him. She felt her eyes water, though she had never been prone to crying. "It has never been so hard to decide anything before in my life. I want to marry you, Okwaho, I truly do!"

Okwaho grimaced. "But …."

Alsoomse sighed. "I am worried about Etienne. He is my friend. I always thought I would marry him … but now … it feels like I am betraying him."

Okwaho stood in silence for several long moments. Finally, he took a deep breath and blew it out slowly. "Prepare your travel pack. Tomorrow we will travel to New Amsterdam and discover if there is any word of your friend. Afterwards, you will give me your answer." With that, he turned on his heal and disappeared into the night.

Okwaho did not come to her parents' home to sleep that night, and Alsoomse felt a sharp pang of fear welling up inside of her. She'd packed her travel sack and had lain awake in the darkness listening to her family breathing slowly and evenly as they slept. Neither Matoaka or her family had asked about Okwaho as they ate or sat talking around the fire. In truth, no one had said more to her than to acknowledge her presence. It was as if everything and everyone in her life was waiting on her decision.

She rose with the sun, after a restless night of little sleep, and gathered food for their journey. There was still no sign of Okwaho. Matoaka approached her as she debated what to do next. The old medicine woman looked frailer than she had even a few days ago. Matoaka reached out her shaky hands to clasp hers. They were so cold! Alsoomse squeezed the old woman's hands and tried to give them a bit of her warmth.

Matoaka smiled. "Your father and mother are accompanying me home today. I am tired and I need to see my husband and my other children."

Alsoomse nodded. "Thank you for training me. I hope I can learn more from you when I return."

Matoaka nodded. "You have learned much, but there is always more that can be learned. I will wait for you ... but you must not take too long."

"I won't," Alsoomse promised.

Just then, Kitchi ran up to her. "Are you ready to go? Okwaho is waiting."

Alsoomse nodded and followed him out of the village. Okwaho was waiting for them by the boats. Kitchi hurried to help Okwaho launch the boat, but Alsoomse did not move.

"What are you waiting for?" Kitchi asked.

Suddenly, Alsoomse turned and ran in the opposite direction.

"Where are you going?" Okwaho asked sharply.

"I must visit Etienne's family. I must know if his mother has heard anything from her son," Alsoomse replied.

Okwaho nodded curtly, and he and Kitchi followed her in silence. As they reached the log cabin, the men followed a pace or two behind Alsoomse as she crossed the porch and knocked on the door. After a moment, the door opened slowly. Etienne's mother stood stock still, eyes wide, as she took in her visitors. Then she smiled in sudden recognition.

"Alsoomse! Kitchi! It is so good to see you both again. And who is your companion?"

"This is Okwaho," Alsoosme said without explanation.

"It has been a long time. Do come in," Mistress Gayneau said and opened the door wider.

The room was warm and inviting with the mingled smells of fresh strawberries and cornbread baking in the covered pot by the fire. Lidie looked up from where she sat entertaining her young brother, Jeremiah, and sister, Sarah. She recognized Alsoosme immediately, bolted to her feet, and sprinted across the floor to embrace her.

Alsoomse knelt to hug the gregarious child.

"What brings you here?" Mistress Gayneau asked. She returned to the kitchen table, picked up her paring knife, and plucked a small fresh strawberry out of a basket. She cut the green top off, dropped it into a pot, and picked up another.

Alsoomse smiled at Lidie and then untangled herself from the girl, she rose to her feet and replied, "Have you had any word from Etienne?"

The woman paused and shook her head sadly. "No. There has been nothing. And I am so worried about him."

"We are heading to New Amsterdam to see if there has been any word. If we hear anything, we will let you know."

"Thank you!" Mistress Gayneau said. She smiled, though her eyebrows were still furrowed with concern. "Here, please take some cornbread with you." She hurried to the hearth and retrieved the pot. Then she cut three pieces, wrapped them in a cloth, and pressed it into Alsoomse's hands.

"Thank you," Alsoomse replied, and they left to continue their journey south.

"It is still early," Kitchi said as they walked. "Only a few ships have returned. Etienne's ship will arrive; it may already be in the harbor. You'll see."

They walked quickly back to the outskirts of their village in silence to retrieve a canoe for the trip to New Amsterdam.

The canoe slid up to the dock and Alsoomse leaned over the bow to tie it to a post. As she did so, she noticed the half-Montauk boy approaching the dock in his own rowboat. He looked more Indian than white man now though. He was more tanned than he had been before and his bare chest revealed that he had been doing a lot of manual labor. His hair had grown long and was braided. He was taller too. He no longer looked like the boy she had last seen. As his boat slid into dock, he reached into his pack, pulled out a clean white shirt, and slipped it on.

She waved to him, and he smiled when he saw her. Then she noticed his eyebrows furrow as he caught sight of Okwaho. He tied up his boat and the four of them met on the dock.

"Abraham, it is good to see you again. You have grown," Alsoomse said with a smile. "This is my brother, Kitchi, and a friend, Okwaho."

A dark look flitted across Okwaho's face, so fast, Alsoomse questioned whether she'd seen it at all.

Abraham looked the men up and down and grunted. Then he looked at Alsoomse and asked, "What are you doing here?"

"We came to see if there was any information on Etienne," she replied. "What are you doing here?"

Abraham told them of his own adventure, of being rescued by the dolphins and of the Usselton family he'd met on Martha's Vineyard. "I stayed with Susannah and her family for a fortnight and helped her father clear the fields and build a root cellar. But every time I saw Susannah helping with her younger siblings, it reminded me of Caleb and Jacob. So, I decided to return home and face my father. When I saw the ship approaching New Amsterdam harbor flying the Dutch flag, I decided to come here first and see if there was any word of Etienne." He shrugged.

"Then we have similar missions," Okwaho said. "Where should we start our inquiries?"

Alsoomse looked around. The dock was busy today. She recognized a friend of Etienne's loading a crate into the back of a wagon. She remembered his name was François. She approached him and asked, "Have you seen Etienne return yet?"

He shook his head. "I haven't seen him, but if I see him or hear anything about him, I will send word. You can be sure of that!"

Then they spotted a large ship, flying a French flag, moored offshore in the deeper water. Small rowboats were shuttling back and forth bringing passengers and goods to the pier. A smaller sailing vessel was docked a few paces down the pier loading their hull in preparation for departure. She scanned the faces of the well-dressed merchants and captains milling around until she spotted Master Carteret. She smiled.

Master Carteret was dressed in a finely tailored burgundy jacket trimmed in gold, with a white ruffled shirt, burgundy breeches clasped at the knees, and long white stockings above highly polished shoes. The large white feather in his felt hat bobbed up and down as he directed the loading of the smaller ship. As they drew near, they noticed a seaman from the larger moored vessel approach Carteret.

He turned to address the seaman, who doffed his cap and handed Carteret a folded piece of paper. Then he returned to his duties unloading the rowboats. Carteret was staring at the paper when they approached. He looked up and his eyes widened in surprise.

"How timely it is to see the both of you," Master Carteret exclaimed. "And you have friends with you too!"

Alsoomse quickly introduced Kitchi and Okwaho and asked if there had been any news of Etienne since they'd last spoken.

"As it happens," Carteret paused. "I have just received this letter but have not yet had the chance to read it. Come, let's find a quiet corner to peruse it."

Carteret led the way down the pier and into one of the taverns facing the docks. The lighting was dim as they entered, and Alsoomse stood for a moment to let her eyes adjust. The room was empty except for a couple of men sitting at the bar. Carteret chose a large table at the back of the room and took a seat. Alsoomse, Okwaho, and Abraham joined him there as an older woman came to take their orders.

Carteret ordered mead for each of them and then carefully opened the note and read it aloud.

Hello Master Carteret,

My name is Nicolas, and I am cousin to Etienne. I hope this note finds you safely, I have received word from Etienne. He has been kidnapped and is sailing on the Zeelandia, *a ship captained by Jacob Janssen van den Burgh, the man who once tried to forcibly impress Etienne onto his ship before being arrested for piracy and smuggling a few years ago. Etienne says he is being held in the brig for failing to follow orders. He has been told they are headed to the coast of Africa to pick up cargo and then will be sailing to the Caribbean, but he has no idea where they will go after that. He asked me to get word to his family. I am to tell them he is safe for the moment, and he will try to find a way to return home to them as soon as is possible. I hope you are able to help me with this commission. Etienne speaks well of you, and I have no one else I can trust with this.*

I will send word if I hear anything else, and please let me know if you hear anything in return.

Sincerely yours,

Nicolas Mestereau

La Rochelle, France

Master Carteret set the letter down on the table and took a large drink from his mug.

"What does it mean?" Abraham asked. "Is there anything we can do to help him?"

Carteret thought for a moment and looked around the table. "There is something I can do. I am sending the *Sparrow* to the Caribbean with a load of grain, pig bellies, and tobacco to trade for sugar and rum. I will ask its captain to make inquiries at the slave markets there. The only commodity the *Zeelandia* could be acquiring from the African coast is slaves," he said and shook his head. "Of course, there is no guarantee that he will learn anything, but at least there is a chance."

"Thank you," Alsoomse said. "You have given me hope. If you hear anything, perhaps you could send word to our village at New Harlem? And I can then get word to Abraham."

"I will do as you ask. And since you are going up that way, perhaps you would take this letter to his family. I know they are anxious for word of their son."

"I will," Alsoomse said. She nodded and took the note Carteret handed to her.

Carteret quickly downed his mug and excused himself. "I'd best inform Captain Jolls of his mission," he said and headed to the door.

Abraham stood too. "I'd better be getting home. Da will be wondering what happened to me."

"May the Great Spirit watch out for you and see you safely home," Alsoomse said and smiled at him.

Abraham nodded and left.

Alsoomse sat for a time caressing the letter she held in her hand. Her eyes closed as she tried to imagine what Etienne would look like now. She sighed softly.

"There is nothing more to do here," Okwaho said. He stood and looked sadly at Alsoomse, turned on his heal, and stalked out of the tavern without looking back at her. Kitchi hurried after him.

Alsoomse stared in confusion at the retreating men. Suddenly, she understood. *Okwaho thinks I have chosen Etienne!* "Wait!" But they were already out the door.

Alsoomse rose and ran after them. She caught up to them as they were preparing to launch the canoe. "Wait! Please, wait," she said. Tears threatened, but she pushed them back.

Okwaho turned to look at her, his arms crossed over his chest. His face was hard as if it was set in stone. She looked pleadingly into his eyes and saw the pain there.

"I will marry you!" Alsoomse said in a rush. "I *want* to marry you."

"Why?" The words fell hard, like a tree falling. Okwaho's face did not change.

Kitchi smiled to encourage her.

"Seeing Abraham again, and listening to Etienne's letter, I realized that ..." Alsoomse paused and took a deep breath. "I realize that … Etienne is my friend. We have shared many adventures together, but he is always the boy I must save from trouble. I confused my concern for him for love, but now I know the difference. I don't have to save you. You and I are equals. We will be life partners. Together, we can conquer any challenge.…"

Okwaho looked at her long and hard. Finally, he sighed. "I will consider what you say." Then he turned and leapt into the canoe without another word.

Kitchi shot her an anxious look, shrugged, and joined Okwaho in the canoe. Alsoomse joined them, and they began their journey up the East River in silence.

Chapter 40

Blood Money

Etienne, June 12, 1664

The captain and I had rowed all night, taking shifts as each grew tired. Somehow, we had avoided the officers of the West Indies Company, who'd been searching both land and sea, though I couldn't avoid remembering the haunted eyes of the slaves as they were each led away. What would happen to them? I remembered Chloe and Po. Their lives hadn't seemed too bad. They had a place to live, clothing, enough food to eat, work. Papa's admonishment still rang in my ears.

God gave us one day to rest, Etienne. You must learn to work hard to provide for your family, put a roof over their heads, clothes on their backs, and food in their bellies. That is the way of life.

But this seemed different somehow. Papa had chosen to be a builder of potager stoves. He had left his father's shop to become an apprentice with another man before he married my mother. He had chosen to become a farmer when there was no demand for his stoves in New Amsterdam. It had seemed a good way to provide, though without our Lenape friends we would have starved. And even now we struggled to make the farm produce enough to feed and clothe us.

Papa also chose to bring us to New Amsterdam, and he chose to take us from La Rochelle. Granted there was danger for him had we stayed, but there were other Huguenots who had chosen to stay. I supposed that was the difference. These people had not chosen to make this voyage. They had been snatched away from family and friends, sold into servitude to people who didn't speak their language, and were taken to a place they never wanted to go.

As I had pondered these things, Captain Janssen had kept a careful watch. We'd almost been caught once, but the captain had found shelter under an outcropping along the cliff. We heard the search party talking above our heads as we floated silently in an alcove beneath the ledge on which they stood. We'd waited a long time until we were sure they'd gone before we continued onward.

We reached the predetermined meeting site as the morning sun broke over the horizon. To our great relief the *Zeelandia* was there, floating at anchor. We were hauled onboard and the ship set sail for safer waters. I'd managed to keep up with my duties, but a growing sense of guilt and despair made me feel sick and disoriented.

I should have done something! But what could I have done? I should have found a way to save him. How? There had to have been a way. I will never forget the way he looked at me.

It was with a relief to finally climb into my hammock and fall asleep, but my sleep was troubled.

I stared into the boy's sorrowful eyes. He wasn't Po. He wasn't my brother, either. But he reminded me of both. I watched as a well-dressed man, carrying a whip in one hand, grabbed the boy with the other hand and dragged him along the dock. The boy stumbled and tripped as he tried to keep up with the man's long strides. Then for a moment to boy turned to face me.

"Why, Etienne?" he said, though I knew he did not speak any of the languages I knew.

I looked down at the heavy purse I held in my hand and gasped in horror as thick, crimson blood flooded out from the draw strings, covered my hand, and dripped like rain onto the dusty ground.

I gasped and opened my eyes. It was still dark and the ship was rocking gently with the tide. I felt around in the blanket until I found my purse. My hand closed upon it. It was heavy, filled with the precious money that would pay my family's debt and give us a new start. Tears came to my eyes unbidden.

I pulled myself upright, swung my legs over the side of the hammock, and quietly dropped to the floor. I clutched the purse as I made my way up the ladder to the deck and crossed to the railing. I knew what I must do, but it was so hard to do it! How could I give up so great a sum, money that would save my family? And yet, how could I keep it, knowing what it was? The ship was quiet. Only the lookouts were on duty, and they let me be. I stared out over the water. Light from the moon glinted off the surface and made beautiful patterns of rippling golden thread. No. It was more like ribbon.

I thought of Magdalena. She was the daughter of this captain, this pirate, this *slaver*! And yet, she was so unlike him. Her smile could bring warmth to the coldest night. She loved her father purely. Did she know of his crimes? She must. Did that make her guilty of them? No, she was innocent. She'd had no part in this deed. But I had. I'd prepared them for the sale. I'd stood by and watched. I'd done nothing to stop it. And then I'd accepted the reward. I looked down at the purse in my hand. I had done nothing to stop it. It was blood money, my thirty pieces of silver…. I pulled my arm back and flung the heavy purse into the sea.

Then I dropped to my knees and wept. *Please, Father God, forgive me! I didn't know what to do. I'm in a mess and I still don't know what to do. Please help me.*

I awoke with a start. I couldn't remember how I'd made it back to bed. I didn't know how long I'd slept, but it had been a deep sleep – the sleep of the absolved.

I rubbed my eyes and looked around. Men were stumbling out of bed all around me and I recognized the clanging of the duty bell, though it was barely perceptible over the howling of the wind. A crack of thunder erupted off to starboard followed closely by the flash of lightning. A storm must have overtaken us in the night and the ship creaked and groaned as it pitched back and forth on the angry sea.

"All hands! All hands!"

I heard the call and rolled out of my hammock. The deck was lurching from side to side and I nearly lost my balance. I looked down at myself and realized I must have fallen asleep with my belt and knife still strapped around my waist, too tired to even remove my trousers. The men were scrambling towards the deck and I hurried to follow them. I left my boots safely stowed in my trunk as another urgent cry for all hands echoed through the hull.

"Hurricane!" Captain Janssen bellowed as we all assembled. "All hands aloft!"

The ship was pitching and rolling violently, and I was thrown into the railing. I grabbed ahold and looked up. The sails were whipping about madly. The mainsail had pulled free of its leads and was thrashing wildly in the wind. I ran for the main mast, grabbed my knife, and held it between my teeth. Then I grabbed the rat line and hauled myself aloft. As I climbed, the mast swung out to starboard over the pitching deck and then swung back to port. I kept climbing and tried not to look down. I lost my footing and clung to the rope with both hands as it swung to starboard again and hovered over the tumultuous water for an instant before it lurched back. My feet struggled to find purchase, but then my feet found the rope again and grabbed ahold with my toes. My breathing was labored as I forced my limbs to reach upwards again.

Breathing heavily through clenched teeth, I concentrated on keeping the mast in my sight and tried to ignore the sights and sounds of the tempest. The ship rolled again and slammed me into the mast. I grunted, clung to the rope, and wrapped my legs around the mast as I tried to regain my bearings. Suddenly I thought of *Maistre* Quintal and the lessons he'd taught me seemingly a lifetime ago. There was one story where Jesus had calmed a storm. The disciples had been afraid, and Jesus had told them, "You of little faith, why are you so afraid?" Then he had gotten up and rebuked the winds and waves, and it was completely calm.

"Where are you now?" I thought.

Thunder rumbled in the distance and I remembered His words. *And surely I am with you always, to the very end of the age.* Carefully, I started up again. The wind ripped my hair from its binding and whipped it across my face. I continued up. The ship lurched again, and the ratline swung out over the churning sea and back again as I clung fast to the rope. A few more knots and I finally reached the yard arm. I wrapped my legs around it and inched out along the beam to reach the end. The sail was tangled in the sheet and I reached out and cut it free.

Just then the ship rolled starboard and I was pitched off headfirst. I reached out and grabbed for the lead lines as my foot became entangled with the sheets and I found myself hanging upside down from the yardarm. I felt panic rising as I swung, helpless as a rag doll. *Please God, help me!*

I felt my leg slip through the rope and flailed my arms wildly, searching for something, anything, to grab. Just as I started to fall, I felt someone grab my forearm, and my hand gripped his. As I was yanked back to relative safety, I looked up into the eyes of the shy seaman who'd given me Magdalena's note, the same one I'd tried to intimidate.

"I'm sorry," I said, "for how I tried to blackmail you …"

"Desperation leads many to do terrible things," he said, cutting me off. "I forgive you. Come we must hurry."

I followed him down the mast and arrived just in time to see lightning split the main mast in two. It fell, crashed through the railing, and plunged into the sea. The sail dragged at us and tried to pull the ship down after it.

"Cut the sheets!" the first mate bellowed. Men scrambled, stumbled, and fell as the ship rolled over onto its side. Several men were swept overboard. Then as the mast tore free, the ship swung back upright. But the sheets were still attached. I could feel the ship start to swing sideways as the sail dragged at the ship.

Again, the order came, more urgent now, and again men lunged for the ropes, knives clenched between their teeth. Again, the ship pitched and rolled. Another mast snapped and tumbled into the sea.

"Abandon ship!"

I thought of Jonah when he had tried to flee from God's mission to Nineveh and the storm that had nearly swallowed the ship that he had taken in his attempt to escape from God. I looked around. Men were trying desperately to lower the rowboats. I felt an urgency. There was something I was supposed to do. What was it?

The slaves! We still had slaves on board chained to the floor beneath the waterline. I ran and slid down the ladder without stopping. I stumbled as the ship lurched again. I kept going, down another ladder. I could hear the screams before I reached them. I grabbed the key off the hook and opened the door. I could see the whites of their eyes glowing in the near blackness. Quickly, I reached the first man and fumbled with the lock. I dropped the key and searched blindly as the ship pitched and rolled.

Please, God, help me! Help me save these people!

I felt something cold, and my fingers closed around the key. This time I inserted it into the lock and it opened with a click. I went to the next person, and then the next. Water was starting to fill the hold. I moved faster. Insert, click. Another. One more. I kept moving. Water was up to my knees. I felt around. There. Twist, click. Twist. Click. The water lapped at my waist now. I kept moving steadily. One more. And another. I was swimming now.

"Ayaii!"

I looked up and saw a man chained to the wall. I pushed through the water and grabbed onto the chain to steady myself. I slipped the key into the lock. Twist. Click. I looked around. It was dark. I couldn't see anything. I could only hear the rushing of the water.

My head cracked into a beam, and I realized the hull was nearly filled with water. Which way was the door? I turned around, and looked, but it was so dark! I started feeling my way along the walls. My heart was racing. Suddenly, a hand grabbed my shirt and pulled me. I followed. He dragged me on. I felt the ladder and clung to it like a dying man clinging to life. I felt a tug. I clung harder to the rungs. I felt another tug, harder this time, and understood. I released my grip and let the man lead me up and up. The water was over our heads now. Up we went. Soon I would have to breathe! Up and up.

Lighting lit up the sky and I realized we were on the deck. I looked toward my rescuer and into the face of a slave. He nodded to me, and I nodded back. I looked around. The ship was sinking. Together we plunged into the sea. I swallowed a mouthful of saltwater and came up sputtering. I swam and swam. Waves crashed over my head. My arms were tiring. I wasn't going to make it. Rain poured down and waves washed over me; it was impossible to tell one from the other. I could no longer tell if I was above or below the water. I was drowning.

I felt a hand groping for me. With all my strength, I willed my hand to close upon the hand that reached out for me ….

Chapter 41

Amends

Abraham, June 15, 1664

As Abraham approached the house, he could see Caleb and Jacob playing in the backyard. The house and yard looked unkept and the fields looked neglected. He walked slowly, not sure of the reception he would receive. Just then, Caleb looked up and spotted him. He was on his feet running and calling to him in an instant. Caleb nearly knocked him over as he collided with him and wrapped his arms around his waist.

"You came back!" Caleb said and burst into tears. "I thought I'd never see you again. You should not have gone."

"I'm sorry," Abraham said and loosened his brother's grip. Then he knelt in front of the boy and pull him into his arms. "I promise I will never leave you again."

"You'd better not!" Caleb said and wiped his snotty nose on Abraham's shirt.

"Come on," Abraham said and took Caleb's hand. "Time to

face Da's wrath."

As they reached the porch, Ralph walked over from the barn. "Da's been so worried about you. Where have you been?"

"I'm sorry …" he paused. "I went to Martha's Vineyard …"

"Never mind. Tell me about it later. We need to tell Da you're back."

Abraham nodded. Ralph put an arm around his shoulder and ushered him toward the back door.

Jacob glared at him as they walked by. He would have to talk to him later. First, he must face Da.

As they entered the house, Abraham saw his father sitting in his mother's chair mending the fishing nets. He looked up and stared at him, his mouth opened in surprise. Before Abraham knew what to say, his father was on his feet, hurrying across the floor to embrace him in his strong arms.

"Oh, Abraham, I thought I'd lost you!" his father said. His voice shook and Abraham could feel tremors running through his father's body. He realized with surprise that Da was crying.

"I'm sorry," Abraham mumbled into Da's chest.

Finally, his father pulled back and looked at him. "You've grown," he said and smiled. "Come tell us of your adventure."

Abraham looked around the room. "Where is your new wife?"

"When I woke up and found you were gone, I … your brothers and I," Da amended, "spent days looking for you. I sent Ralph and Samuel over to Gardiner's Island and then to the mainland looking for you." Then after a long pause he added, "I have not remarried."

That night, Abraham lay in bed, stared up at the rafters, and listened to his older brothers' snores. Caleb had curled up under his right arm. Susannah had been right. His father did love him. He was needed and missed. And his father had loved his mother too. He'd sat drinking, he'd abandoned his duties, and had spent too much time at the tavern out of grief and despair. Abraham realized that he had been so wrapped up in his own anger and grief that he hadn't seen it. His heart ached. He'd added to his father's loss by leaving. Guilt pricked at him.

Then he thought of Susanna and her family. He had learned so much from them. Maybe he'd needed to go. Maybe he had experienced his own *huskanaw* ceremony. He did feel different now. More confident. More certain of what he wanted and who he was.

He stared at the rafters and sleep stubbornly refused to come. He wondered what adventures Etienne was having. Would he ever see the brave seaman again? He hoped so. He still missed Mum. He blinked back the tears that formed behind his eyes and sighed. But the tears kept coming. He rolled over, buried his face in his pillow, and gave in to the sorrow. He cried until he had no more tears left. As he started to drift off to sleep, he felt Jacob crawl into his bed and snuggle up to his left side. He put his arm around him. It was good to be home.

Chapter 42

Wedding Day

Alsoomse, June 24, 1664

Alsoomse walked with her mother dressed in a newly finished white buckskin dress. Purple and white wampum beads had been strung together in short strands and then sewn around the neckline and again at the hemline of the dress. She wore a wide belt of wampum around her thin waist. Long fringe hung from the sleeves of her dress. Her feet were clad in new beaded moccasins. In her hands she carried a large, lidded basket woven in a checkered pattern of alternating dark and light fibers.

As they approached the long house, she looked up to see the wedding wheel hanging over the doorway. It was made of a birch branch bent into a circle and then woven with white deerskin in the burnt feather design, or in the shape of a dark-tipped white feather. It represented cleansing and good fortune.

Alsoomse stooped and followed her mother into the longhouse. The room was packed with family, friends, and tribal leaders. She carefully made her way toward the bench in the middle of the room and took her seat next to Okwaho. His mother sat on his other side and her mother then sat on her other side. He too held a large covered basket in his lap. He turned and smiled at her, and she smiled back. The room was warm and stuffy from all the bodies pressed together in the confined space. Her heart was beating rapidly, and she felt a bead of sweat roll down her side.

One of the council chiefs stood and came to face them. He turned to her mother and asked, "What is your daughter's name?"

"Alsoomse," her mother replied.

"To what clan does your daughter belong?"

"The Turtle clan of the Lenape."

"Do you think your daughter is capable of fulfilling the responsibilities of marriage?"

Her mother turned slightly to look at her a moment and then replied, "Yes, my daughter will fulfill her marriage duties."

The council chief nodded and continued. "Are you satisfied with your daughter's choice?"

"Yes," her mother replied without hesitation.

"If hard times come, and your daughter and her husband become homeless, would you open your home to them and their children?"

"Yes."

Then the chief turned to Matoaka and asked, "What is your son's name?"

"Okwaho," she replied.

"To what clan does your son belong?"

"To the Wolf clan of the Mohawk."

"Do you think your son is capable of fulfilling the responsibilities of marriage?"

"Yes," Matoaka said proudly.

"Are you satisfied with your son's choice?"

Matoaka looked at Alsoomse and smiled warmly. "Yes, he has made a fine choice."

"If hard times come, and your son and his wife become homeless, would you open your home to them and their children?"

"Yes," she said and smiled.

Then the council chief looked at Alsoomse and asked, "Are you prepared to be the wife of the man you have chosen for the rest of your life?"

"Yes," she replied without hesitation.

"Will you prepare food for your husband and children?"

"Yes."

"Will you care for your husband if he becomes ill?"

"Yes."

"When it is dinnertime and your children are out playing with others, you are to call *all* the children in to eat. If they have dirty faces, you will wash all their faces, just as if they all were your own children. Do you accept this responsibility?"

"Yes."

"As a wife and mother, it is your responsibility to prepare and bring your children to all group ceremonies. Do you accept this responsibility?"

"Yes."

"Marriage is a partnership, and no one has the authority over the other; you do not dominate your husband, nor does he dominate you. Do you accept this?"

"Yes."

The council chief then addressed Okwaho. "Are you prepared

to be the husband of the woman you have chosen for the rest of your life?"

"Yes," he looked at Alsoomse and smiled.

"Will you provide food for your wife and children?"

"Yes."

"Will you care for your wife if she becomes ill?"

"Yes."

"When it is dinnertime and your children are out playing with others, you are to call ALL the children to eat. If they have dirty faces, you will wash all their faces, just as if they all were your own children. Do you accept this responsibility?"

"Yes."

"As a husband and father, it is your responsibility to prepare and bring your children to all group ceremonies. Do you accept this responsibility?"

"Yes."

"Marriage is a partnership, and no one has authority over the other; you do not dominate your wife, nor does she dominate you. Do you accept this?"

"Yes."

The council chief then returned to his seat and another council chief, this time a woman, rose and approached them. She looked at Alsoomse and Okwaho and then held up a long ceremonial wampum belt with both hands. She began the Thanksgiving Address.

> *We who have gathered together are responsible that our cycle continues. We have been given the duty to live in harmony with one another and with other living things.*
>
> *We bring our minds together as one and give thanks for the people gathered here, that everyone is at peace here*

where we live on earth ... now our minds are one.

We bring our minds together as one and give thanks for Mother Earth. She has given us everything we need to live in peace ... now our minds are one.

We bring our minds together as one and give thanks for the food plants. They help us when we're hungry ... now our minds are one.

We bring our minds together as one and give thanks for fruits and especially strawberries, the head of the berry family ... now our minds are one.

We bring our minds together as one and give thanks for the grasses. Some we use as food and some as medicine ... now our minds are one.

We bring our minds together as one and give thanks for water; the rivers, the lakes, the oceans, and that clean water keeps running all over the earth. It keeps our thirst quenched ... now our minds are one.

We bring our minds together as one and give thanks for the fish. They give us strength so we don't go hungry ... now our minds are one.

We bring our minds together as one and give thanks for medicines, that they still help us when we are sick ... now our minds are one.

We bring our minds together as one and give thanks for wild animals, that they still help us when we are cold and hungry ... now our minds are one.

We bring our minds together as one and give thanks for the trees, especially maple, the head of their family, that it still creates sap as the Creator made it to do ... now our minds are one.

We bring our minds together as one and give thanks for the birds, that we still hear the nice singing they bring, especially the head of the bird family – the eagle is its name ... now our minds are one.

We bring our minds together as one and give thanks for our grandfathers the thunderers, that they make new waters ... now our minds are one.

We bring our minds together as one and give thanks for the four winds, that they still do what the Creator has asked them to do ... now our minds are one.

The council chief now gave a speech about marriage and explained their duties to one another and how it would make their marriage strong over a lifetime. Alsoomse listened and wondered if she was ready for this marriage. She felt fear tighten around her heart and panic clutch at her throat. She thought she might faint and glanced up at Okwaho. He met her gaze and smiled so warmly, she felt the fear and panic leave her. She smiled back.

The speech finally ended, and she and Okwaho stood and faced each other holding their baskets. Hers contained folded buckskin and clothing to represent that she was committed to Okwaho and their future children.

Alsoomse handed her basket to Okwaho and said, "I will do all that is required in marriage. I will tan the hides to make clothing, cook the food you bring to feed us, make the reed mats and blankets to keep our house warm and comfortable ..." Then she paused, glanced quickly at her mother-in-law and added, "and I will make the medicines to keep our family and community well."

Okwaho smiled and handed her his basket. She didn't have to open it to know it contained a cake baked from white cornmeal sweetened with honey and strawberries. Even though it was women who grew the corn and harvested the honey and strawberries while the men hunted and fished, the cake was a symbol representing all food.

Okwaho said, "I too will do all that is required in marriage. I will fish in the lakes and rivers and hunt in the woods. I will protect our family and our community from enemies. I will carry on the traditions of our ancestors and teach them to our children."

Then the council woman handed one end of the wampum belt to Alsoomse and the other to Okwaho. Together they pledged to the Creator and Great Spirit that they would uphold their marriage responsibilities.

Both of their mothers stood along with the remaining five council chiefs, including her father and Okwaho's father. They all gathered around her and her new husband as the wampum belt was passed around the circle and then to every person in attendance. As each person took hold of the sacred wampum belt, he or she offered up words of encouragement or advice to her and Okwaho. As the belt was passed back to the presiding council chief, a cheer arose from the crowd. Her mother quickly took the basket from her hands and pushed her way outside to cut the cake for the guests, and everyone in attendance jostled around them to offer congratulation and more advice.

Finally, the crowd dispersed and Okwaho led her outside as the wedding cake was distributed first to them and then to everyone else from the several tribes in attendance. When the cake was finished, Okwaho smiled at her again and turned to lead the men and boys in the Feather Dance to honor the Great Spirit. Alsoomse smiled and walked forward to lead the women and girls in dancing. Then a huge feast began with food and dancing late into the night. Her family stayed for a few days and then returned home. She and her new husband would remain a few days more and then they would also return to Manahatta to take their rightful place in her tribe.

Chapter 43

Medicine Bag

Alsoomse awoke with a start to the sound of her mother-in-law moaning softly in her sleep. She had overslept. The long house was nearly empty, except for her and Matoaka, who was lying in her bed, covered with a beaver blanket, despite the warmth of the morning. Alsoomse rose and hurried to her mother-in-law. Matoaka opened her eyes and smiled as she knelt beside her.

"What is troubling you, Mother? Shall I make some medicine to ease your discomfort?" Alsoomse asked.

Matoaka shook her head slowly. "There is nothing more to be done for me, Daughter. I have been ill for many seasons. It is my time."

"But I never knew …," Alsoomse said, alarmed.

"I did not want you to know, Daughter. I was already doing all that could be done. I wanted to see my son married, and I have. Now the pain is spreading. I can no longer eat, nor drink. Soon I will join my ancestors, but before I go, I wanted you to have this. …" She reached her thin arm up toward a bag hanging on the wall above her, but when she couldn't reach it, Alsoomse stood and retrieved it. It was her medicine bag.

Matoaka held it to her lips and closed her eyes briefly. Then she held it out to Alsoomse. She took it as tears began to form in her eyes.

"Don't cry, Daughter. It is the way of things – it is the circle of life. You must become the medicine woman now. Remember what I have taught you. Listen to the nature spirits. They will tell you which plants are good for what ailments and how to prepare them. Use the songs the Great Spirit gives you. You have the healing power. Use it to help our people."

"I will," Alsoomse promised.

"Now fetch my son, Okwaho."

Alsoomse rose quickly and went to find him. When they returned Okwaho knelt beside his mother and took her frail hand in his. Alsoomse came and sank onto her knees beside him.

Matoaka looked up at her son. "Protect her, Son of my Heart. The White Men will keep coming and one day they will take over all the land. We will have to adapt to their ways, or we will be forced to leave, or else we will be destroyed. You are wise and will know what to do. Listen to your spirit wolf. Follow him and he will show you."

Okwaho nodded and leaned over to kiss his mother.

"Now go," Matoaka said. "I am tired. Send your father to me."

Okwaho nodded and rose. He helped Alsoomse up and together they left the house. He saw his father standing near the men's lean-to lost in his own thoughts and hurried toward him. Alsoomse waited. Okwaho spoke to his father, and she watched them embrace. Then her husband returned with her father-in-law. She went to him. He took her hands in his and squeezed them. She nodded and let herself be led away by her husband as her father-in-law disappeared into the house.

Okwaho picked up a pack and slung it on his back. Then he took another and handed it to Alsoomse. "Where are we going?" she asked.

"We must hurry and warn your father," Okwaho said. "I have heard rumors from our northern brothers. The English are coming.

Soon there will be no place for your people on Manahatta. We must lead them away to new lands farther north and west where they will be safe for a time."

Together Alsoomse and her husband started down the path toward home. They hadn't gone far before they heard the sound of white men's boots and horses crunching along the path, recklessly breaking every stick they came upon. Alsoomse and Okwaho paused, crouched in the undergrowth, and waited.

Soon a dozen men on foot and three mounted on sleek dark horses came into view. They had an unfavorable look to them, with guns slung over their shoulders or packed within easy reach with their saddlebags. They did not march in formation like soldiers, but came on in a disheveled, undisciplined manner. Many wore malicious or hardened looks that bespoke of trouble. They seemed to be heading in the direction of Manahatta.

Alsoomse and Okwaho waited until the white men passed and disappeared around a bend in the trail before they came out from hiding. Okwaho looked at her and shook his head. She nodded in agreement. The men were clearly up to no good. There was no time to delay.

They traveled quickly, stopped only to eat or rest, and made good time.

Finally, they reached the canoe they'd hidden in the reeds of a quiet inlet. Her husband helped her into it, shoved it out into the water, and leaped into it himself. She marveled again at his great agility and strength as they glided out into the rapids. They would have to maintain control of their lightweight vessel as they crossed the current to reach the island, tiring work requiring balance and steady nerves, but made easier by the help of another. She was worried for her family and it gave her strength. Okwaho paddled in unison with her strokes and made steering corrections now and again to avoid a floating log or a submerged boulder.

Mosquitos buzzed around her ears as they reached the sheltered waters of the inlet near her village. She was grateful for the sunflower oil infused with sweetgrass she'd found in Matoaka's medicine bag, now her medicine bag. The sun was high in the sky; it was another warm day. They reached the shore, climbed out of the canoe, and secured it to a tree along the water's edge. Alsoomse felt a knot in her chest and looked worriedly at her husband. He smiled, squeezed her hand, and together they went to find *Noshi*. She didn't know if they could convince him of the danger, but they had to try.

Chapter 44

English Frigates

Abraham, August 24, 1664

Abraham spent several days showing his brothers how to harvest the sweet corn and the green beans. Then he explained how to store them for use in the short term. He'd reminded them to leave some to dry in the fields for next year's seed. The flour corn, squash, and stewing beans would also stay in the fields longer to dry out or harden for long term storage and winter use.

Ralph willingly listened to his instructions and learned quickly, but Sam fought him every step of the way until Da intervened, belt in hand. Sam worked then but glared at him darkly whenever Da was not looking. Even Da came out to help with the harvest. Abraham was grateful for the training Mum had given him. He sighed and looked down at the basket she'd made, now brimming with sweet corn. But there was still work to do, so he quickly scanned the fields and spotted his younger brothers as they worked. He nodded to himself and bent back to the work.

Suddenly, they heard horse's hooves galloping up the road to their house. Da stopped his work and went to greet the visitors, followed by Ralph and Sam. As they crossed the field, Isaac, Jacob, and Caleb dropped their baskets and ran after their older brothers. Abraham looked around. He shrugged and followed his brothers up to the house.

When he arrived at the front porch, he found Uncle Thomas speaking urgently with Da.

"Come, Brother, let's go inside," Da said and ushered Uncle Thomas into the house. Abraham and his brothers followed.

"Abraham, fetch some ale for us, please," Da said. He and Uncle Thomas took seats by the hearth, and after they were settled with their drinks, he asked, "Now what has gotten you so rattled, Brother?"

Uncle Thomas took a swig of ale and said, "I've received word that four English frigates have been spotted headed toward New Amsterdam. Word is that they mean to take the Dutch colony. They've sent word asking for support from the militia."

Da sat back and rubbed his chin, deep in thought. "King Charles is trying to control the North American trade routes."

"Why should we care about that?" Sam asked. "We are still Englishmen, aren't we?"

"We are," Da agreed. "However, we currently live in Dutch territory, and up until now the Dutch have let us alone to live as we see fit. But if the English are determined to take this land, that may change, and likely not for the better."

"Why would it be worse?" Sam asked.

"Ever since Parliament passed the Navigation Act of 1660, they have restricted the trade of sugar, tobacco, cotton, wool, indigo and ginger to ensure they are only shipped to England or English provinces. It has hurt the businesses in Boston, Virginia, and Carolina. That is why we are seeing more smuggling up and down the coast. If England now takes over New Netherlands, will they want control of the oil industry too?"

The room was silent as the weight of Da's words penetrated everyone's thoughts.

Uncle Thomas stood and handed his mug to Abraham. "Thank you for the hospitality, but I must go now. Just wanted you to know the word. We've got men keeping an eye on the English and will let you know what results."

"Thank you, Thomas," said Da. "Send my love to Alice."

"Will do," Thomas said. He nodded, strode to the door, and left.

Abraham listened to the sound of horse hooves retreating down the road and wondered what would come of this surprising news.

"Abraham." Da's voice jolted him out of his thoughts, and he looked up. "Don't you have a Lenape friend on Manhattan?"

"Yes, Alsoomse."

"Perhaps it would be prudent to warn her of the English arrival. I know they've been living peaceably with the Dutch, but the English arrival may change the situation for them too. It may not, but at least they will be alerted."

Abraham nodded and stood. "Should I leave now?"

"If you want to get there before the English arrive, I recommend haste." He paused. "And while you're in New Amsterdam, check to see whether the new harpoons we ordered have arrived."

"Can I go too?" Sam asked.

"No. You can help Ralph bring in the harvest."

"But why send Abraham?" Sam and asked, angrily. "He's just a kid, and it could be dangerous. Why not send me instead?"

"Abraham is a young man now. He has proven himself capable.

Your actions last time we were there proved to me that you cannot be trusted."

Abraham swelled with pride that Da had trusted him with this task. He pushed the boat out into the water and leapt in. It took a couple of days to reach the Lenape settlement on the northern end of Manhattan. It was midday when he reached the shore of Manhattan, he jumped out, pulled the boat up onto the beach, and went in search of Alsoomse, but Okwaho found him first.

"Is Alsoomse around?" Abraham asked after the proper greetings had been exchanged.

"Come, I will take you to her. Do you have news of Etienne?"

"No, but I have other news that may concern you all."

Okwaho nodded and let him into a long house in the center of the village. Alsoomse was sitting by the fire with an older woman Abraham assumed to be her mother, and a man he assumed was her father.

Alsoomse rose to her feet when she saw him. "Is there news of Etienne?"

Abraham shook his head, as Okwaho made the introductions to his in-laws.

"I have news that may affect all of you," Abraham said in his Montauk dialect.

"Please sit," Alsoomse's father said. "Kitchi fetch a bowl of *sappen* for our guest and something to drink. I can see that he has had a long journey and we will extend hospitality. Then we can talk."

Kitchi stepped out of the shadows, nodded, and left. Alsoomse,

Okwaho, and Abraham sat down by the fire, and Kitchi returned with the food. He handed it to Abraham and then sat down beside him.

"You look well, Abraham," Alsoomse said. "Your reunion with your family must have gone well?"

Abraham smiled. "It did."

"That is good. I am happy for you."

Abraham finished the turkey and corn porridge and set the bowl down beside him. Then he addressed the elder man. "I have come to warn you that the English are coming. They have plans to take this land from the Dutch. I know that you have lived in relative peace with them for many years. And peace may still be possible with the English, but it is also possible that they will want the whole land. My father says he thinks they intend to control the trade in this region. I don't know what that will mean for your people, but I wanted you to know."

The elder man nodded with respect. "Okwaho has also brought us news of the English arrival and a further warning from his mother. She was a medicine woman and had a vision foretelling of the English and their lust for our land. Okwaho and Alsoomse have urged me to take the tribe from this place, but until now, I have resisted." He paused and his eyes closed in thought. "The English must first take the land from the Dutch. And perhaps peace is still possible. I will stay a little longer. Soon, it will be time to move north for the winter. Let us wait and see what the English will do."

Abraham nodded. "Thank you for your hospitality. I must go to New Amsterdam to check on some supplies before returning home."

It was getting dark as he had approached the settlement of Gravesend on the west end of Long Island. He took refuge in the small inlet south of the town and as evening fell, he watched as five companies of soldiers disembarked from one of the frigates and, as darkness fell, started to march across Long Island in the direction of Manhattan. It did look like the English were planning an invasion.

The next morning, Abraham ate his remaining biscuits as he tried to decide what to do. It was unlikely that the English soldiers would bother with a lone rowboat, especially one carrying a half-English boy. So, he decided to chance it and continued his trip toward the harbor of New Amsterdam. It took several hours, but as he neared the docks, he saw that one English frigate had anchored off Governor's Island, just off the tip of Manhattan. Two more frigates were sailing around New Amsterdam to block the mouth of the North River.

He tied his boat to the dock and climbed onto the dock. He looked around. There was a great deal of commotion, and even panic, as men assembled along the pier and women and children hurried toward the safety of the blockhouse. As he scanned the people moving along the dock, he spotted the fur trader's son, François, and hailed him.

"What's going on?" Abraham asked.

"The English are here to invade us!" François said. "They've sent a note to Director-General Stuyvesant informing him that they 'knew of no New Netherland but that the land belonged solely to England.' And it doesn't look like they are going to wait for an answer either. We've had news that a militia from New England is approaching from the north. We will soon be surrounded!"

"What can I do to help?" Abraham asked.

"Come, the men are gathering near the fort."

Abraham hurried after François. They reached the gate to the fort, breathing hard, and were quickly admitted. Townsfolk were crowded in the bailey. Women clung to their children or each other. Men held muskets or swords and spoke together in low tones. Finely dressed councilmen were gathering atop the curtain walls of the fort.

Abraham noticed a door opening in one of the buildings and out stepped Director-General Peter Stuyvesant, easily recognizable by his purple cloak, wide pale-blue sash, and peg leg. He held a cane in his right hand, the same side as his peg leg. In the other hand, which hung down his side, he held a rumpled piece of paper. Several people moved to intercept him, as he walked slowly through the bailey.

"Please don't fire upon them!" one woman pleaded.

"They will burn our houses and kill our children," another woman said, clinging to the arm that held his cane.

Many more people approached him as he continued walking, as if in a trance, toward the steps leading to the battlements. Stuyvesant climbed the stairs and joined the councilmen mulling around the base of pole where the large GWC flag flapped back and forth in the wind.

"Come on," François whispered. "Let's see if we can see what is happening in the bay." He hurried toward a stairway leading to the top of the outer walls. Abraham followed quickly after him.

As they reached the walkway atop the wall, Abraham noticed that a several canons had been set up in defense around the battlements. A few canons had a barrel of powder standing along-side, but some did not. He looked around.

Several men were gathered around the Director-General as he ascended the stairs and walked toward the crenellations to gaze out at the English Men-of-War anchored in the harbor. The frigates were broadside to the sides of the fort with their gunnels open showing their canon in the ready. François and Abraham joined the crowd of anxious men.

"What are we to do?" one man asked.

"Even if the city were fortified, which it is not," Stuyvesant replied, pausing before continuing, "we don't have enough men to defend the city. We could line them all up around the perimeter, but there would be a four-foot gap between each man. We don't even have sufficient powder to fuel the canons."

"But, sir, we can't simply hand the city over to them!" another man said.

"Do you see another option?" Stuyvesant replied glumly.

A low mumbling spread through the men, but the Director-General seemed not to hear it, lost as he was, in his own thoughts.

"We cannot expect any relief or assistance," Stuyvesant said. "I've received word that the New Englanders have been joined by six hundred Esopus Indians and one hundred fifty French privateers. We cannot win this."

The men fell silent as the awful realization hit each of them. They would have to surrender the city and beyond that, the entire colony.

Finally, Stuyvesant spoke. "Send word to the English that we will receive them to negotiate our surrender. They are to receive safe passage ashore. Bring them to the council chamber and we will meet with them there." Then he turned on his heel and descended the stairs in silence.

The city surrendered to the English. People returned to their homes with the promise that the English would allow them to continue as they had before. For now, things seemed to be returning to normal. Before returning to the docks, he made a stop at Master Carteret's house after leaving the fort. There was still no word of Etienne, though Robert Jolls had made inquiries at several port stops. He hoped his friend was safe.

As he approached the docks a large black raven landed on a mooring, cocked his head to look at Abraham, and squawked. Abraham felt an omen chill his heart just as it had done in Boston nearly a year ago. He tried to shake off the feeling as he made his way toward the warehouse at the pier. He inquired about the harpoons and was rewarded with the news that they had arrived. He admired the deadly sharp tips and carried them to his boat. He stowed them inside, covered them with a tarp, untied the rope from the mooring, and dropped down into the boat. He rowed past the English frigates anchored in the harbor and hoped for peace and safety for everyone.

Chapter 45

Heading North

Alsoomse, September 11, 1664

Leaves rustled in the trees as the wind blew through them, and a rabbit scurried into the undergrowth as Alsoomse moved along the narrow deer path. She found an old willow tree bending over the stream, walked over, and gently laid her hand on the bark. Moss had grown up one side leaving patches of soft green. The bark had been hacked away on one limb leaving a patch of naked wood stark against the surrounding bark and moss.

Alsoomse moved her hand to cover the wood. *The year had seen so much hurt and loss, and yet there had been happiness too.* She turned and hurried along the path toward Etienne's family's farm. When she arrived, she noticed a man she did not know, dressed in the Dutch military uniform, talking to Etienne's father, Mr. Gayneau, in front of the house. She hid in the bushes at the edge of the woods and listened.

The soldier stood facing her and speaking in urgent tones. "The English have taken New Amsterdam. Johannes de Decker has sailed north to warn Fort Orange, but the English troops are close behind him."

"What will this mean for us?" Mr. Gayneau asked.

"The English claim that they will honor our property rights, tolerate our religious practices, and allow us to continue with our trade networks. Some are skeptical though."

"Well, so long as the English allow us to live in peace, I don't care whether the government is Dutch or English. I certainly do not wish to move without knowing the whereabouts of my eldest son. I'd expected him to return from his voyage by now, but word has been slow in coming. His mother is quite beside herself with worry."

"I hope you will receive news of him soon then, and I hope you are right. I fear the change. It is true that the English want to benefit from the successful Dutch trade networks in this region and that may well lead to interference."

"Perhaps you are right, but there is nothing to be done in any case," Mr. Gayneau said. "Thank you for the news. I wish you a blessed day!"

Alsoomse watched the visitor turn to leave, and wondered what all of this change would mean for her tribe. As the soldier retreated, she stepped out into the clearing and approached Mr. Gayneau.

He turned to look at her and smiled. "Alsoomse! What a pleasure it is to see you again."

She smiled back at him. "I have come to tell you that my tribe is heading north. I had hoped to hear more of Etienne's well-being before we left."

"There is no news," Mr. Gayneau said and shook his head sadly.

Alsoomse grimaced. "When you do see him again, tell him that

I miss his friendship and hope that he is well. I hope to see him again someday, but he should know that I have taken a husband. I don't know if our tribe will return next spring. A lot has changed, and we must decide the best paths to take."

"I understand and I wish you all well."

Alsoomse turned to leave, paused, and looked back. "And tell him that Kitchi misses him too."

"I will," Mr. Gayneau said and raised a hand in goodbye.

Alsoomse hurried back down the path and wondered if she would ever see her friend again. *Stay out of trouble Little Brother. And come home soon.*

Chapter 46

Whaling

Abraham, November 20, 1664

The weather had turned cold, and Abraham was huddled under a blanket by the fire in the small shack they kept near the beach. He'd been on lookout duty since before the dawn, and now that it was well into mid-morning, he'd been relieved by Isaac. Jacob and Caleb were playing with the crude wooden whale he'd carved from driftwood. They used pieces of bark as boats and were simulating a whale hunt. A small fire crackled in the hearth behind them.

Just then the door banged open, and Da strode inside. "Have you warmed up now, Abraham?"

"Yes, but I'm not ready to go back on watch. Isaac has barely been on duty!"

Da blinked and then smiled. "I want you to row one of the boats with Pannoowau. A couple of men have fallen ill and I think you're ready."

"Really?" Abraham blinked and stared up at Da with his mouth hanging open.

"Hurry, Son. We must be ready when the call comes." Da said and turned toward the door.

"Thank you, Da!" Abraham said. He sprang out the chair, dropped the blanket on the floor, and ran to hug his father. "I won't let you down!"

"Come. I need to introduce you to the crew and explain what you need to do before there is a sighting."

Abraham followed his father out of the cabin and down to the beach where he entered the middle tent with his father. Pannoowau was there with Ralph and five other men.

"Ralph is the harpoonist," Da said. "Frank is on the tiller, and the rest are rowers, like you. You will be paired with Pannoowau, since you are both about the same height now, to keep the rowing even."

Abraham looked at the Indian boy and met his returning glare. He forced himself to smile and extended his hand. Pannoowau looked at his extended hand but refused to take it. Abraham let it drop to his side.

Just then the call rang out – blows! The men sprang to their feet and ran past him toward the water's edge. Abraham quickly turned and followed. His ankle had healed well, but he still ran with an awkward lilting gait. The boat had been pulled up out of the surf and the men all grabbed a side and pushed it toward the water. Abraham found his place opposite Pannoowau in the middle of the rowboat and grabbed the side. As the boat slid into the water, the men jumped in and took their places at the oars. Ralph sat in the bow and gripped a harpoon which was tied to a rope coiled in the bottom of the boat. Abraham took his seat, facing backwards, and began to row. Frank was sitting in the stern holding a wooden lever which he used to steer the boat.

At first his oar kept clashing with the rower in front or behind him. Pannoowau yelled at him.

"No, Stupid! Watch your rhythm. Keep pace with me."

It was easier said than done, but within a few strokes, Abraham had found the beat and pulled in time with his partner. The boat skimmed across the surface of the water, and bounced up and down on the waves. They rowed, and rowed, and rowed. Abraham's arms were already starting to tire, but still they pulled and heaved. Hours seemed to pass before, finally, the boat shuddered as Ralph stood up and hurled the first harpoon. It missed as the great whale dove into the water.

They were told to stop rowing and waited in tense silence to see where the whale would surface. Abraham saw a dark shadow pass beneath them. It was huge — many times the size of their pitifully small rowboat. Abraham suddenly felt exposed and vulnerable, like a tiny, insignificant feather on the great expanse of the sea.

The whale breached and rolled on its side as it passed. Abraham saw its great eye studying him as if to see if he had the courage to challenge him. Abraham felt a shiver roll down his back and he gripped the oar tighter. As the whale slipped past, Ralph launched another harpoon at it. This one stuck, and Ralph quickly grabbed another harpoon and thew it. Dark red blood mixed with the churning water, and the heavy scent of iron filling Abraham's nostrils. The whale cried out in pain as another harpoon stuck, and the whale disappeared beneath the waves. The water looked as dark as ink with red foam bubbling on top, a sickening stew of death and destruction. Suddenly, the rope played out and Ralph fell back into the boat as it lurched forward after the fleeing whale.

Men from the other two boats were yelling and pulling at their oars, trying to follow the scarlet trail. Abraham's boat was propelled farther and farther out to sea at a dizzying speed. And then just as suddenly, they stopped as the whale dove. Sharks began to circle the rowboat, drawn to the whale's blood. The other two rowboats were struggling to reach them, but they were only tiny specks on the vast, grey sea. A nervous tension radiated from the men, and still there was no sign of the whale.

Then in a great eruption of saltwater and warm mist, the whale launched itself out of the water and fell onto the surface of the sea. A great wave of fringed water flooded the small ship and soaked everyone, just as a great tail caught the keel, flipped the boat upside down, and spilled everyone into the sea.

Abraham, still clinging to his oar, jabbed it at an approaching shark.

"Turn it over!" Someone yelled as the sharks continued to circle.

Men kicked and splashed as they tried to turn the boat right-side-up. Abraham could only stare at the sharks circling ever closer. He jabbed at another and then took his eyes from the sharks and dared to look around. The whale was gone. The water was so cold. His arms and legs felt sluggish. The other two boats were still several leagues away. It would take them too long to reach them. He jabbed at another shark and then noticed one coming up at him from beneath. He took a deep breath and slipped under the water. He swung at the shark, fought the resistance of the water, and thumped the shark on the nose. It moved away, but it would be back.

Abraham surfaced again and saw that the boat had been righted and men were scrambling to get back inside. He started to swim, but more shark fins were approaching. He wasn't going to make it! He was trapped. Shark fins were all around him now. He clutched his paddle, treaded water, and looked for a way out. Suddenly, he heard a chattering noise. He looked toward it just as a dolphin leapt out of the water and swam straight for him, followed by its entire pod.

As the dolphins approached, the sharks retreated. Abraham tucked the paddle under his arm and swam for the boat with all his strength. He reached the boat, moved alongside, and handed up his oar. He thought that he was be the last man to reach the safety of the boat, but where was Pannoowau? He looked around and finally saw him drifting far out. He yelled to him and waved his arm frantically. He started to swim, but Pannoowau seemed to drift farther away the harder he tried to reach him. He heard Ralph yelling his name and turned toward his brother. Ralph beckoned him frantically, but Abraham shook his head and kept swimming. A dolphin surfaced, head above the waves, right in front of him, and seemed to be chiding him.

Abraham pointed toward where Pannoowau floated and tried to make the dolphin understand. "I must save Pannoowau!" But the dolphin continued to block his path. Abraham looked back to where he had last seen Pannoowau. Other dolphins were moving toward the Montauk boy, but before they could reach him a great white shark lunged at the boy and clamped down on his torso. The Pannoowau's face contorted with horror and then slipped below the inky red water.

In panic, Abraham turned and started swimming back toward the boat. He swam with the single-minded fervor that only terror can bring. He was exhausted and freezing as strong arms caught him and pulled him over the side. He lay shivering and crying, curled up in the bottom of the boat, unable to move, as slowly the rest of the men began to row back to shore.

Chapter 47

Executor Arrives

The morning had started out like most mornings. Abraham had gone out to muck out the horse pens and give them fresh hay. He was just coming back to the house for breakfast when he saw a man on horseback ride up. The man looked familiar. He had an odd resemblance to a grey herring, too slender with knobby joints and a long, pointed nose. His clothes were drab and hung from him like empty flour sacks.

Abraham walked over to meet the visitor. The man held the reigns of his horse as he dismounted and nearly fell when one over-long foot became stuck in the stirrups. Abraham watched in amusement as the man dislodged his foot and hopped back on the other with his arms flaying in the air. Then he steadied himself, attempted to brush the wrinkles out of his jacket, adjusted his hat, and finally, pulled a ledger from one of the saddlebags. Suddenly, Abraham recognized him. The clerk from Mr. King's financing business in Boston here to collect the mortgage payment.

The clerk turned to Abraham and said, "I am looking for Mr. Samuel Dayton. Is he at home?"

"Yes. Come with me. I'll show you in." Abraham led the way up the porch and opened the door. Da was sitting in his chair by the fire. "Da, you have a visitor."

His father looked up and recognition registered on his face. He stood, regained his composure, and walked over to shake the clerk's hand. "What can I do for you?"

"The agreement you made with Mr. King stipulates that you were to pay," he looked at his ledger, "seventeen pounds, two shillings, seven pennies by December 1st of this year. Failing that, your house and property would be transferred over to Mr. King. Since we have not received your payment, I have come to claim the deed and evict you from the property."

"The whaling has not been as productive as we'd hoped, but it is only the start of the season. I'm sure we can make some arrangement," Da said.

"Arrangements were already made, and you have failed to uphold your end of it. There is nothing left to do but resolve matters."

Da looked helplessly around the room. *Maybe he was searching for a miracle*, Abraham thought.

"Come, Mr. Dayton. We must go before the magistrate to settle these matters. The court will be closed tomorrow for Christmas, and I do not intent to stay in this desolate, backwater village a moment longer than necessary."

"Abraham, go and saddle my horse, please," Da said and followed the clerk outside.

It had been hours since Da had left with Mr. King's assistant. Supper was simmering over the fire and the sun had nearly set, but still Da had not returned.

"When can we eat?" Caleb whined. "I'm hungry!"

Abraham sighed and rose to set the table. "We can eat now. I guess Da will eat when he returns … whenever that will be."

After dinner, Ralph and Samuel left to bed down the animals while Abraham cleared away the dishes. He had just sent his younger brothers to bed when the door opened and Da slunk inside. He looked old, like he'd aged ten years in one day. He hung his hat and coat by the door, walked over to the fireplace, and slumped into his chair. Abraham grabbed a clean bowl and spoon and walked to the hearth to fill it. He handed the food to his father, and he took it gratefully.

"Do we have any ale?" Da asked as he wiped stew from his beard.

Abraham nodded and retrieved a mug. He filled it from the barrel standing in the corner of the room and handed it to his father, who drained it quickly and handed it back for more. As Abraham returned with the second mug, his father said, "Help Jacob and Caleb pack their things. They are leaving tomorrow."

"What?" Abraham looked at his father in disbelief. "Where are they going?"

"They've been sold to pay the mortgage."

"To whom?" Abraham said. His voice cracking, but he ignored it. "Why would you do this?"

"What would you have me do? Make us all homeless in the

middle of winter?"

"But Da? Why this? Why them? It isn't fair! It's not right!"

"I need Ralph and Sam … and you to help with the whaling. Isaac is getting old enough to start helping with the household chores. But Jacob and Caleb are still more of a burden than a help. And they will be cared for. Your Aunt Alice and Uncle Thomas have bought Jacob's apprenticeship. They will raise him as their own. They are well respected in town. Thomas is the Deputy now and Jacob can help Alice in the shop."

"And what of Caleb?" Abraham asked.

"He'll work for Mr. Garlick and his wife on their farm."

"But Da, tomorrow is Christmas."

His father stared into the fire and did not speak. Abraham saw tears filling his father's eyes and turned away from him angrily.

"We'll hand them over after church," his father said in a shaky voice.

Abraham grunted and left to pack his brothers' few belongings.

Abraham hadn't heard anything the pastor had said in the sermon. He hadn't sung any of the songs either. The whole service had passed as a cacophony in his ears. He hadn't even noticed his cousins. He could no longer think or feel anything but disappointment and anger – at his father, at Mr. King and his clerk, and at the whole world. At God too!

The service ended and as they walked outside into the crisp air, Jacob turned and hugged Abraham tightly.

"It's okay. We'll still see each other. You'll just have to come to town more often," Jacob whispered in his ear.

Abraham pulled back and tried to smile. "Be good for Aunt Alice. I'll come as soon as I can."

Jacob nodded and then ran to join his aunt and uncle. Abraham watched them walk away. The crowds were thinning now. Abraham looked around and saw a shabby-looking farmer approaching with his plump wife. The man was scowling under a sloppy hat rimmed with sweat. The man spotted Da and strode over.

"So, this is the lad?" he said and squinted down at Caleb.

"Hello, Mr. Garlick," Da said and extended his hand. "Yes, this is Caleb."

Mr. Garlick ignored the proffered hand and studied Caleb. "He looks kind of scrawny, don't he? What can he do?"

"He planted seeds in the garden with me," Abraham said. "And he helped harvest the beans, corn, and squash."

"Humph!" Mr. Garlick felt Caleb's arms and turned him around. "We'll see. Come, Boy! There's work to be done."

Caleb burst into tears and Abraham knelt and embraced him. His own eyes were watering, and he blinked hard to keep the tears at bay. "Be good and do as you're told. Don't worry. I'll come check on you."

Caleb nodded and Abraham wiped his face with a handkerchief, then he pressed the carved whale into his hand.

Caleb looked at it and smiled up at Abraham. Tears streamed down his face.

"Boy! Hurry, time's awastin'."

Caleb hugged Da and his other brothers quickly and then ran after the Garlicks. Mrs. Garlick took his hand as they walked to their horse and wagon, climbed in, and drove away. Abraham stood and watched them until they disappeared around the bend.

Epilogue

Etienne, June 15, 1664

Was I dead? It was dark. This was not what I'd thought it would be like … to be dead. Heaven was supposed to be bright and joyful, with streets paved with gold and angels singing praises to God. But then, I was probably in Hell. I'd accepted blood money, and even though I'd later thrown it into the sea, I'd still accepted it in the first place. I hadn't stood up for what was right. I'd watched all those people sold into slavery. And how many had I helped bury at sea when they'd died of dysentery or scurvy? But this didn't feel like Hell either. Where were the lakes of fire? A chill ran through me. I strained my senses for clues.

I felt wet. Water was lapping at my bare feet. I felt sand beneath my hands. I opened my eyes. The moon was still visible just above the horizon, though the sky was beginning to lighten. Dawn would be breaking soon. I sat up and looked around.

The beach was deserted. Palm trees lined the narrow stretch of sand, and dense jungle filled in the space behind them. The sea lapped at my feet in low rolling waves. I tried to remember what had happened. There was a storm, and the ship was sinking. I'd tried to free the few remaining slaves chained below decks. Had I gotten to them all? How many people had drowned in the angry sea? Had my efforts even mattered? I sighed. At least I'd given some of them a chance to survive, however small. I hoped I was not the only one to make it.

I looked around again. Where was this place?

Then I heard a noise from the jungle behind me. I jumped to my feet and looked around for a weapon. I still had my wampum belt tied around my waist. I felt for the sheath. Miraculously it was still there along with the knife my father had bought for me in Holland. I drew it and turned to face whatever horror was approaching.

An African man burst out of the bushes. He was dressed in a loin cloth. He beckoned urgently for me to come with him. I approached him cautiously. He looked familiar. The man beckoned me again, more urgently. Suddenly, I recognized him. He was the last slave I had freed from his chains. Then I heard men's voices coming closer. I listened. Dutch. The pirates! I bolted toward the freed man and took cover with him in the jungle. Jacob Janssen van den Burgh had survived!

THE END

The story concludes in ***Charting a New Course.***

Reviews are important to helping others discover books they might like. If you enjoyed this books, I would be honored if you would leave a review on the site where you purchased the book.

Sign up for my newsletter at
https://books.bookfunnel.com/CFC_Free_Gifts
to receive a free short story and updates on my current projects.

Check out my website at http://www.amandamcetas.com.

A Note to My Readers

When people think of whaling in North America, they generally think of Nantucket. However, offshore whaling had already been occurring on Long Island, first by the Montauk and Shinnecock peoples, and then by the European colonists who settled there in the 17th century. The first small-boat whaling venture recorded was in 1640, off the coast of Southampton. It wasn't until 1675 that whaling was introduced to Nantucket by James Loper of East Hampton, who was asked to teach the men of Nantucket the whaling business. Drift whales, whales that died for one reason or another, would occasionally wash up on to the beach, where native peoples and colonist would then divide up the spoils. But drift whales were a rare find so, enterprising Native Americans and colonists developed techniques for hunting the whales from the shore using rowboats.

Form the beginning, Montauk and Shinnecock were hired as whalemen by the colonial entrepreneurs. The Montauk and Shinnecock willingly took these jobs to earn the money necessary to purchase European manufactured products, such as iron tools, iron pots, knives, guns and ammunition. The colonial entrepreneurs also hired the native whalemen for their experience and because of a severe labor shortage. In fact, at the end of the whaling season owners would provide a sizable signing bonus to any whaler willing to sign on for the following winter. These contracts were then recorded in the township records.

In March of 1664 King Charles II grants the territory between the Delaware and Connecticut Rivers to his brother, James. The problem was that this territory already belonged to the Dutch as part of New Netherlands. Tensions had been on the rise between the major European powers of England, France, Netherlands, and Spain. King Louis XIV signed a mutual defense treaty with the Dutch Republic, agreeing to provide military support if the English attacked the Dutch. In return, the Dutch agreed not to interfere with French actions involving the Spanish Netherlands. The French king also feared that an Anglo-Dutch war would draw Spain into the conflict.

On May 25, 1664, Colonel Richard Nicholls sailed from Portsmouth with four frigates and 300 soldiers and arrived in Gravesend Bay on the east end of Long Island on August 27th. War would not actually be declared until March 4, 1665.

Nicholls sent messages to the militia in New England and asked them to join him from the north to surround New Amsterdam. Nicholls sent a letter to Director-General Peter Stuyvesant and offered him good terms if he surrendered. King Charles I granted New Netherlands to his brother, James, the Duke of York, and James was anxious to preserve the profits coming from what would become New York. Despite a lack of powder for the cannon, Stuyvesant was inclined to resist the British invasion, until he was confronted with ninety-three burghers concerned for their property.

On September 4th, the British warships began maneuvers to surround and take the port city, forcing Stuyvesant to accept surrender. Consequently, several merchants met with Nicholls's representatives on the Stuyvesant farm on September 6th to draft the Articles of Surrender, in which the current inhabitants of New Netherlands were guaranteed their property rights, laws of inheritance, and religious freedom.

On September 10th, Johannes de Decker sailed north up the Hudson River to warn Fort Orange just ahead of the troops Nicholls sent to order the fort to surrender. On September 24th, Johannes de Montagne surrenders Fort Orange to the English knowing that since the English controlled the mouth of the Hudson, the fort would be cut off to resupply and trade networks.

The slave trade during this period was controlled through treaties with the major European countries. The treaties controlled where and the number of slaves each country was able to ship. Up to this time the Treaty of Tordesillas, established on June 7, 1494, divided up the American continents between Portugal and Spain and essentially gave them control of all the trade to and from the Americas for over a century. After the British defeated the Spanish armada in 1597, Queen Elizabeth I authorized privateers to attack the Spanish galleons returned from their colonies in the Americas. This weakened the power of the Spanish Empire and eventually opened the door to the Dutch, English, and French to compete for colonies and trade in the New World.

Trade wars between the Dutch and the Portuguese from 1624 to 1654 resulted in Dutch control of parts of Brazil. In 1621, the Dutch States-General issued a charter to the Dutch West India Company, *Geoctrooieerde Westindische Compagnie* in Dutch (GWC), which gave them a monopoly on the Dutch slave trade between West Africa and their territories in South America. One of their major trade ports was on the Island of Curaçao off the northern coast of present-day Venezuela.

Jacob Janssen van den Burgh was a Dutch sea captain who originally sailed for the Dutch West India Company until the 1660s when he became a privateer in the slave trade on the *Sinjoor*, and later, on the *Zeelandia*. He was convicted of piracy but somehow managed to buy his way out of the consequences. His is listed as one of the survivors of the *Zeelandia* when it sank in the West Indies, also known as the Caribbean Sea. He continued trading slaves and later, applied for a captain position with the West India Company on the *Middleburg.* Not much is known about him after this.

The genealogical records provide a lot of information about the Dayton family. Ralph Dayton, grandfather to the Abraham portrayed in this story, was born in 1528 in Ashford, Kent, England. He emigrated to New England with his family in 1634 and settling in Hartford. Ralph was a shoemaker, and along with the blacksmith, miller, copper, and tanner, was an important member of the agricultural community. He was also an interpreter to the Native Americans. He moved to Long Island and became one of the founding fathers of East Hampton and a progenitor of a number of descendants. Samuel seems to have moved around a lot in his youth. He married Wilhemina Medlyn (no surname), who was born on Long Island in 1628. It is believed she was a Montauk and other records indicate that she was involved in land sales in the area, which indicates that she may have been associated with an important family within the tribe.

Samuel tried his hand at farming and worked as a cobbler (a shoe repairman) when he ran low on money. He got involved in the "whaling design" while living at North Sea. Records indicate that he took a loan with Jonathan King in Boston in 1663 listing his property as collateral, and when he could not repay the mortgage, he sold indentureships on his two sons Jacob and Caleb on December 25, 1664.

It is presumed that Wilhemina Medlyn died sometime in early to mid-1664, though no specific date was recorded. There are also indications that she had a daughter in 1663, but again, there are no specific dates or records available to indicate what happened to her.

It is known that there was an epidemic of smallpox that broke out on Long Island early in 1664 and killed significant portion of the native population that spring. The rest of what is known of this family, I will save for the next book.

Atlas van der Hagen, 17th century map of London, originally started by W. Hollar, student of German engraver Mattheus Merian. Published after 1688. Geheugen van Nederland/Memory of the Netherlands, Koninklijke Bibliotheek. Public Domain.

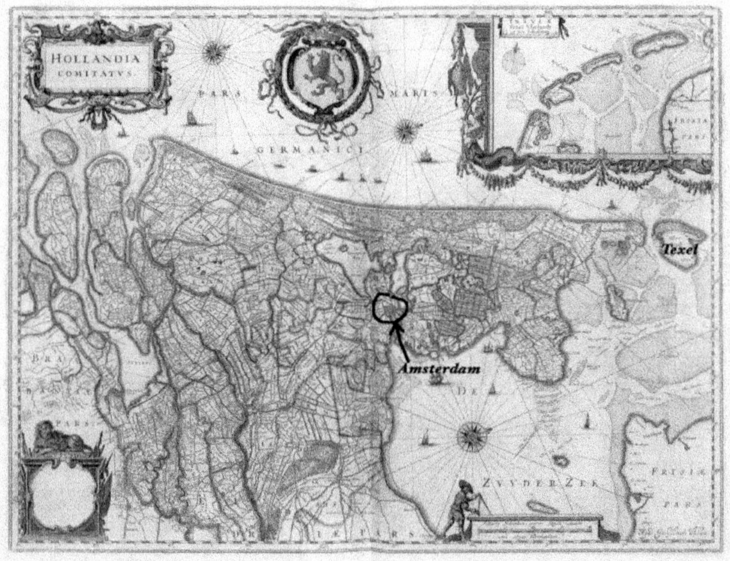

Hollandia Comitatus, by Willem Blaeu, 17th Century
Media donated from Koninklijki Bibliotheek, Public Domain.

Amanda M Cetas

Homan Heirs Map of the Local Slave Trade in West Africa, from Senegal and Cape Blanc to Guinea, the Cacongo
and Barbela rivers, and Ghana Lake on the Niger River as far as Regio Auri (1743)

File provided to Wikimedia Commons by Geographicus Rare Antique Maps. Public Domain.

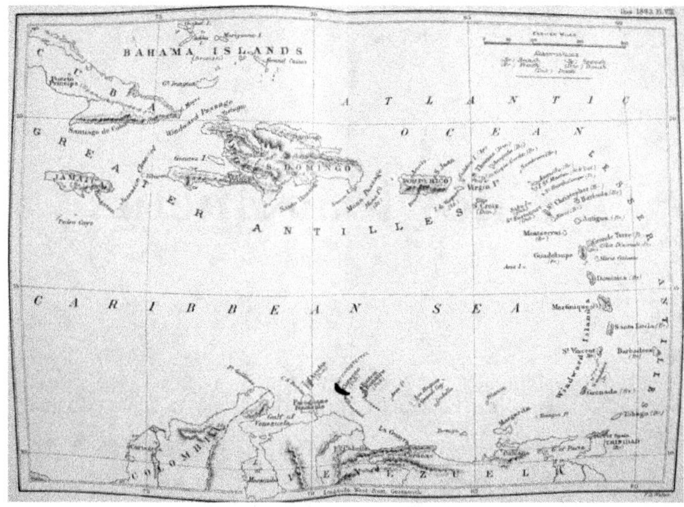

On the Birds of the Islands of Aruba, Curaçao, and Bonaire by Ernest Hartert, 1893
Contributed by Smithsonian Libraries. Public Domain.

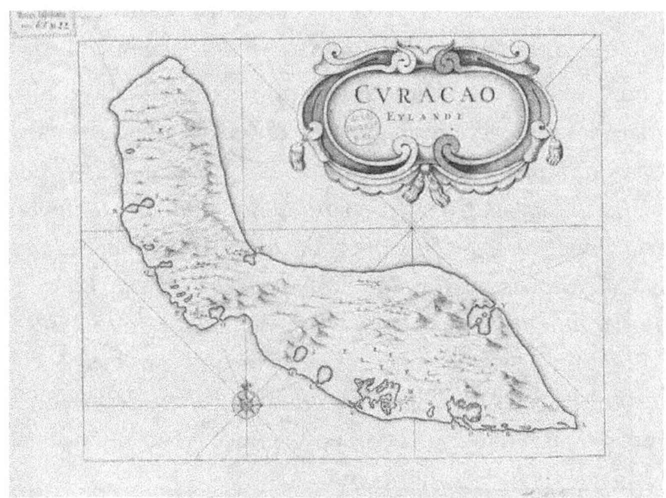

Curaçao Eylandt, ca. 1670, author anonymous.
Contributed by Creative Commons. Public Domain.

Acknowledgements

This book is the culmination of three decades of research into my family genealogy and various court records, newspaper articles, journals, land grants, family records, historical maps, and numerous other primary and secondary sources. *The Early Daytons and Descendants of Henry Jr.* by Donald Lines Jacobus and Arthur Bliss Dayton has been an invaluable supplementary source for information on the Dayton family. There have been so many other invaluable sources that is impossible to acknowledge them all.

Some of the most important primary and well researched secondary sources were found in *David Zeisbergers History of the American Indians (1910)*, *Records of the Town of East-Hampton, Long Island, Suffolk Co., N.Y., with Other Ancient Documents of Historic Value.*, Vol. 1, "Address on June 12th, 1890," *Addresses at the Celebration of the 250th Anniversary of the Village and Town of Southampton*, *Narratives of New Netherland 1609-1664* by J. Franklin Jameson, and John A. Strong's *America's Early Whalemen: Indian Shore Whalers on Long Island, 1650-1750.* For a complete annotated bibliography, please visit my website at https://www.amandamcetas.com.

Once again, I give my eternal gratitude to my editor, Laura Edge, Melissa W. Kelly for the line-editing, and my husband, without whom this book would never have been completed. Finally, I want to thank my beta readers for their input.

About the Author

Photo by Jim Irish, 2019

Amanda is the author of the historical action & adventure series *A Country for Castoffs*, which combines her family history with the larger historical context to educate and entertain a new generation of readers. She has researched her family genealogy for decades and taught middle and high school history for fourteen years. She loves the fragile beauty Sonoran Desert where she lives most of the year and the vibrant Willamette River each summer. Though her best inspirations reside with the ever-changing Sea of Cortez, where she has watched her three children grow up over the years, and now enjoys watching her grandchildren making new discoveries for themselves!

Join her mailing list at the following subscribepage.io/Amanda-M-Cetas-Author-Newsletter to receive updates on her current projects.

Visit the author's website at www.amandamcetas.com. Follow her on Facebook at Amanda M Cetas or Instagram at Amanda M Cetas Author.